n*e*

It's over. Don't go there.

Poet and novelist Kathrin Schmidt was born in 1958 in Gotha in the former German Democratic Republic and lives in Berlin. She trained as a psychologist and later worked as an editor and a social scientist before writing full time. Her first poetry pamphlet was published in the famous 'Poesiealbum' series by the GDR publisher, Verlag Neues Leben, of which Christa Wolf had in earlier years been editor-in-chief. Two further collections were published in the GDR. After the fall of the Berlin wall, Schmidt represented the anti-reunification United Left, the most left-wing of several newly-formed groups in the GDR, at Berlin city's round-table discussions. Schmidt's eight poetry volumes and five novels have garnered a host of residencies and awards, notably the 1993 Leonce-und-Lena Poetry Prize, and in 2009 her novel Du Stirbst Nicht was awarded both the annual prize of the reputed Südwestfunk Radio Best List and the German Book Prize, having been shortlisted alongside Nobel Prize winner Herta Müller. 'You're not dying' has since been brought out in fifteen languages including an English translation by Christina Les published in 2021 by Naked Eye.

Kathrin Schmidt is a member of the worldwide association of writers known as PEN International which advocates for freedom of expression. In claiming her own right to express non-mainstream views in today's Germany, Schmidt is never far from controversy.

Also by Kathrin Schmidt

Poetry
Poesiealbum Poetry Series, Issue 179, 1982
Ein Engel fliegt durch die Tapetenfabrik, Neues Leben Verlag, 1987
Flußbild mit Engel, Suhrkamp, Frankfurt am Main, 1995
Go-In der Belladonnen, Kiepenheuer & Witsch, 2000
Totentänze, with Karl-Georg Hirsch, 2001.
Blinde Bienen, Kiepenheuer & Witsch, 2010
waschplatz der kühlen dinge, Kiepenheuer & Witsch, 2018
sommerschaums ernte, Kiepenheuer & Witsch, 2020

Novels
Die Gunnar-Lennefsen-Expedition, Kiepenheuer & Witsch, 1998
Koenigs Kinder, Kiepenheuer & Witsch, 2002
Seebachs schwarze Katzen, Kiepenheuer & Witsch, 2005
Du stirbst nicht, Kiepenheuer & Witsch, 2009
Kapoks Schwestern, Kiepenheuer & Witsch, 2016

Stories
Sticky ends, (science fiction novella), Eichborn, 2000
Drei Karpfen blau, Berliner Handpresse, 2000
Tiefer Schafsee und andere Erzählungen, (short story collection),
Leipziger Bibliophilen-Abend, 2016

It's over. Don't go there.

short stories
by
Kathrin Schmidt

translated by *Sue Vickerman*

Naked Eye Publishing

First published in the German language as
"Finito. Schwamm Drüber." by Kathrin Schmidt

© 2011, Verlag Kiepenheuer & Witsch GmbH & Co. KG,
Cologne/ Germany

© 2011, Kathrin Schmidt

First published in English translation
by Naked Eye Publishing 2021

Book design, typesetting and front cover by Naked Eye.

ISBN: 9781910981153

nakedeyepublishing.co.uk

Translator's acknowledgements

'Cut to shreds' was a finalist in the Summer/Fall 2021 **Gabo Prize for Literary Translation** and was published in *Lunch Ticket* Issue 19, 2021 and in *Rritobak Krorpatro*, Calcutta, June 2021.

A further sixteen of these translated stories have been accepted for publication in the following print magazines and online journals.

In January 2021 'O snore, all ye faithful' appeared in *Dreamcatcher* 42, and three stories appeared in spring 2021 issues: 'Under wraps' in *Metamorphoses Journal of Literary Translation* vol. 29:1, 'Balder and Sons' in *nomansland* 15, and 'Line of vision' in *The Los Angeles Review*. In July 2021 'The Death Wish' appeared in *Asymptote*, and 'Lord of the Cherries' in *Apofenie*. In September 'On thin ice' appeared in *The Green Mountains Review*, and in October, *'On the point of a knife'* in *The Mulberry Review*. Five more stories published in 2021 were: 'The fish dish' in *Air/Light*, 'Tadeusz. Full stop.' (as 'Tadeusz. Period.') in *Trafika Europe* 20, 'The whiner in the diner' in *The Queen's Quarterly*, 'Norwegian Formula' in *Southword* 41, and 'Pulling the wool' in *The Interpreter's House* 76.

In 2022, 'Buttonholed', 'Frau Bestov and Herr Luck', and 'The demise of Herr and Frau Blumner' will appear respectively in *World Literature Today*, *The Shanghai Literary Review*, and *Stand Quarterly of the Arts*.

I am grateful for the help of German friends who demystified terms for me, and to Kathrin Schmidt herself for answering many questions. Special thanks go to Christina Les and Mike Kilyon for editorial support and especially to Jutta Heinen for the native-speaker eye she cast over every story. Most of all I am indebted to Keith Vickerman, my uncle, for meticulous proofreading, hours of discussion and the benefit of his awesome encyclopaedic knowledge.

Contents

It's over. Don't go there.

I'D FIRST BECOME AWARE OF POPESCU, without knowing his name obviously, when he was playing football with the three Dittman kids in front of my house on the dusty, rarely driven-on unmade road (I don't live in one of the streets of fancy villas but down one of the alleys that go off). The Dittman kids were what you might call 'local stock', meaning, anyone who went back a long way. In other words, they'd lived round here from before our absorption into the West; Germany's 'Reunification'. In their case, 'going back a long way' obviously applied primarily to the Dittman mother, who over the years had acquired children somewhat unconventionally, as you might say. She was bipolar and had got pregnant several times during her manic episodes, then gone into a deep depression that made her unable to say who was responsible. Old Mrs Zurwacke who lived in the Dittman mother's building, one floor above, had kept not just me but plenty of others well informed, wearing a face that shifted between sympathy and a kind of grim pleasure in telling of her neighbour's troubles. Management of her medication over time had reduced the extremity of her mood-swings, and no-one had ever persuaded the authorities to take the Dittman mother's kids away from her, even though there had been a few tries by her relatives who'd reported on her as an unfit parent. Each morning the Dittman mother – petite, quiet, nicely turned out – would walk to her job at the bank, and in the late afternoon – petite, quiet, nicely turned out – would come home again. The children, two girls and a boy, all primary school age, were so far from causing any disturbance to the old folk in the building that it was rumoured the Dittman woman dosed them with her medication to keep them quiet. When she was out shopping with a couple of the kids in tow, she came across to me as very self-possessed and always a little bit anxious. The children hardly spoke to each other and seemed to be in their own peaceful little world which they had no inclination to leave. I appreciated they had chosen a way of being that made them feel safe and secure; at the same time I shuddered to think of the price they were paying for it.

The Dittman mother lived alone with the children. The grandparents on their mother's side wanted nothing to do with them, while none of the paternal grandparents had a clue there were any grandchildren out there to love. Sometimes I sat in the garden with a cup of coffee and saw the Dittman mother going for a walk by herself. I could have called her over. I actually had imaginings of creeping inside her skull; of managing to feel something of the tension I suspected was in there. But I just sipped. Greeted her as she went by.

On the day I first noticed Popescu playing football with her children, I had written a contemptuous review of a contemptible book, and was fretting about whether I could send in my piece to the magazine editor who'd lumbered me with the job. In my agitation I was pacing back and forth by the kitchen window, when I saw the dark-skinned, sweating Popescu climb over the fence and reclaim the ball from my front garden. I went down the front staircase to open the garden gate for him because I was worried about the perennials

I'd planted by the fence in the autumn. What a nerve – looking me up and down like that. The impudence. As I stood before him in my unprepossessing red velour loungewear (a cheap sweatshirt and matching pants, strictly for wearing at home) Popescu gave me a downright once-over, an arrogant laugh escaping from between his teeth, his look seeming to linger on my cleavage. I was about to throw him out, but then I saw the trio of scared-looking children by the fence, pathetically peering up at their ball partner. Not wanting to upset them, I therefore just turned round to go back in the house. Popescu meanwhile didn't use the garden gate but climbed over the fence a second time. In so doing, he left evidence. Though he wasn't especially heavy, the metal spokes got bent outwards. For anyone walking by, especially at night with the poor street lighting, he'd created a hazard. Words failed me... Which was Popescu's problem too.

Hours later I was out there, looking furtively right and left before using all my strength to bend the spokes at least partway back to their original position. When my husband got home from work he presumably noticed some remaining irregularity; at any rate he stood outside with his bicycle at that part of the fence, feeling along the spokes with his hand, looking puzzled. Undecided about whether there was something to moan about, he chose not to. At least, there was no mention of it after he came indoors. Likewise, I kept silent.

The next I day found myself waiting for Popescu to appear. I kept having another look out of the window, and even decided to do my work at the kitchen table so I wouldn't have to leave the study at the back of the house every few minutes to check out the street. It was three o'clock before Popescu showed up with the Dittman kids. Having been distracted by my anticipation, I'd got little work done.

Amazing, how much those children relaxed through playing

ball! Instead of the timidity, the hesitant little steps, they were soon tearing about, wild and free. They didn't shriek, or anything like, but their expressions showed the pleasure they were getting from their unfettered leaping around. They were wiping sweat from their foreheads and upper lips and laughing – albeit almost noiselessly, but definitely laughing. Their relaxed faces held only a hint of the serious, controlled expressions I'd believed were in their nature, but which they'd dispensed with once I was no longer looking at them. I found this distinctly unsettling.

In the evening when I popped out for more shopping, the Dittman mother was in front of me in the check-out queue. She greeted me in a friendly way. Smiled.

I was quite taken aback.

Walking down Rembrandt Strasse the following Sunday I spotted my dark-skinned football player disappearing into a tenement, of which I knew two of the three occupants. This meant that the third name (which I read on my hastily redirected stroll past the panel of doorbells) must be his: Mircea Popescu. Strolling further, I paused at this and that fence, remarking aloud on the glorious summer flora and taking advantage of any opportunity to casually make inquiries. The answers I received related closely, I found, to the mouths that uttered them. A purple-ish lipsticked pinched mouth spoke in a lowered voice of a load of nasty gypos that regularly met up there. A mouth with downturned corners set in a disdainful-looking male face made it known how surprising it was that there hadn't been a shooting by now. In contrast, a full-lipped female mouth painted deep red talked about the good-looking guy, which Popescu indisputably was; and an old lady's wrinkled little mouth said that the way Popescu looked after folk in his building set a good example; what a shame (said the owner of the little mouth) she didn't live there herself... This didn't leave me confused: I'd have expected nothing else.

One afternoon when Popescu was once again playing football with the Dittman kids in front of my house I opened the window, making a bit of a performance of it on purpose, and called loudly to my husband who was working in the garden. My cheap red sweatshirt and pants were hanging out on the line. It was a matter of regret that the ball had not yet flown over my fence today. My husband clearly hadn't heard me. I made as if to call him again, but instead a loud 'Popescu!' came out. Which was in fact what I'd really wanted to shout. Now that it was out, I had to go with it. Popescu opened the garden gate and came to my kitchen window. I invited him and the children in – might a little rest from their football game be in order? – and put orange juice and mineral water on the table along with the large watermelon. The children were polite, their steps after playing football already timid again, but they didn't seem anxious. Seeing the melon the little boy actually whooped. My husband came in and sliced it up as if everything was absolutely normal, and I realised I'd forgotten how much I loved him doing things like this. I was amazed at how uncomplicated it can be to form bonds. Somehow, over the years, I had lost this knowledge.

The Dittmann kids seldom spoke, and even then only quietly, but when Popescu encouraged them with a gentle cuff, their eyes sparkled just like other children's. And he encouraged them so often, it felt almost like we were sitting in the shower of a sparkler. We arranged to meet two days later, in the evening.

And that's how it went on. We were never round at his place without the Dittman mother being there, who would have cooked something tasty. He was never at ours without the

Dittmann mother, who would praise my husband's creamy ragout. When Popescu married her it didn't seem right to him to take away her name when she had lived here so long, and replace it with one that didn't belong around here. He preferred to take her name. With his wife and three kids he moved into a bigger flat exactly halfway between his and their former homes.

During that time, Mircea Dittman would wordlessly pass me newspaper cuttings to read. The regional newspaper: police report section. The city's newspaper: page three, features. Lots of readers' letters. The whole lot going back nine years. At the time of one long article from the local paper, he'd apparently been living in Germany only semi-legally for the previous five years, having got here in what might be termed an 'underground' way. As a member of the Romanian minority in the province of Voivodina in Yugoslavia, he had deserted as a junior officer when hostilities broke out, in full knowledge of what desertion meant. But even in Germany, where he ended up, things weren't good. Desertion was not recognised as grounds for asylum. In the event of deportation, one shuddered to think of what penalties Popescu might be subjected to as a member of an ethnic minority, including – in areas whose administration had been taken over by Serbian Volunteer Regiment paramilitaries – execution. His parents had therefore sold the greater part of their possessions to fix him up with false documents, giving him the identity of a Bosnian. One who'd fled his burnt-out village. A believable story. Refugee status. But according to the Dayton Agreement, as a young single male he was supposed to go back. In his distress he produced his real papers, daring to reveal that he'd entered the Federal Republic with false ones. The case went through the press. Dzenan Galic was once again Mircea Popescu, the officer who had deserted the Yugoslavian army. As such, he was not eligible for the amnesty for deserters and conscientious objectors that came into law in 1995. But they could hardly refuse to grant him asylum. Yet this status then invalidated his work permit. The general public expressed their opinions in conflicting letters to the editor. Some felt that an officer is an officer, and he should be subject to whatever the punishment for desertion is in his homeland. Send him back. Others said it was obvious his desertion signified his refusal to commit crimes against humanity. Asylum was the least Germany could offer, considering the uncertainty of what might happen to him if he returned. There were letters – some anonymous – complaining that a person like Mercea Popescu was benefiting from a decent job in a German locksmith's shop while they, the workers, were on the dole – it was taking the mickey. One piece was full of total lies, saying Popescu was probably one of those so-called 'poor' gypsies who, in the time just after the two Germanys reunited, came driving round all the villages in the area in their great big Mercedes loaded with stolen carpets. The editor, of course, had no opinion. The storm Popescu had stirred up raged on and on. But you can't halt the turning cogs of an asylum procedure, and in the end it all came out well.

To sum up, Mircea Popescu had lived on false identity papers and had put himself in danger through an attempt to make them serve a genuinely good purpose. He was truly brave to have ventured into my neighbourhood, a typical middle-class east Berlin suburb of villas on avenues lined with grand, well-established linden trees, where the faces looking on from behind the ancient iron railings expressed, rather than contentment, an ambivalence. He had dared, and he had won – albeit by the skin of his teeth.

But he never talks about it.

It's over. Don't go there.

The twilight hour

WHEN THE SHADOWS WERE SHORT AND TIME WAS LONG, Brigitte Bambosa would always be on her sun-lounger in the garden's remotest corner. To anyone passing by, the modern detached house at the heart of the garden announced itself straightforwardly, leaving little to speculation. But the type of person who'd be taking a walk in this newly-built housing colony probably wouldn't be curious anyway. Lying on the sun-lounger Brigitte Bambosa would sometimes reflect on this. Only rarely did she herself set foot outside the front door. Her husband did that, on her behalf. He worked in the big city, beyond this commuter-belt development. As she lay on the sun-lounger Brigitte Bambosa lifted the little straw hat she'd pulled over her eyes and blinked in the sunlight. In recent weeks, time had been yawning on at ever greater length, though at the age of just thirty-seven she was – damn it – still young. Her husband insisted on taking care of the garden – he needed it to offset his sedentary office life. As for the little trees on the small patch of lawn behind the house, they took care of themselves. Having finished furnishing their new home, culminating with the bedroom, she would now sometimes stand on a chair in the morning and stroke a finger along the top of the fitted wardrobes. Too seldom was there a speck of dust to wipe away. And too often, Brigitte Bambosa would fixate on time's ever-greater length, the way it stretched between one day and the next. When you tried to return chewing-gum to a ball after chewing it soft, it would stretch to an ever greater length. Lately, Brigitte Bambosa no longer tried. This thing that stretched between the days – even she had to concede it was 'boredom'.

She got up, intending to fetch a bottle of water. On reaching the door round the front of the house, she saw an elderly couple hurrying along the treeless new road, albeit pausing here and there. She opened the front door, stepped inside and closed it behind her. Surprised, she found herself behind the curtain of the hall window, watching the two old folk. The man was indicating in her direction with his right hand. Brigitte Bambosa didn't move. He couldn't possibly have noticed her. What comment was he making to the woman? The latter was shaking her head dismissively anyway and – Brigitte Bambosa thought she could see from a distance – pursing her lips. The clock showed ten past twelve.

Five hours later her husband came home. Brigitte Bambosa had prepared a Tuscany salad, uncorked a chilled white wine and toasted a baguette. They ate on the terrace behind the house, talking about the upcoming local elections. Her husband was, as she knew, rather too keen on voting Left. But apart from her, no-one was allowed to know that. She herself had in recent years always voted Green out of a desire to salve her conscience, and she felt good about this, even if, two weeks at most after the election, the warm glow had entirely dissipated. The secret Left-Green Alliance tipped wine-glasses at each other: the current state of the world was tolerable. Later, when they were side by side in the bed of the newly-furnished bedroom, she smoked another cigarette, observing him after he'd long since fallen asleep.

The next morning, the climb onto the chair after her husband's departure once again showed up too little dust on the top of the wardrobe. In an effort to make her second coffee-break feel at least a little bit less long, Brigitte Bambosa reached, sighing, for what was number three on the bestseller list. And gazed out through the window. Heck – that old couple was standing there again. The man was scrutinising each window in turn, like he was searching for something in particular. The woman, bent and haggard, was having some trouble raising her head far enough to follow his look. The clock showed three minutes past nine.

In the following days, Brigitte Bambosa started watching out for the elderly pair. They walked past the house on average four times a day.

They always stopped contemplatively before the Bambosas' new-build, looking from the name-plate by the bell to the front door, then at each other. Brigitte Bambosa thought she also detected slight shrugs of their shoulders. Then they'd walk on. It seemed they had a regular schedule. For example on Wednesday Brigitte Bambosa saw the couple coming down the road at around ten o'clock loaded up with shopping – though they hadn't gone up it. On Thursday they came down the road twice without having previously gone up it even once. Brigitte Bambosa puzzled over this. On these two days they probably took a circular route. On other days they'd go up the street, each carrying a small bag, and after twenty minutes come back down. They were always holding hands, which stirred Brigitte Bambosa somewhere deep inside. Day after day for three weeks, she waited for these old folk. The shadows were now getting longer again, which not only shortened the time between morning and evening, but the time between the days also began rushing on, rather than sedately limping by. Brigitte

Bambosa almost forgot her boredom.

At last, on the Monday of the fourth week, she dropped her wallet in the street shortly before she expected the old couple to pass by, and lay in wait behind the front garden's still-flimsy hedge. Obviously she didn't literally lie there, but (despite its negative consequences for her husband's wellbeing) busied herself with weeding out weeds that had hardly grown back yet. The two came along; the woman saw the wallet, the man bent down to pick it up. Brigitte Bambosa had placed her identity card in the very first bank-card compartment so the oldies would have no problem working out the owner's name and address. They approached the gate to the front garden, and, seeing Brigitte Bambosa, called out loudly. She looked surprised, brushed off her soil-sullied hands on her shorts, and went over. The woman was brandishing the wallet and when she saw it, Brigitte Bambosa held her hand to her mouth in horror. No, when did I do that? How stupid! Thank goodness it's been picked up by honest folk like you! Do you want to come in for a few minutes? I'll make you a nice cup of coffee to get over the shock! It transpired that the two old folk wouldn't like a nice cup of coffee, not having in fact suffered a shock, however they wouldn't mind coming in for a cup of tea. The little bent-over woman pushed her husband before her. As Brigitte Bambosa now saw, he evidently had only one working eye. The eye nestling in the other socket was made of glass. She had some difficulty addressing him. Although intending to look him straight in the face she felt impelled to stare at the glass eye, then found its lack of reaction unnerving. The woman had a drooping mouth-corner and on the same side, a drooping eyelid which obscured a third of her iris when she looked too far to the left. Brigitte Bambosa's instant thought was – total crock. The elderly pair didn't let go of each other even when they'd been sitting for some while. It was as if he could cope with whatever infirmity so long as he held his wife's hand. An old-established team.

Brigitte Bambosa talked a bit too much. She noticed this but couldn't rein herself in; she just couldn't cope with the pauses, when even the air seemed to stop moving. While making the tea she talked about how hard the local water was; while cutting the cherry cake baked yesterday, about how pitted fruit such as these cherries could upset some elderly people's gall bladders (looking at the old woman inquiringly); putting a jug of milk on the table she wittered on about the udder disease in the herd of a dairy-farmer not far from the housing colony. But when the man started talking she instantly shut up, knowing this was what she'd been waiting for.

He asked tentatively if he could have a sweetener. She didn't say yes but swiftly turned, took the dispenser from the cupboard and placed it on the table in front of him with a wide and sparkly grin. The tiny woman stirred three spoonfuls of brown sugar into her tea. Brigitte Bambosa silently noted the old lady's shyness. It gave her a feeling of having the upper hand.

She asked the old couple their names. Frischer, said the woman, Max and Hildegard. And she stressed how nice it was to make Frau Bambosa's acquaintance. They exchanged saccharine smiles. Brigitte Bambosa had never spent any time in the company of geriatrics before. Her parents were long gone, having died in a traffic accident twenty years ago, and her husband's parents were only sixty.

She sighed audibly.

Anyway, we must be off now. Duty calls! the man declared. Brigitte Bambosa guessed the pair to be well over eighty, and wondered what duty might call. Did they want to take a piece of cherry cake with them? And just in general, it'd be really nice if they popped in more often, since they passed by such a lot! The couple smiled embarrassedly but were nodding – perhaps a little too keenly.

Two days later they rang the bell. Brigitte Bambosa had seen them coming and was right behind the door. Needing a time-lapse she tidied her hair, then sprayed herself with the perfume her husband had given her for Christmas. When she opened the door she acted pleasantly surprised. The old woman thrust a bouquet of scarlet carnations at her.

Today they were curious enough to want to see the house. They seemed particularly interested in the very few photos Brigitte had put up here and there. Her parents; the three brothers with their families. Did she also have a photo of her husband? She thought a moment, then searched for the old album. When she found it, the couple were practically burning with curiosity to take a look. They'd only just reached the third page, Socialist Naming Day, when the man triumphantly looked at his wife, then at Brigitte Bambosa. The surname... he stammered excitedly, it's such an unusual surname, we thought straight away that we'd found them again!

Brigitte Bambosa was at first totally in the dark.

An hour later, she was beginning to get it.

Her in-laws had been Party members in the same chapter as the couple (Hannelore and Gerhard Bambosa had never let on they'd been in the Party. Her husband, too, had kept this back from her.) They'd been doctors in an outpatients' clinic, as had these two. After the wall came down the older couple had retired, while the Bambosas had opened a community practice, which they were currently intending to run for another three or four years. Only when Brigitte's husband had felt sure of her commitment to him had she been permitted to meet her in-laws. The Bambosas, while polite, had always been distant, and the daughter-in-law had never wanted to step over that invisible line that was drawn around them. The Frischers, on the other hand, were transparently open, talking about former times not as if they had come to an end, but as though to affirm their ongoing reality. Sharpen the memories, not put them away. For Brigitte Bambosa, it was all new. She wondered why she had never sought to open the door to the senior Bambosas' former lives. Not even so much as a tentative knock. For the rest of the day she pondered this thought, unpacked it, rearranged the contents, but came no closer to her parents-in-law.

She eventually accepted a return invitation. The following Friday she set out. The Frischers lived in the first block one comes to in the old residential area that borders the housing colony. Brigitte Bambosa thought she recognised the oak-effect chipboard wall-cabinet, terminally creaking, its shelves sagging beneath the weight of books. An ancient carpet competed for the most perfect shade of grey with an equally ancient couch, and the furnishings were completed by two nineteen-seventies armchairs. They offered her one of these. The man sat on the couch; his wife bustled into the kitchen to get the coffee. If she blanked out the books, Brigitte Bambosa felt like she was back in her parents' living room. Though it had been much tidier than the Frischers'. Through the door to the porch she could see stack upon stack of newspapers, while neat news-cuttings were set out on the table arranged by topic and held down with smaller or larger stones. Herr Frischer tore up a sheet of paper and placed a piece between each pile of cuttings as he cleared them off the table. He wiped the waxed tablecloth with a warm dishrag and fetched a coffee cup from the cupboard, then tea glasses for his wife and himself.

Once seated at the table, there was, for a moment, no

conversation, as if they couldn't decide how to begin. But then Herr Frischer cleared his throat and said they were walkers, do-ers and thinkers. The pair of them actually walked past Brigitte Bambosa's house more often in one day than Brigitta would leave the house in an entire week. She thought of the chair she climbed on in the morning in search of dust. Her in-laws contributed money so that she didn't need to work but was 'paid' to make a home. No-one else got paid to do that, and she'd thought it was good, even though at first her husband couldn't understand how she could happily give up her teaching job. In this day and age? But the in-laws offered them the prospect of a considerable inheritance, and that definitely outweighed the prospect of thirty more working years standing in front of over-sized classes full of unmotivated and uninterested pupils. So you reflect on things a lot? She said. And go for walks, and do activities? Semi-consciously she was paralleling this with her own state, but the Frischers of course had no idea of that. They were now talking about The Party, of which they had been members for more than fifty years. The local chapter meetings, the campaigns, the contentious elections. They'd taken up campaigning for the environment, which had sometimes caused friction. It helped them, that they could carry on being involved, because the 'change-over time' – by which they meant the months between the opening of the border and Reunification – had completely knocked them sideways, with Frau Frischer's stroke coming out of the blue on the fifth of January nineteen-ninety, a day never to be forgotten, and shortly thereafter, Herr Frischer's detached retina that had made him blind on one side. He'd had the eye taken straight out because of a persistent infection, and in the beginning was actually pleased at not being forced to watch what was going on all around. The displays in the shops had changed practically overnight; he was away at a rehab centre with his wife during that time, thank God, otherwise there was no way they'd have been able to take it all in at that speed. They seemed almost grateful (to whom, though?) that the aforesaid misfortunes had befallen them back then, allowing them to remain cocooned in cotton-wool until Germany's 're-set' was complete. They had then just taken the new social order as given, and begun campaigning against it. That had been something new: until then they'd always have stuck to the Party line, but it no longer existed. For a heartbeat Brigitte Bambosa wondered – though too fleetingly for an answer to come – whether this 'line' bore any relation to the forbidding line her in-laws had drawn round themselves. The Frischers were saying how they no longer needed much, and so used their decent pension for Third World projects and to keep the roof over their heads. Their faith in the Party was absolute, though they'd never concede that it was 'religious'. Whatever. Old folks have their beliefs. In their twilight years, these two wanted no more changes.

Brigitte Bambosa ate some of the chocolate-and-biscuit layer cake. Her mother had made her this classic East German concoction on birthdays when she was a child. The coconut oil made her feel sick, but there was nothing else for it but to swallow down the nausea.

What about your in-laws?

Herr Frischer's question hung, hologram-esque, in the air between them. From Brigitte Bambosa's side it looked like a giant steam-iron whose on-switch she dare not flick for fear of it coming down devastatingly hard, whereas from the Frischers' side the question looked like a pristine, freshly-laundered pillowslip flapping innocently on the breeze and billowing into its neighbours, thus happily being reunited with fellow linens of similar hue. Eager to hear about their former comrades, they were waiting to pick up any 'stray pegs', so to speak, that Brigitte Bambosa might let drop. She played for time. The last crumbs of the chocolate-and-biscuit layer cake allowed her a minute of delay, which she indicated by wagging her hand in front of her mouth. But eventually the crumbs were swallowed, her thinking time over – but her mind was totally empty. She was stuck for an answer. No matter; Frau Frischer was now embarking on a reminiscence: how, in June 'eighty-nine when the Tiananmen riots were happening at the Gate of Heavenly Peace in Beijing, they had sat down with the senior Bambosas and watched Western television pictures. The Frischers watched in distress, hardly believing it as they actually witnessed the Chinese army attacking students, whereas the Bambosas' perception of those same scenes was totally different: in their view, what they actually witnessed was the students attacking the army. And then in a stern voice Frau Bambosa had come out with, what else should the soldiers be doing but fighting back against those counter-revolutionaries? And in that moment, the Frischers had come to appreciate how pre-conceived ideas can profoundly affect what one sees. They'd parted company that day without another word, what with feeling upset on totally opposite counts. I bet those two die-hards are as Red as they ever were, are they?

Brigitte Bambosa was aware that she herself was red. As in, red-faced. In a rush she leapt up and took her leave – the conversation had been so interesting she'd almost forgotten her urgent dental appointment! The Frischers looked surprised, and stood and watched as she crossed the road in a great hurry and, at the turning after the next-but-one house, disappeared.

She stopped.

Took a deep breath.

While she didn't exactly approve of the Frischers' loyalty to the old, now reconfigured Party, she at least found them consistent. They were presumably committed to the new Party's stated aims; furthermore it provided a context in which they might retain at least a little recognition of their service (which is what it had been); it wouldn't all just be forgotten. As to their serious illnesses during the years of transition to a new, united Germany – it was almost as if they saw these as the price they'd had to pay for persisting unquestioningly with their 'misguided' views. While the former State was no more, it was still somehow deeply embedded within them. Furniture held no value other than for its basic functionality; all of it, including their crockery, dated back to the former regime. Brigitte Bambosa thought of her in-laws' porcelain displayed in the brass cabinets they'd purchased upon moving into their house, and how they bought a whole new service every two to three years. It had been fun to inherit the coffee- or tea-sets herself once in a while, when the latest arrived and Frau Bambosa passed on the "old" one to a homeless charity or wherever. Was it better to remove any semblance of continuity? Even from how you served your coffee? Were the Frischers the die-hards, stuck in their 'twilight hour', whereas her in-laws had woken into the bright new dawn, in terms of adapting to the new order of things? Brigitte Bambosa felt giddy. Whenever she came close to an answer, her mind failed to take hold of it, pull it into the light. Her legs were twitchy as though she needed to climb on the chair. At last, she stumbled off down the street. Dark times can also be good times. And good times can be dark. This hit her with full force when, in the twilight, she saw her in-laws' car pulling up outside her house.

Later, as they dined together, of the Frischers she spoke not one word.

Koenigsberg Meatballs

SENTA HABERBERGER SPLUTTERS A POCKET-SIZED HOLE into the stagnant air, then refills it with little regurgitations and a big belch. The air-pocket is soon dense with the stink of onions and pickled sick. Senta Haberberger has just eaten traditional meatballs boiled up with capers, served in a sour-cream sauce enhanced with a liberal slosh of white wine. It is Senta Haberberger's birthday. Due to being born in 1899, Senta Haberberger has for ever been a year ahead. When starting infant school she'd been one year older than the (also infant) century. The year she'd had to drop out of school is likewise long, long ago. Two years longer ago than that first spark of maternal feeling that had given her the balls to conquer the meatballs. The ensuing decades saw Senta Haberberger rise to become a formidable lady, then decline. Senta Haberberger is remembering her birthdays. She relives having her ears boxed so hard, her skull is left jangling. Turning two, three... eleven... right through to thirteen, each birthday bringing her mother's ear-boxings. This being due to Senta's stomach churning at the very sight of meatballs cooked with capers. There, on her plate, every year, the dinner specially prepared for her birthday – a mush of sauce, potatoes and something like vomit. Having to force it down, owing to her mother threatening to box her ears. Senta Haberberger is reliving the retching. The mush spewing back out. At fourteen she gives birth to a child. As punishment her mother doesn't make her a birthday dinner that year. The

Children's Court registers the child as residing in the grandparents' household. Senta Haberberger gets a job polishing silver for a toff with a kiss-my-ass swagger who uses her to polish his cock. But these days Senta knows how to handle this, rinsing herself with vinegar the minute the toff with the swagger is done with his polishing. At her parents' house her little boy is learning to walk. The swaggerer gets out of being conscripted; turns out he is also a bed-wetter. Senta Haberberger changes his sheets. While she is doing this, Swagger pokes his finger inside her from behind. Once the bed is made, Senta Haberberger bends over to pick up the soiled bedding and deftly flips up the back of her skirt to help him with access. She holds herself steady on the bedside cabinet while Swagger polishes himself. He withdraws, dripping, and orders her into the bed, but Senta goes for the vinegar. Swagger is an idiot. For doing the polishing, he gives her meat, fresh cream, capers and milk. She takes these home to her mother who uses them to cook a meal for the little boy's birthday. Senta Haberberger's child is whimpering, the sour cream dribbling out of his downturned mouth-corners, and at last, she feels something for him. Her child must not suffer like she did. He must not let the loathing take a hold – they must conquer the meatballs! Cautiously, Senta Haberberger starts eating them, spooning a tiny heap of meat and potato onto her tongue. She pauses. The child (whose ears her mother is threatening to box) is looking sidelong at Senta with a doubtful expression. Senta is afraid she'll retch, but it doesn't happen. She swallows, and does a little roll of her eyes at her child, widening them in secret communication. As his mother feeds him the mush, the boy smiles – then vomits. Senta has had enough. She goes back to Swagger's villa. He asks if they liked the dinner and fucks her for supper. From this time on, Senta has no further difficulties with Koenigsberg's traditional meatballs. Aged twenty she has another child. Swagger is very put out that she's found a man to marry and doesn't need the job of polishing his silver any more. Nowadays she eats meatballs she herself has cooked. Following the marriage, her older child, her boy, is allowed to come and live with her too. Senta becomes a housewife and orders capers from the grocer. The man who has taken her on is a blacksmith with a red hot poker. Senta periodically submits to him. By the time he's had a slap-up dinner and a good session with his red hot poker in the local brothel, he can barely get it up with her. Furthermore she needs less vinegar with Swagger these days than she used to. She is able to buy quality foods for her children, which makes it all worth it. Her only problem is her daughter, who doesn't like the traditional meatballs with capers. Losing her memory and her temper in the same savage moment, Senta Haberberger boxes the girl's ears till her skull is jangling. The blacksmith joins in too if he's there. When the child has finally been subdued they put her to bed, then the blacksmith leaves the house to go and use his red hot poker, and Senta Haberberger takes her daughter some peppermint tea. Senta is worn out, but not yet ready to fall asleep. She needs some stimulation. Sometimes she's even tempted to run off to Swagger's villa. She doesn't, because the food is better at her house than anywhere else in the entire neighbourhood. The blacksmith certainly can't be accused of stinginess. By the time he dies (due to a cancer that has eaten away his bollocks) another war is on. Senta Haberberger writes to her son on the Eastern Front. At home in Koenigsberg, every birthday is marked by the preparation of traditional Koenigsberg meatballs, though the war has made the sauce watery. Senta Haberberger works in the Army Catering Service where she steals a bit of food now and then. She still quarrels over meatballs with her daughter who detests them. Senta can be as vile as the vile capers-and-cream, but her daughter is tall and strong and fearless – until the end of the war, when she must learn to be fearful. She flees westwards from Koenigsberg into Germany's east, taking all her worldly goods, including her mother. The son has already had quite enough of the east, and writes home to his mother that the sky over Koenigsberg isn't a patch on the blue skies of LA. Senta has already turned forty-seven when her daughter gives birth. Her daughter is over thirty and is delighted. Senta boils up the traditional meatballs with capers. Her daughter boils over, and in her screaming rage finally discloses the child's father: a Russian, who hooked her with his herring – a lush, blue, briny herring. Woman! Fuck! he yelled, and chased her from pillar to post with his herring till she swallowed his lush blue fish and her virginity. The Russian was blond. A bit Aryan looking, then? inquires Senta of her daughter, though times are of course not what they were. Her daughter ignores her. Senta spoons a tiny heap of potato topped with meat in sour cream into the mouth of her daughter, who chews and swallows. And in due course her daughter, too, in one savage moment, loses her memory and her temper, so that her daughter's daughter, detesting traditional meatballs with capers, goes to school with cowed head sunk between her shoulders. Whenever cream appears on the barren shelves of the state-run co-operative, Senta's daughter cooks Koenigsberg meatballs. When it is Senta Haberberger's birthday she invites her daughter and her daughter's daughter to eat with her. The child throws up on the carpet. Senta Haberberger shrieks and tells her off. Still retching, the child mops at the carpet. When Senta Haberberger starts drawing her state pension, her daughter's child is thirteen years old and has a stepfather. Her daughter helps the stepfather get back on his feet. He shows his gratitude by treating her daughter's child with affection. The daughter's child proudly adopts her stepfather's views on things. The stepfather does not like blacks with their dark purple dicks. In Senta's daughter's child's class at school there is a brown girl whose father is a soldier in America. When their teacher tells them which soldiers are good and which are bad, the daughter's child starts bullying the brown girl. The brown girl moves to America. Bully for her, says the teacher. Bully for you your mum's soldier was a Russian, the stepfather says to the daughter's child. Otherwise I wouldn't have touched you with a barge-pole. The stepfather laughs, stroking the daughter's child's hair. It's the child's birthday. Senta Haberberger is dishing out the food at her daughter's house. The retching starts. In the afternoon, a handful of children, all born since the war, come for apple pie. The daughter picks up a pebble and throws it. The children born since the war dive after the pebble and the one who brings it back gets a stick of liquorice. Brown liquorice juice runs from the corner of the daughter's child's mouth. The child wipes away the dribble with her plait and falls over into the nettles. Meanwhile Senta Haberberger is telling the stepfather about the old days. About Koenigsberg that is now Kaliningrad, where she grew up eating the traditional meatballs. The stepfather scoffs at this, considering her daughter's child is still green in the face after the lunchtime incident. Her daughter's child's complexion only improves once she moves to the city to train for a job. The rosy cheeks of her daughter's child, who is now adult, appeal to a spiv with an Elvis quiff. He kisses her neck. Some months later, the child of her daughter's child endeavours to bring itself forth into the world far too early. It kicks and pushes, it tears open its eggshell, it departs from her daughter's child before its appointed time, survives, and becomes an obedient child of the Republic, obtaining, one December, its blue Young Pioneers neckerchief. Her daughter's child recalls when the daughter's child's child would refuse to eat her meatballs. Whoever heard of such a thing? Children are starving in Biafra while over here they're turning their noses up at meatballs. The daughter is determined not to spoil her little granddaughter, and the daughter's child, similarly determined, takes her turn at losing (in one savage moment) her memory and her temper. Her raised hand threatens to set the child's skull jangling. Until, that is, the daughter's child's child sings a little song through her sobs. I'm still too small to cook the tea, my little hands can't pod a pea, so all day long I'll dust and dust, how happy will my Mummy be! And Mummy is forced to smile because the daughter's daughter's child's burbled song is barely understandable. She kisses the child on the lips, clasps the child to her bosom. But the retching doesn't subside. The daughter's daughter's child brings forth a creamy capery mush into the world. Senta Haberberger is shaking her head now, remembering Swagger. So very long ago. Everyone older and wiser. At school the daughter's child's child paints a picture for Senta's birthday, rolls it up, parcels it in gift-wrap and goes visiting. Senta Haberberger has just finished eating and opens the door to her daughter's child's child, spluttering, as she does so, a pocket-sized hole into the stagnant air and refilling it with little regurgitations and then a big belch, the meatballs repeating themselves, as ever, and causing a terrible stink. But her daughter's child's child is well acquainted with all this.

Lord of the Cherries

It was back in the time when, day in day out, the only thing I cared about, thinking now, was being an Exemplary Child of the German Democratic Republic; the time when our schoolbooks contained a verdict on the previous war, but only as a thing long in the past – a past which surely couldn't have been the one our parents had lived through, at least not in the mind of the Exemplary Child of the German Democratic Republic with perfectly knotted neckerchief, cheerfully patriotic mother and father, and a leather satchel containing an apple, round and red, and a slice of buttered bread. That was the time when Herr Barz, the school teacher in the village of Sodern, was preparing himself for a final act, the nature of which remained unforeseen by anyone who was close to him.

The fierce heat of that shimmering and, right from the start, intense summer has blurred my memory. The shadows of the past have obscured things; what I did and didn't see. A child will block impending pain before its onset, hiding it behind the 'thirteenth door', like in the fairytale. The child's parents will take care to lock that door, and keep the key at their bedside. The child in the other room may then sleep peacefully. Quite rightly, the child will eventually start asking questions, and begin to build up a picture from the answers. And quite rightly that picture will fill out with ever more detail and end up framed on the wall: an altarpiece of Virgin and Child shows who the martyrs, wrong-doers and victims are. Like the schoolbooks, the picture might offer some 'verdicts', which will cause that child's own children to speculate...

Each year we would suspend the Lord of the Cherries among the green foliage of early summer. We'd make his hands and feet out of rags and leather scraps, loop necklaces of tinkling milk-bottle tops over his straw head, fetch the black hat of some elderly relative from the cellar, and string the ugly creature up. Our Lord of the Cherries hung there in the breeze, the object of other kids' envy and jealousy: it was such brilliant fun. They'd call him 'Worzel' or 'Lump', but he was our God, beckoning to us from the cherry leaves. His wizened brown gaze heralded the start of June. When it rained he looked like a sad, bloated bag. In better weather, dried-out and lighter, he transformed in the breeze into a cheery peasant who could coax the very chirrups out of starlings. His fingers, made out of braided electrical cable, had grown as long as his whole form. We'd done that on purpose. Through him, we too had grown. In among the branches, we had become little gods ourselves. He was hanging there for us – we who were trying to follow in his image.

This all took place every year in the garden of Herr Barz the teacher, entirely on the initiative of us children. Barz's own plump, cheerful offspring were the stars, in this world of starlings and sticklebacks. They invited us in; they had open house, and their garden was our favourite place. Ten-year-old Hanne, whom I sat next to at school, and four-year-old little Karl, whose eyes converged to a point about twelve inches from the tip of his nose. The rest of us – we were sometimes five, but typically a foursome, usually me and our nearest neighbours Christina, Gerhard and Ralf – had no idea what was really going on. We'd be handed out spicy biscuits and apples, and didn't particularly wonder why it was only ever on birthdays that our own parents would invite the other children round and give them sweets. Barz the teacher, a silent, serious man, didn't really match his cheerful children. They took after their mother who was as plump and cheerful as they were. Their mother was the only person in the world who could look little Karl in both eyes. Her own eyes converged to the same point before her nose, hence when mother and son looked at each other at close range her eyes met little Karl's pupils. In such moments Karl would be very still, and his round eyes would begin to swim. His mother would dry them with the sleeve of her blouse, then move away, and Karl would be alone again and dependent on his right eye with which he saw the world, while the left eye remained dully half-closed, only having any purpose when under his mother's regard. Sometimes we tried to force little Karl's eyes to look into our own by holding either a stick or a finger vertically in front of our noses and squinting at him, but using this method we couldn't actually see Karl ourselves. When the time came for the Lord of the Cherries to be strung up, we took him along. He watched the procedure with wonder. Wooed by our teacher's cherries, we gave the Straw Man on high our devotion.

Our parents said nothing. But the teacher's family seemed to be excluded from any little social meet-ups. While they didn't try to make us stay away from the teacher's garden, they never sent us there, even though on Sundays they ideally liked a bit of slap and tickle after the midday roast and would bribe us with money for the movies or with apple pie (provided we stopped moaning and bickering) so that they could withdraw to the bedroom for a while and get on with it. We didn't disturb them. We would trail into the teacher's garden and sprawl below the fruit trees, whether they were just blossoming, or the fruit was ripening, or else was dangling, mature, among the leaves, or due to a frost was no longer to be had.

More than twenty years after that summer in Sodern, the locals began to speak up about having stayed silent, saying things hadn't been how they looked. That deep inside, those "cheerfully patriotic parents" of the past had always been bitter, and distanced from the state; that when they'd received awards from the hands of the district secretaries, their smiles had actually been for show only. The knot of the children's neckerchief by no means perfect – its slackness just cleverly hidden, that's all, through all those years of childhood. The apple round and red, but the sandwich tasteless. And Bartz the teacher, despite his taciturnity, was secretly respected. In 1956 he had come home from the Bautzen prison – a place that threatened them all, had they spoken freely. He'd been a serious man of few words, one of the city's sons whom the occupying forces had seized and interned ten years earlier for being a member of a Christian party which was not, at least at that time, deemed to be a friendly ally. Eight years after his disappearance, his elderly parents were notified that he was in Bautzen for spying for the American secret service. At this, they gathered up their courage and wrote letters of petition, which went unanswered. Meanwhile, our (only-pretending-to-be) "cheerfully patriotic parents" were chewing timidly on their tasteless sandwiches and adhering to a 'truth' that went only as far as the country's borders, then stopped. Barz the teacher, whose return was scheduled for a sunny day in May, was going to have to spend a further year doing unpaid work in a furniture factory before being allowed to work with a primary school class again. According to our parents he probably hadn't spied at all, otherwise he certainly wouldn't have been permitted to teach children. In the end Barz the teacher must have come to the view that what had happened to him was due to an error made in the heat of whatever the latest (and by no means last) fray had been.

Years later he was still thanking his plump, cheerful wife for taking him on after his belated return; even for agreeing to the wedding, which had been attended by only a few locals. His cross-eyed wife's plumpness was what he'd longed for on his terrible Bautzen nights. The teacher's plump, cheerful wife recounted this more than twenty years after that summer. She told it with sadness to Hanne and Karl, who suddenly recollected how their father, when he thought he was unobserved, would push their mother's pumpkin breasts apart with his head and try to clutch her backside. In the tenth year after Hanne was born, that summer in Sodern, teacher Barz, silent and serious, had become a quite normal, ordinary man who was able to sleep well again, and speak the way other people spoke. On his curriculum vitae, with which he applied to a high school that took pupils through to the school-leaving certificate, he wrote of "oversights" and "disorderly periods"; of his "own errors" and the "educational time in Bautzen" which had turned him into a committed supporter of the State System.

When I recall that summer in Sodern, Christina is missing from the picture. Gerhard and Ralf were there, with their perpetual grins, but Christina had gone to Hungary with her parents. Back in May she'd told us she wanted to bathe in Lake Balaton. When she returned, the event giving rise to this story was long past. Christina's return from Lake Balaton ended up taking some time: Czechoslovakia, which was between us and Hungary, had become a theatre of war where some sort of conflict was playing out. "Friendly" neighbouring countries had sent in tanks because, as we heard at our breakfast tables, "the Czechs are never satisfied" and "are a danger to us all".

Christina was forced to return via Ukraine and Poland since no tourist trains were running through a warring country; she was therefore missing from the little tableau we formed that morning, entering the garden near the beds which Hanne and little Karl thought their father would be weeding. He was nowhere to be seen. The holidays had started and we were intending to sprawl under the fruit trees and watch our Lord of the Cherries swaying in the breeze. Little Karl reached the tree first. Jabbing his plump finger up at the branches, he spoke just a single word. There. Barz the teacher was strung up, a mighty Lord of the Cherries among the foliage, his eyes wide open; to the future turned, as our country's national anthem ran. Meanwhile somewhere in Ukraine, Christina was travelling through history on a hard wooden bench. The cheerfully patriotic parents made us forget the whole thing, and these days, their verdict on how it all was has become set in stone.

Buttonholed

FOR HOW LONG, NOW, had these uniform green days been marching by? Reenie Schnitzel had completely lost track, by the time she undertook to 'buttonhole' one – pull it out of its rank and undo those gold buttons; those buffed-up, glinting buttons that made them all look so uniformly superior. She needn't feel particularly guilty about pulling one of the squad out of line and leading it astray: it was not she, after all, who had issued the command for the days to merge; to become a single monolithic army, goose-stepping past, monotonous and interminably green. At the end of the day, all she wanted (once she'd had her way with it) was to re-dress that day in slightly different clothes. Just a different colour, or something.

Reenie Schnitzel was sitting at her wooden table on a metal chair. Before her on the table was a yellow plastic pot of cold custard. Reenie Schnitzel knew more about plastic pots of custard than she did about uniforms. Indeed a whole army of custard-pots had taken up position in Reenie's refrigerator, only moving from their posts if Reenie herself moved them; as in, when she'd take one out, peel back its foil lid and put in a spoon (also plastic). Or when she'd pull a whole attachment of them off the supermarket shelf, place them in her trolley, marshal them to the checkout and, after due procedure, pile them into the boot of her car and take them on a tour of duty. This would always entail a short diversion: she never headed directly for their final destination (her fridge) without first having picked up a newspaper, a pack of cigarettes, and one of the many rather unusual key-rings they sold at the kiosk. Reenie Schnitzel had never felt threatened by ranked custard pots, whereas the uniformly green days were beginning to unsettle her. More and more, actually. So she decided, as the aforementioned pot of custard slid down into her tummy, to force the following day to desert. This needed to be well planned.

First of all, she'd have to get over her shyness about undoing buttons that weren't on her own clothing. In the late morning, Reenie Schnitzel chose a nice café with dim lighting and a table not far from the row of coat-hooks beside what was the café's only door. She ordered a Viennese coffee. Read the newspaper. Opened the cigarette packet. Fastened the house key, bicycle key, garage key, toilet key, mailbox key and car key onto a cute sheep whose rubbery belly you squeezed till its raspberry-sized silicone eyes popped out of its eye-sockets. She tried it out a few times. The instant you let go of the sheep's belly, itself the size of maybe five average raspberries, the eyes shot straight back inside. Reenie Schnitzel found this most amusing. The sheep key-fob was taking over from a dog one whose rubbery belly – also the size of five raspberries – you squeezed till a brown silicone turd amounting to about three raspberries came out of its anus. As soon as you let the dog's belly go, the emergent turd shot back in. Reenie Schnitzel wasn't sure she found turds quite so amusing. She placed the redundant dog beside the ashtray in the middle of the café table and dropped the sheep, six keys and all, into her handbag.

The pleasure of eating the thick cream on top completely absorbed her, but then, as she sipped the black, alcohol-laced coffee below, she remembered that this was not why she was here. But she wasn't making much headway in her quest for buttons that were not her own. Her gaze lingered on two adolescent girls dandling spoons in their ice-creams at a table further to the back. They were definitely bunking off school. Some school pennants hung from their elastic-waisted mini-skirts which fluttered in the draught wafting between café door and kitchen. Reenie Schnitzel was forty-five years old, and due (presumably) to the hand of fate, or something like that, had remained childless. She was remembering, though, how keen she herself had been to wear the pennant flags awarded for being an exemplary young communist, while her father had just as keenly forbidden it; also, how the utterance 'Half mast!' had been his command to lengthen her skirt by at least ten centimetres. Sometimes it had been possible to just let down the hem, but more often she'd had to match it up with a different fabric and add a piece on, which sadly stopped the skirt from having that nice flutter. Envy crept up Reenie Schnitzel's calves to the hem of her heavy blue pleated skirt. She was aware of its weight, the depressing reality of it, on her still shapely and supple knees.

The coffee was distinctly stewed. With the dog back in her hand where it was receiving a further knead, Reenie called the waitress over and ordered a bowl of raspberry ice-cream. At the very least, she'd succeeded in leading this day far enough off-track from the relentless march of the rest of the squad for it to come with her to the café! In her exuberance over this achievement, she leapt up as the waitress was teetering away and unbuttoned the back of her tight-fitting blouse from the neck down. She justified the attack by saying in horror that a wasp had just settled behind the waitress's left ear and then due to the woman's abrupt movement when she'd turned to go back to the counter had fallen down inside the neck of her blouse, where it was likely trapped above her waistband and possibly about to sting her around that area, which is known to be especially painful. While contending all this, Reenie Schnitzel was clawing deep inside the waitress's blouse, feeling around for the insect, then – at the waitress's own insistence – undoing her bra and sliding her hands all over the liver-spotted, acne-scarred lumpiness of her back. Eventually Reenie yelled out, cupped her hands and at top speed transported her supposed captive outside into the air. When she came back in, feigning breathlessness or else indeed breathless with astonishment at her own courage, the waitress had withdrawn behind the till where she was able to refasten her bra in a relatively calm manner. The waitress, too, was feeling astonished – both at the customer's determined intervention, and her own insistence that her bra be undone. This was something new to her; something quite out of the ordinary for a day like today, or indeed for any of Reenie Schnitzel's days either, which were ordinarily – or at least, the way they presented themselves to Reenie – as uniform as an army. Though the waitress couldn't know that.

Reenie Schnitzel sat down again at her table and grabbed the silicone sheep, squeezing its eyes out quite a few times before managing to collect herself and think about what to do next. It had been lovely to get as far as the waitress's underwear. For the moment, her shyness had returned, and she felt awkward when she again addressed the waitress, requesting a slightly less strong coffee and a little more of the cream. She also felt awkward about looking the waitress in the eye, though the latter was now waiting expectantly for this. An onlooker might well have got the impression that they were each waiting for the other to make the next move. Reenie Schnitzel persisted in gazing beyond, rather than at, this female stranger who, for her part, was watching for some sort of sign in Reenie Schnitzel's eyes, or a twitch of her mouth, or a signal from any other part of her. The dark blue skirt silently absorbed the drops Reenie Schnitzel spilled as she drank, while pulling itself even more tightly round her knees, as though to protect her virtue – a virtue which precisely three men had tried, but woefully failed, to claim. Suddenly, from some dark recess of Reenie Schnitzel's memory, it all surged back. Her memory of those men's faces was close to making her laugh. There was Harold, the computer whizz-kid she'd met when she herself was still in computers. Which had been more hideous – his ludicrously high forehead or his ludicrously small eyes? The noises – both oral and nasal – from the lower half of his face forced your attention away from the competition in hideousness going on in the upper half, so that there was never a moment of calm in which to make straightforward eye-contact. Reenie hadn't even tried, and, after half an unsuccessful evening with Harold, had unceremoniously left, which to this day she saw as Deliverance. The second had been Mr Tenderman, her boss at the supermarket where she'd been temping on the meat counter. Tenderman, with his sweaty attentions, ruddy cheeks, miserly ways and excessive excitement when a female victim landed in his net. Reenie nearly became one until, when he started fingering her, she had the idea of grabbing the meat tenderizer and – as perfectly befitted his marvellous name – tenderizing Tenderman's face. The next day she was out of a job. And the third attempt on her virtue has come from Knobson, her long-time neighbour, whose wife has recently run off and who recently asked Reenie for an evening's company, and recently came round to discuss condoms and show some to Reenie Schnitzel, which she recently very nearly succeeded in re-purposing (as she told him) for the administration of an enema. All this effort, to protect her virtue.

The laugh in Reenie Schnitzel's throat subsided, having been stifled by her plump fist. Her palms were now involved in a mutual massage, like two lovers… And suddenly, Reenie Schnitzel felt sheer joy at being offered this chance. The waitress at once saw the shine in her eyes, and needed no further sign. That look was her command: she jumped clean off the tracks along which her own days had been interminably chugging. Untying her apron she turned to Reenie Schnitzel, took her arm and, with utter disregard for the remaining customers, strode out of the café door, seeking the land of promise she had seen in Reenie's eyes. They walked quite a long way without speaking, Reenie kneading the silicone sheep with her left hand while her right one curled round that of the waitress, who wanted to go on gazing into her eyes (though this proved impracticable since Reenie stared at her toes when walking), until, without having planned it, they found themselves on Reenie's doorstep. She stopped short. The uniform green days came back to her; how she'd been intent on making one of them desert. To be achieving this with the help of a woman seemed quite incredible. She did, now, look into the eyes of the waitress, whose expression was dazed, her eyes hungry; hungering for the passion that was building in Reenie with every minute. Having entered the flat, Reenie, with an air of command, pulled from the fridge an entire attachment of yellow plastic custard-pots. The women, quivering, their appetites raging, pealed back row after row of lids, taking turns to drip the stuff into each other's mouths, kissing it from each other's cheeks, from each other's belly buttons; at first only removing their blouses, but then stripping off altogether. And Reenie realised that losing her virtue was going to be as light and effortless as the fluttering of those little skirts of old. At the peak of her orgasm, the days broke from their ranks, right before her eyes, and scattered. An army in defeat. Later on, when one of them –

dressed in the waitress's clothes – took a seat beside the two women (who were down on Reenie's kitchen floor having a smoke), a shiny gold button suddenly bounced across the floorboards.

Learnin' the blues

THE WORD 'CRUEL' IS MORE A WORD YOU WOULD USE OF WINTER, but that year Artyom, the children and I suffered a cruel summer that ended with us limping through autumn's gate like worn-out soldiers, hoping for some respite. Artyom had only started his new job in May, as a mathematician at the district co-generation power plant in Berlin Mitte; going on holiday was therefore out of the question. At one and a half, the twins were at the toddling stage and constantly wanted their hands holding. I only had two hands, I had no other option but to put them in the big playpen I'd set up a bit away from the pear tree in the back yard. I spent morning till night staggering between the baby-cage and my mother, endeavouring to feed or change the nappies of one or the other of them. My mother was seventy-two, exactly twice my age. If I spent time trying to draw her out, whether pointing to the sun dappling through the pear tree's foliage, or whatever, I'd have no resources left for my girls, and could only hope that having each other to play with was enough stimulation. Actually I called them my gremlins, though it bore no link to their real names, Chloe and Phoenix. When Artyom came home in the evening I would hand them over, exhausted. Artyom was what you would call a good father. He engaged with the girls, speaking to them now and then in Russian. Sometimes when they were around him they seemed already to be babbling in his language. At these times my mother would appear to return to her old self. She had been a Russian teacher, and often a light of recognition would pass over her face. I kept a camera to hand so that I could photograph her at one of these moments, with that light in her face, but each time, it was gone before I could press the button. Days of utter exhaustion.

"Sweetheart – have you baked the peach tart for tomorrow?" Artyom asked, this particular evening, in his relaxed manner; he'd readily do it himself if I hadn't managed it. But it was the very relaxedness of his tone that irritated me, making me retort with another question: "Did you bring home the potatoes and toilet paper?" He sprang up, setting the girls on his hips, and went into the hallway where he had cursorily dropped his bag and the shopping when he came in. As ever, faultless. Four-ply loo roll and baking potatoes. I fetched the peach tart out of the fridge and set it on the table before him. My mother grunted from the armchair. A gremlin started to cry. The other was whooping ecstatically for no apparent reason. Artyom evidently enjoyed the notion that this was a fully functioning family; at least that's what his broad grin seemed to suggest. The biscuit base was my speciality. I had spread peach slices on it, soaked the whole thing in a mixture of quark and gelatine, left it to cool, and finally coated the top with yellow jelly. Artyom happily put the kids to bed. I had enough to do every night with my mother who, when it was time for her, too, to go to bed, would lead me a merry dance.

Once she was asleep I took a very long shower. During which I didn't give Artyom a thought. In truth, I seldom thought about Artyom. Fact was, he had put a picket fence around my life, all safe and secure, with his good salary and his conscientious helping-out with the twins, but somehow I'd lost sight of this in the whirlpool of daily activities in which I spun, unable to get a foothold. Eventually I stood in front of the mirror with wet hair and scrutinised myself as I drew a dark lipstick over my lips and mascaraed my eyelashes. I looked just how my mother used to look. In making that observation, it came back to me how much she had loved dancing. At weekends she'd often go to the dancehall with my father. She had probably loved dancing even more than she loved my father. At this thought I was suddenly reminded of Artyom after all, and it felt out of the question to get into bed beside him without first having gone dancing. On warm September evenings you can leave your hair to dry naturally in the street. I pulled on jeans and a flowery top, seventies retro, and my lightest pumps, grabbed my gaudy little handbag and quietly closed the door.

The inky blackness of night was now setting in, usurping the dusk. For a moment I just stood there, enjoying how a September night can smell. In a daze, I put one foot in front of the other, wandering to Ehrlichstrasse, where I got on a tram. Two, three stops. Bar Havanna. I put my head round the door. Till three years ago I had spent all my spare evenings and all my spare money in this bar. Now I couldn't spot any friends any more among the young clientele who were probably, like me back then, still students, still single and looking for a partner. For the first time I had the distinct feeling of being old. Irked, I withdrew my head from the door, went up the steps into the metro station and headed off. Seated opposite me was a young man, glasses, medium-length hair; he was reading a book in English: *The Kite Runner* by Khaled Hosseini. In my bag I had the German version of the same book. I got it out and pointedly opened it. The man briefly glanced up, spotted my reading matter and smiled. Before he got off at Jannowitzbruecke, he looked at me with a distinct question in his eyes. I got off with him. Our books now being stashed in our bags, he took my hand. There was nothing to say. He was silent, like me. We walked south, down Brueckenstrasse, finally ending up in Kreuzberg. I pulled him into a bar, we drank beer, ate a hot-dog. Eventually I tugged at his sleeve; the bar's standard ambient background music had just turned into something you could dance to. The landlord turned it up louder when he saw we'd started smooching, there among the tables. We were so intimate with each other and yet at the same time, completely lost in our own thoughts; entwined, eyes closed, holding each other really close and swaying to the beat. *Learnin' the blues* by Katie Melua. God alone knew how this music-track had found its way into this bar. We only noticed how the other guests were staring at us when, at the end of the song, the landlord switched it off and we opened our eyes. Somewhere way behind, someone began to applaud. We paid, and found ourselves out in the street again, but it wasn't that easy to say goodbye. Something was standing open between us; not unfinished business as such, but definitely something that was stopping us from letting go of each other's hands. I knew I needed to have sex with him before I could bring myself to return home. His back felt taut, just like Artyom's taut frame right before he would let himself go. We interlocked in a doorway; it was an assured, forceful encounter. When a drunken woman arriving home late made the light go on, my jeans were already pulled back up. The muscles of his back felt relaxed now under his skinny-fit tee-shirt. I kissed him on the forehead. He picked his bag up from the ground and left. I chose the opposite direction.

The new day was two hours old when I got home. For a second time I took a long shower, then removed my mascara and lipstick with baby oil and got into bed beside Artyom. He moved his left thigh onto my belly and snuffled contentedly.

The next morning I sprung the peach tart out of the baking-tin and sliced it. Lastly I laid a circular tart-tin over it to protect it, chuffed I'd had this idea. Artyom came through to drink the coffee I'd made. He kissed me on the forehead just like I'd done to the young man the night before. It was doing me good, this knowing something that Artyom didn't know. I wished him a nice birthday celebration with his colleagues and gave him last night's book, *Der Drachenlaeufer* by Khaled Hosseini. He sandwiched the book between his papers in his bag, popped his head in on the girls in the living room one more time and left the flat. Once downstairs he placed the tart on the passenger seat. The gremlins were calling. As always, I had things to do.

Later, when I finally looked in on my mother, who usually woke up long before the girls, she was dead. Dr Heal, our local GP, said it was a heart attack. The staff of the funeral home packed my mother up in a grey nylon shroud and zipped it closed. I thought about how I'd seen her in the mirror the previous night. Even when they were carrying her downstairs I didn't feel like crying. To phone Artyom on his birthday didn't seem right. In the yard I knelt beside my children in the playpen and felt steady again. I wanted to sleep at long last, but the girls constantly brought me back round with their dolls, plastic cars and little sand-buckets. Later I picked two lovely fresh fallen pears out of the grass for Chloe and Phoenix, to cut up for them in the kitchen. My mother would always have been sitting right there on the little bench under the pear tree, lost inside herself. With her lying dead, I couldn't stomach the ripe pears.

In the evening Artyom and I ate the two left-over pieces of peach tart. He held me safe and secure in his arms. We talked about my mother.

Thirteen teachers – the staff who were still at her school –

attended the funeral, plus Artyom's siblings and his parents who hailed originally from Omsk in Siberia. His father would later nail two further small wooden batons onto the cross, positioned diagonally, as my mother had always wished. If you visit the graveyard today, there is an Orthodox cross on her grave. Luckily, till now nobody has noticed. Or at least no-one has ever asked questions.

Even after her death my mother continued to occupy the little bench. I couldn't sit on it and rest or read a book, and when the twins kept on staring in surprise at the empty bench each time they toddled out of the house into the yard, I knew they, too, could see my mother sitting there.

For Sale Idyllic Plot!
(subject to flooding)

WHEN MY GRANDMOTHER WAS TALKING TO HERSELF I'd just hear this whispering noise coming out of her old biddy's mouth in that old biddy way. I didn't love her, which was no wonder, given her splayed legs, the stubbly chin of her furrowed face, the way she smothered me with her pervasive smell. She'd do things like backing her behind into my ribs or pushing her rounded back against my drawn-up knees while I just sat there, or her muttering lips would dribble into the palms of my hands till mentally I was throwing my guts up. The internal retching would reduce me to a mush which she'd then gobble up with relish. Muttering 'bless my cherry' she'd stick her fingers in my mouth, trying to catch hold of my tongue, which repeatedly slithered away. It was always an effort, when she did that, not to actually vomit, which could have got me into bad trouble. My parents had always taught me to be nice to my grandmother; to love her, because that's how all people should be treated in their Old Age. In my grandmother's case, Old Age meant a state of advanced dementia. Unfortunately my grandmother's awareness of her own body made her interested in my female parts, which she called my honey-pot or cherry or muff, and which she sometimes tried to have a feel of. In her hand would be a slim crochet hook with which, when still in her right mind, she had crocheted many a lavender bag for our household. I was seven years old and was a sturdy child with chunky calves that Grandma took great pleasure in, leading as they did to similarly plump thighs which ended where Grandma's body had a particular affinity with mine. At midday, which was when I got home from school, Grandma would be lying quietly in her bed. It was my first year of school and I had picked up the habit of poking out the tip of my tongue while writing. I now had to watch out for my grandmother quietly getting out of bed behind my back and snapping at my tongue with her own mouth. But even when she did this I wasn't allowed to run away. I was supposed to go on loving her. It wasn't easy. My dim little parents had no clue what it was like, always having to be on the look-out to protect your tongue. In fact they were pretty clueless about everything. For example there was the time my attention was caught by a railway carriage that had been whitewashed and set on concrete foundations and made available to the German Red Cross. It was apparently a carriage dating from the Nazi regime, and I remember that they kept some things secret from the child I was then. I'd been called in for the MMR jab and was standing five metres from the actual syringe, wondering at the scragginess of the woman next to me's neck. Thick veins wormed down the backs of her hands, and having pondered on how the syringe might navigate one of these bulging canals, I announced I was *going under* (into a deep faint). My mother caught me and started doing something with my coat; it was unbuttoned, anyway, when I came to a few seconds later, my gullet wide open and gasping for air. It struck me that my dim little parents had no clue what it felt like to be called in for an MMR jab. An MMR jab, however, was still better than the quest for seven guarantors for the Idyllic Plot (subject to flooding) my grandmother went on and on about. It really must have been an idyllic plot, because my grandmother was attached to it like a withered apple that had been overlooked when the rest were picked and which still hung there stubbornly, winter after winter, right to this day. At some time she must have called the place home. What she always wanted to know was, how I'd managed to CROSS THE MUDFLATS when I'd fled. There was no point asking what 'the mudflats' was, what with the bless my cherry, the snapping at my tongue and everything else. She called me by my mother's name, but my mother, being so rarely at home, never heard this. It must have been idyllic indeed, this flooded plot, because my grandmother begged me with exaggerated enunciation to find seven guarantors so she could get the money for it. She said she would use the money to buy herself a little girl; one with a juicy cherry to bite into, a honey-pot to lick the honey out of, a muff as soft as velvet. She took the crochet hook, scraped some flaky skin from her greasy hairline, sucked it off and minced it between her toothless gums. I was constantly thwarted in my quest for the seven guarantors because my requirement wasn't taken seriously. There wasn't a single person willing to underwrite the Idyllic Plot (subject to flooding). When I told my grandmother, with whom I shared a bedroom, she was furious and put me over her knee. And spat. My hopeless parents hadn't the faintest clue about Grandma's Idyllic Plot (subject to flooding).

I was known for being bowlegged. At one point my mother took me to the orthopedic surgeon to try and remedy my condition. The surgeon stuck steel inner soles with leather wrap-arounds into my shoes and sent me and my mother to another doctor. He looked at my honey-pot, talked about bad blood and chronic boils, and cut out the lumps I'd had between my thighs for ages. I screamed, and walked home with my mother with my legs even more bowed than before. My mother had to go to work. It was my grandmother who took care of the house, and her mornings were now entirely taken up with me and the necessary cold compresses. Grandma dripped chamomile onto the incisions in my crotch. I was feeling a little bit of love for her, making a special effort, only throwing up internally, but my grandmother was anyway oblivious, and stuck her tongue in my belly-button. I was forced to giggle, and Grandma talked about how nice it would be once she'd bought the little girl with the velvet-soft muff. At this I announced I was about to *go under* (into a deep faint). She promptly bit me awake. Her mouth reeked of carbolic. My dim parents had no clue about the seven guarantors, and they finally sent me back to school, even though the boils continually grew back and would erupt all over again and stink. My grandmother's horrid spitting was so bad it was unbelievable. In town there was an old people's home. We should put Grandma in it, my father said to his wife one evening, but she threw up her hands, rejecting this outright. People would think this that and the other, wouldn't they. Thinking this that and the other wasn't, in my view, a bad thing; I was constantly thinking this that and the other in my endeavours to find the seven guarantors, a topic my dim little parents refused to hear about. While learning my very first letters I asked Barbara Kaltwasser if she'd be able to bring her six brothers and sisters over after school some time. Barbara Kaltwasser was a bit surprised as her brothers and sisters were little and noisy. Luckily for me they had become, in a sense, old beyond their years, due to her parents' plan to move them all to a foreign country – to Bielefeld, in the west. The final farewell was imminent, so for Barbara this was a welcome opportunity to escape from the stress of packing and closing down her life. For her, it was just a visit to a school friend. But I'd at last managed to find seven guarantors – Barbara Kaltwasser being the eldest. One Wednesday they all came crowding into the room I shared with my grandmother.

Barbara had brought me the blouse and blue neckerchief of her Young Pioneers uniform. It's not the fashion in Bielefeld, she said, and put the bag of things on the side-table. My grandmother checked Barbara's pockets to see if they contained the money she so urgently required for the little girl. I was slightly worried my grandmother might take a liking to Barbara and want to keep her. However her six brothers were making one hell of a rumpus around the room, so she couldn't possibly get bitten. I counted them for my grandmother. See: there are six of them plus Barbara, which makes seven. Exactly seven guarantors, Grandma, for your Idyllic Plot (subject to flooding)... It grew late and my grandmother dozed off, having not even acknowledged the presence of the seven guarantors. That night I told the whole story all over again to my dim parents who had no clue about anything, and my mother made a long phone call to Dr. Zeman, our paediatrician, who sent my mother and me to Dr. Krummhaar because he knew more about these things. Anaemic. I'm prescribing iron, was Dr. Krummhaar's verdict the next day to my mother, who was clueless. But I understood: every week I helped fold the clothes after my grandmother finished ironing them. I imagined how flat I'd become with this iron medicine, and almost felt a tiny bit pleased. On the way home I collected little pieces of green, red, blue and yellow glass. There were some jewelry and fancy goods retailers in the town who would give away any glassware that got smashed to people with allotments and gardens to decorate the paths between the beds and borders. The owners of these businesses were Dlouhy, Martinek, and Ribarsch & Effner, and they had come OVER FROM GABLONZ, as my grandmother would say. OVER FROM GABLONZ meant that these people had probably, like her, been forced to abandon an Idyllic Plot (subject to flooding), but once here had done very well for themselves over the years. When I showed Grandma the little pieces of glass she sat down on the bed, saying she was green with envy. OVER FROM GABLONZ and giving themselves all those airs and graces. And my Idyllic Plot still under water, oh deary dear. How *did* you manage to cross the mudflats, my girl? Grandma snapped at the tip of my tongue. Bless my cherry you cheeky little sod. The pieces of glass tumbled to the floor and my hands reacted by forcing back Grandma's head. I should be loving her, I hadn't forgotten this. My fists bored into her eye-sockets till she started crying and got away from me, shouting for the seven guarantors she required for her happiness. In my mind, my homework required the colourful glass as visual aid (we had to find out and write down what businesses there were in our town), so I picked up the pieces, bruised my grandmother's shin with a cruel kick, and ran into the garden, where I hid myself and my treasure behind the gooseberry bush. OVER FROM GABLONZ, my mad grandmother screamed from our bedroom. The windows were wide open. I called out goodnight, even though the clock tower was just bonging midday. My hand was by now bleeding, covered in cuts. I calmed down. When my dim little parents arrived home that afternoon I was still sitting there behind the gooseberry bush, where, in repose, I'd painstakingly written the names of the jewelry firms in my exercise book. Terrified of Grandma coming prowling through the garden in search of the seven guarantors, I couldn't tell at first that they were my parents' footsteps and not hers, and started screaming, a hoarse shriek emitted at full throttle. My dim mother heard it without reaction, whereas my father declared they should finally put Grandma in a home. My parents then found me, and my mother heated up some elderberry juice in the shiny silver saucepan that was always used as my morning milk-pan but turned completely black and blue with the elderberries. Elderberry will bring down your fever, sweetheart. My dim mother wiped the sweat from my brow, droplet by droplet, and said her heart fluttered whenever she thought of me, but as to understanding me she really hadn't a clue. Later on, it must have been that same month, we went on a nice outing to the nearby reservoir where I was due to learn how to swim. On seeing the deep waters into which my father was intending to throw me, I wanted to *go totally under* – into a deep faint – but luckily my grandmother was delving into my honey-pot on the back seat of the new car. Without this incident our nice outing would have been curtailed, because nothing upset my dim parents more than my black-outs, which they had more trouble coping with than anything else I did. My mother had herself come ACROSS THE MUDFLATS, I knew that much at least. She'd had to swim to leave the idyllic flooded plot, when she can't have been much older than I was now, standing fearfully beside the reservoir. My dim father was soft-soaping me before throwing me in. Grandma was trying to snatch my towel and was rubbing against me like a dog that I would never actually allow to be that friendly. Then suddenly she bit hard into my dim father's left calf. Shortly after which, I was to be looking at Grandma from close quarters for the very last time. She was lying on the ambulance's stretcher, her blood-stained mouth trying to kiss me. For once my dim mother wasn't quite so clueless, guarding me behind her as they put Grandma into the vehicle and took her to the clinic that she was never to be allowed out of and which I was not permitted to enter.

When my dim parents weren't there to notice, maybe because they were working late, or else picking berries from the gooseberry bush in our garden, I'd run off to the clinic. From the railings around the clinic's garden I'd sometimes see my grandmother standing at the window. She'd be waving to me, as if I were OVER FROM GABLONZ, or had come ACROSS THE MUDFLATS; or perhaps she wasn't waving to me at all but at the Idyllic Plot (subject to flooding), or at the seven guarantors who now lived in West Germany; or perhaps, there behind those windows, she had even found herself a little girl with a velvet-soft muff. I almost hoped she had.

Pulling the wool

IT NEARLY UNDID HER. Watching his toes emerge from the bottom end of the quilt, little by little, as she gradually pulled it up towards her felt like being unravelled. The further she pulled it up, the more sensitive his reaction – presumably to the chill wafting in. Even in winter she never had the heating on in their bedroom. The way the dark hairs on his legs went erect never failed to give her a slight, silent *frisson* of desire. Sadly she always had to get up much too quickly, while he slept on. The warmth of the bed held him captive, trapped in blissful, all-enveloping darkness, while she, due to her paper round, had to rise barely two hours after midnight.

With a sigh she switched the lamp back off so as not to wake him, brewed coffee in the little kitchen and had a slice of toast, spread with her favourite jam. Red jam. Sometimes, if he'd done the shopping, there was only yellow jam or plum jam. She then went hunting for a piece of cheese or a bit of left-over sausage, and if she succeeded in finding anything would eat it knowing she'd now have to go shopping again for their supper. Shopping was one of the most hated jobs she could think of – that feeling of exposure, when she put special offers or products that were especially cheap on the conveyor. There wasn't enough money for more, despite her newspaper deliveries, which she did with the family car. This job was why they hadn't got rid of the car, though she sometimes wondered if it was worth it since the job made her only slightly more money than the cost of running it. Her four children were by now 'out of the woods' in terms of all the initial expenses, as Herr Laurer the neighbour would blithely trot out, but 'the woods' had only meant dirty nappies and bed-wetting, whereas they couldn't be deeper 'in the woods', now that they all attended school, in view of the things that went on there. She'd told her youngest son there was no money to buy Yu-Gi-Oh cards. Though on that score she was glad, because in her view those cards were quite clearly damaging to children's brains – the way they got them then swapped them, only to get more and swap more, their fierce battles not stopping at deception and theft.

Finally, two hours after midnight, she put five breakfast plates on the table and the things that children and husband would need to start their day. They made their sandwiches themselves. If the sausage and cheese were all gone, as today, she'd quickly fry them some egg patties which would have cooled down by morning so they could be put between slices of bread. When she came back, after seven o'clock, she'd go back to bed and would sleep throughout the morning, getting up with thoughts of lunch around midday. When the children came home from school she'd try to be bright and gay with them. But didn't always manage it.

Today she came home dripping wet, having got totally drenched in the penetrating rain, even on the short sprints between car and mailbox. Hoping to ward off the cold which was already beginning to announce itself with shivers and a runny nose, she took a hot bath, after which, to wrap up warmly, she grabbed one of the three or four knitted sweaters she owned but would ordinarily avoid like the plague. She quite simply detested them. They made her itch, even through the blouses she made a point of wearing underneath. Even when her mother gave her the wool to approve before knitting the thing, and she rubbed it on her neck to try it out, the resulting item was always itchy. *Snuggly!* – she'd say, on receipt of these gifts. She alone knew what she really meant by that. She had secretly given the sweaters to friends, keeping just a couple, which she'd only wear if her mother came over. Due to this guilty conscience she kept her wardrobe firmly locked, usually keeping the key on her in her trouser pocket. Her mother had even passed on her knitting machine, a monster of a thing that for a long time had been residing, ignored, half-hidden in the gap between the wardrobe and the wall. Her mother had given up machine-knitting when her eyesight failed and it became too much effort to wind the thread around the hooks for casting on. This had turned her into an even more enthusiastic hand-knitter. The children were actually delighted by this: they'd sometimes even commission a particular design. Hadn't their youngest boy just asked Grandma for a Yu-Gi-Oh sweater, in fact? Which Grandma would knit – try stopping her! She smiled. She had put on a long-sleeved angora base-layer under the chosen batwing sweater. Glancing in the mirror she saw a pink, fluffy kite.

Sifting through the advertising leaflets she'd taken from the mailbox downstairs she came across a small red flyer. A scrap merchant was collecting in the area. When she saw the date was today, she thought of the old machine. She got it out. The accessories were stowed in a box on top of the cupboard: an assortment of weights, combs and 'transfer tools'. On a smaller box she read the words *intarsia carriage* which, when she opened it, contained something unidentifiable. But she liked the words. Images of a carriage inlaid with tiles came to her: images of ornamentally carved wooden doors, with exquisite mosaics decorating the internal sides and roof. For a moment she smiled. She had finished separating the scrap-metal machine parts from the plastic components that she would dispose of following the recycling instructions, when the absent-minded act of sliding her fingers across the many tiny needle-hooks suddenly triggered the astonishing thought: she had never ever knitted anything in her entire life. At the very bottom of the wardrobe, below the skirts and trousers hung neatly on the rod, was a stash of machine knitting yarn. Looking through the box she found a perfectly acceptable red, and hunted for the instruction booklet she'd already set aside for paper recycling. It took two and a half hours to assemble the twin-bedded knitting machine with its every bell and whistle, and when she was done she fell asleep, worn out.

The children came home from school. No lunch was waiting for them and after a wary look into the parental bedroom, they took things into their own hands and cooked pasta, the supply of which was always plentiful. They ate it with butter and Maggi sauce, which would have prompted a rant from their mother about the importance of a wholesome diet with vitamins and protein and which would probably have ended with the food being forbidden. So they were happy. To celebrate the day they got themselves ice-creams from the freezer too, and if the youngest had been more careful and hadn't slipped over on the tiles as he closed the freezer door, or had been able to hold back his yells, she might not even have emerged from her den till suppertime. But suddenly she was standing in their midst, her eyes heavy with sleep. *Dumpling eyes*, as her husband called them. The little boy immediately stopped howling and looked delighted to see her, pushing his head into her lap. 'All better', she said. She sat down and took a plate of pasta, adding ketchup. It had cooled down too much, anyway, for butter and Maggi, though she had entertained the thought, today, of quite simply joining in with the children's pleasures. The fact was, she too was happy: the children had cooked for themselves, letting her sleep. Their chatter was riotous. Too much effort to join in. So she just quietly watched her thoughts which, like little white mice, latched onto the curtains, scurried up to the pelmet, waved her goodbye and headed out through the open window. A lovely, cold day, in which peace prevailed. Her mother had given them the little house in the middle of a former colony of allotments when she herself moved into a small new-built flat with a kitchenette and communal heating system. Because the dimensions of the allotments went far beyond the prescribed allotment size, it had been declared a 'development area', and new houses had been conjured up out of the clay all around their little old house. Luckily they had had the heating replaced while they were both still breadwinners. But a further ten years had gone by since then, here in this outlying area of Berlin. The windows were all warped and leaky and needed replacing. The outside walls, grey and crumbling against today's blue sky, were still un-insulated, and the garden fence dated from the early years of the previous century. It was actually a beautiful wire fence with fine trellis-work and an entrance that curved in a great arch above all who came through it. But this too required major repairs, needing patching in many places, and in some cases replacement of the posts that supported the trellis. She felt perfectly capable of this task: even the job of mixing concrete was not new to her. But with sleeping through the mornings, and seeing to the children in the afternoons, there was little time for it. She sighed, watching her thoughts as they scurried back in through the window. But they didn't stop with the children, running instead in a herd right out of the kitchen, across the hall and into the bedroom, where the knitting machine was all set up. She had to admit, that old table was of some use now after all. Her husband had wanted to chop it up many a time. After sending the kids to do their homework she went and consulted the instructions on how to get the monster going. After some time, the first rows were knitted – with varying tensions, since she had adjusted it a few times, trying it out. She was amazed. The red yarn had turned itself into an astonishing two-dimensional item. The uneven sizes of the holes between stitches made you want to peep through them. She finished by turning the knob to the position that promised the tightest knit, and began to work with the transfer tools, weaving a little jacquard pattern right across the width of it, trying out a right-to-left design. By the end she'd knitted a piece that measured almost three metres long and eighty centimetres wide. But she hadn't done the shopping... She made semolina pudding using two cartons of long-life milk, placing sugar and cinnamon alongside it on the table plus some homemade apple sauce.

Her husband came home over-tired. He worked as a rep for a small Westphalian manufacturer of men's and women's orthopaedic footwear and travelled all over East Germany selling his wares. Today all he'd had to do was drive to Cottbus, taking in some small shoe-shops in the towns and cities along the way. He didn't get enough sleep. Even when he'd bounced into the Volvo (a company car) in the morning, he'd invariably come home jaded. He too was now in his late forties. Perhaps age was already taking its toll? This didn't diminish her sexual desire for him, and he, in turn, normally couldn't resist her familiar charms when he felt her bare breasts on his back or her buttocks in his lap. It's good with him, she reflected, taking another plate from the cupboard. The two litres were just enough. She herself only took one or two spoonfuls.

Next on the menu was a game of Yahtzee. Playing this game

with six people required some forbearance but the children stuck with it enthusiastically. When at last their kids stood in rank and file before them, washed and with their teeth brushed, saying goodnight, they were both, as ever, completely overwhelmed by parental emotion: the mother proud; the father feeling so humbled he actually dabbed a tear from his eye. And when the kids were in bed, he said how much he loved her, and they kissed and rolled on the floor, incapable of getting up until they were (for the time being) done.

The room was dark by now, and when he stood up he cracked his head on the carriage-rest of the knitting machine and swore, but she just laughed over the egg that swelled up, and fetched the steel knife-sharpener from the kitchen because it felt sufficiently chilled to use as a compress. When, a little later, they went to bed, he opened a bottle of white wine and they had a drink. By the time they were done with their second round of sex it was after midnight. Swearing herself now at the thought of having to get up in two hours, she lay on her side and, with her feet tucked between his legs, fell asleep.

The alarm rudely awoke her from brief, racing dreams, the episodes succeeding each other at such high speed that on waking she couldn't recall them. Before she was fully alert he had kissed her, and as she pulled the quilt up little by little to watch the hairs on his legs go erect, it came to her: she could 'undo him' in wool! She imagined a onesie knitted in soft red wool, in a loose, loopy jacquard pattern, with two little strands of wool right at the bottom that could be pulled to unravel him! The fantasy of the ensuing ball of wool growing ever larger made her feel momentarily rather dizzy: for a minute she had to sit on the edge of the bed with singing in her ears. But she then leapt up and started on her day's work, which was now to take such a very different turn: no sooner had she delivered the newspapers than she was sitting at the knitting machine. It wasn't easy to get to grips with the techniques of increasing and decreasing, and it took a whole week to learn to do circular knitting. But then she cheerfully got on with it, starting at the top and knitting a tube. At what she guessed was the right point, she divided this into two tubes, subtly tapering them according to the shape his legs had in her imagination when he wasn't there to look at, then closing them up at the foot. She hadn't worked a gusset into it. At the shoulders she sewed on four hand-crocheted tapes that could be tied closed. After the unravelling, they'd be all that was left. She was now really excited about his birthday.

Since it fell on a Sunday the children had made him his breakfast. Bacon and eggs, red and yellow jams, plum preserve and honey – they must have pooled their pocket money – and even a bottle of sparkling wine in the fridge. They waited for their mother, who would be home from her job around nine in the morning today, then brewed the coffee right on time and sat in front of the television. She had nothing to give him other than the red onesie, but didn't dare for him to unwrap it in front of the children and, when she got home, kept the parcel back, giving him a meaningful look. He understood. After a long and plentiful breakfast as a family, they sent the foursome off to the matinée as their Sunday treat. When he unpacked the parcel he was dumbfounded, incredulous, but she was smiling, and since he was still in his bathrobe she put him straight into the onesie, tying the tapes on his shoulders. He looked down at himself, speechless with dismay. Spotting himself in the mirror on the wardrobe door he was transfixed. With a gesture of command, she ordered him to lie down, then started by loosening the strand of wool at the tip of his left foot – the first act of undoing. Slowly, very slowly, one by one, the rows unravelled. It was exactly as she'd imagined it: her sexual desire increased unstoppably with the size of the ball of wool in her hands. For the right leg she started a new ball. Two further pauses in her mounting desire were due to arriving at the torso, when she started a ball from nothing again. And now, as the knitting dissolved, so too did his initial feeling of dismay. As he watched her hands roll the balls he was having more and more fun; indeed some little way from the balls in her hands he could feel something else going on. It was almost like a little snake was darting its tongue at his calves, his thighs; as if, as he lay before her entirely at her mercy, the flames of some hastily-gathered and lit kindling were licking round his buttocks, belly and chest. And when, in this extreme state of pent-up tension, she finally, silently put down the wool, something inside him erupted. He grabbed a ball and slowly began to wind the wool around her body. She stood up, letting her legs be wound round individually, while her arms got bound tightly to her sides. By the end her head looked like a mummy's, bound in a red husk. She closed her eyes and, with no option of moving further than onto their bed, waited, feverish. And at last felt him. Sharp. In the moment before the climax, which they approached in unison, it was as though they were being swirled into each other like two active chemicals that were going to ignite and shoot to a new high – and in that instant she got hooked, in her mind's eye, into the up-down, up-down of the little needles in the rope-lock until all her senses were subsumed, in its rapping, rhythmic judder…

Frau Bestov and Herr Luck

Frau Bestov was carrying a moulinette — a gadget for chopping fruit and vegetables — when she spotted the newspaper fluttering gently in the refuse bin just in front of her. It bore today's date. Frau Bestov could see this clearly because her distance glasses were on her nose as she walked by. She looked around furtively and, seeing there was no-one nearby who might take exception to her act of purloining a used newspaper out of a public bin, she went ahead, stashing it one-handedly into her shoulder bag, the other hand being taken up with the moulinette. The saleswoman had tied a string around the cardboard box containing the moulinette and knotted it in a loop, which Frau Bestov now had around her wrist. She loved to shop at Mayer's Hardware and Fancy Goods store. The way they tied string around your boxed-up purchases, just like the old days, made a wave of special memories wash over her and ripple out in circles from the middle of the shop where she'd be standing, and she'd see the goods all around her lift ever so slightly on the swell, then come back down to rest. She'd get waves of goosebumps too, seeing herself in Mayer's with her mother, standing at the counter. That would be fifty years ago now: her mother finally taking home a cardboard box containing a moulinette for which she'd been saving up for ages. Last week, more than twenty years after her mother's death, the moulinette had fallen apart altogether. A crack had developed, making the gadget unusable, hence her purchase of this new one. She too had had to save up for a while, because it was a proper Moulinex made of stainless steel, not just a cheap thing on which the first spots of rust would appear after the first half-dozen rinses.

She no longer sunscribed to a daily newspaper since being out of work, which she suspected would go on being the case until her pension kicked in. But that was at least seven or eight long years away, so sometimes when a newspaper showed up in a refuse bin, she'd snatch it out and have herself a nice little coffee break. The timing of these occasions would always be between five and six pm. She had given up coffee, in fact, after calculating exactly how much she'd been spending on her two morning cups. Blood pressure was a good enough reason to change this habit (though she had no idea how hers was actually doing since she so rarely went to the doctor). But if the day had gifted her a newspaper, complete with puzzle page, entertainments section and political commentary (which she also very conscientiously read), it was an enormous pleasure to treat herself to two large cups of coffee in the late afternoon.

Early this morning she had already boiled potatoes and steamed a bunch of greens for soup, all the while looking forward to trying out the moulinette. She ended up making a wonderful potato soup, with salt and Maggi seasoning added for taste. To mark the special occasion, she opened a carton of long-life whipped cream and stirred it in. The coffee was brewed using the old Melitta filter her mother had once received from her sister across the border in West Germany. The flower-patterned soup plate and the coffee pot now arrived on the placemat on the table. She reached over and poured some coffee, savouring the aroma, further deferring the moment of gratification, and she opened and laid out the newspaper before either a first spoonful or first sip. Then revelled in the multiple delights.

On page one, surprisingly, the American war in Iraq was being criticised. Frau Bestov would have expected such commentary only on page two or three. Where it belonged. When she let her thoughts run away with her, she could imagine herself in a city like Fallujah: having to get by as an elderly spinster, and yet giving out food to women and children. Potato soup, made with the new moulinette. Or sausages served hot with mustard. Since her television had broken down and she had postponed its repair month after month because of other (mostly unforeseen) expenses, she was lacking in mental pictures of foreign cities. She accepted as real what her mind conjured up, and if, as today, a photo in the newspaper served to introduce a bit of authentic reality, she would from then on visualise herself wandering around in the scenes shown. Till a newer photo in a further newspaper provided a replacement. Her teacher had always called her *a good soul* because she had brought in her brother's hand-me-down trousers for Gunter Goatherd and had bought an ice cream with her own saved-up pocket money for Lutz Muller, who had seven brothers and sisters. Now, once again, she could feel proud of herself: a bringer of salvation to Fallujah.

She took a spoonful of soup. Her mother used to say *to eat is a treat*, but that wasn't exactly correct, because as Frau Bestov gradually became full during a meal, the "treat"-feeling would leave her, or turn, rather, into a quiet, replete satisfaction. Indeed there was sometimes no room for the final spoonfuls, the last bit thus ending up back in the pan for the next day. Today, however, she managed to finish off her little bowlful. Finally she got to the second cup of coffee, and skimmed through the sports pages — the only ones that didn't really capture her interest. Unless they'd printed a proper feature on women's rhythmic gymnastics. But this rarely happened, because this country had hardly any rhythmic gymnasts left, and major international championships only took place twice a year. It was most unlikely she'd manage to get hold of a newspaper covering such an event any time soon. When Frau Bestov came to the marriage adverts, as her mother had always called them, she was intending to pass over them with the usual prudishness and dismissive sniff, but her eye was caught unexpectedly by a black-framed ad with an emboldened first word: **Stop!** And she actually stopped, and read on: *Herr Luck, 55, nicely built, Vietnamese, seeks partner of similar age. Eventual marriage not ruled out.* A strange disquiet took hold of Frau Bestov, who had never thought of marriage in her life. Not even when Burkhart had been after her and had almost managed to get her to go dancing with him. When the day was almost upon them, she'd gone down with severe nausea, so Burkhart had had to go alone — and the next day he paraded in front of her with the girl he'd met there. She had looked at him with entirely neutral interest, and been taken aback by the contempt in his eyes.

* * *

Herr Luck. Vietnamese. She suddenly saw herself in Ho Chi Minh City. She actually had a clear picture of this because in former times, when it was still called Saigon, she'd seen a film about its seizure by the North Vietnamese that had stuck with her, firmly imprinted in her memory. Herr Luck was gripping her arm and pulling her along with him, and they were now disappearing down a narrow alley. His hands were over her eyes; she wasn't allowed to look until they arrived at his parents' house. A little old lady, dragging her right leg behind her, came out of the house to greet them and wept, so moved was she to see her German daughter-in-law. She called out for her husband who'd been sitting behind a screen, apparently playing a board game with another old man, and the two old folks bowed to Frau Bestov countless times. A little later, having set up a small table outdoors beneath the house's awning, they served tea, of which Frau Bestov partook. With the first imagined sip, she returned from her flight of fancy, no longer noticing the taste of the coffee she still held in her hand. She put down the cup, fetched a sheet of her good, rarely used writing paper and an elegant envelope — the kind with a tissue lining — and began writing to Herr Luck. Yes, she was the same age, and no, she didn't mind whether or not he was "nicely built." She was suddenly struck that she had no children and therefore, of course, no grandchildren — something that had gone quietly unnoted in her conscious mind all these years. Even now, what struck her was her surprising relaxedness about it and lack of regret. She was completely and utterly freestanding. And freesitting and free-lying-down, too, for that matter. There had been few people in her life with whom she'd had regular dealings other than former colleagues (who'd nearly all been laid off by the savings bank, since almost none had the certificates in bookkeeping they were required to have since Reunification). Frau Mayer from the hardware and fancy goods shop was one of her few contacts, the still-youngish wife of the grandson of the Frau Mayer who had actually served her mother fifty years ago. She went to her once a week to browse the shop's very frequently rearranged displays and have a chat. They both had time for this because not many people strayed into the small premises. The fact that she had bought a moulinette today counted as an extraordinary event in her ordinary life, and now the letter another. She signed the sheet very cordially — *sincerely yours, Frau Bestov,* folded it in three with the help of a ruler, tucked it into the already addressed envelope, and stuck on a red stamp. She always kept just one of these in the house. No reason to have more in. After dropping the letter into the box in front of the post office she did the third extraordinary thing of the day: she went to the Bayerischer Hof bar at the top of the market square and allowed herself an advocaat.

From then on, she waited, thinking *you never know* and keeping the newspaper to hand on the side table next to her favourite armchair.

Her thoughts now wandered less often around Fallujah or Baghdad, but rather sauntered through Ho Chi Minh City and Hanoi, Hue and Da Nang, stopping in small fishing villages on the Mekong Delta and searching in the mountains for members of the Hmong minority, about whom she had once read when she was still getting her newspaper. A reply from Herr Luck was not forthcoming. Nonetheless his features slowly became clear; she recognised him each morning as the elderly gentleman of whom she had taken her leave shortly before falling asleep the night before. As she went about her daily cleaning, cooking and knitting, he'd every so often put in an appearance, whereas whenever she went out to stretch her legs, he was constantly by her side and they would talk. This gave rise to some sniggering behind her back, if not outright laughter, among the people Frau Bestov encountered during the day. Once, when the head of the local Association for Solidarity with Citizens in Need crossed her path, the latter stopped short, took out her notebook and wrote down *Frau Bestov — senile?*, aiming to check this out in the near future with the help of the local GP. But with each day of Herr Luck's companionship, Frau Bestov gained ever more self-assurance and dignity. Her formerly hunched shoulders had risen, making her stand two and a half centimetres taller, and her stride was longer and more purposeful. She didn't look at the ground as she walked, but held her head up high, repeatedly turning it to attend to Herr Luck walking beside her. Herr Luck, moreover, was becoming more handsome and distinguished with each day. Almost as tall as Frau Bestov, his legs were impressively muscular, and his hair, which had initially been short and grey, had grown into a real mane that was now coal black. A handsome couple.

It was the end of the third month since posting the letter, and Frau Bestov had just ensconced herself behind a pot of tea, when the doorbell rang. She was so shocked that she froze, momentarily, on the *Celebrity News* page, barely registering the picture of Maxie Popdoodie who had remarried and wanted to step out of the spotlight for a while. Frau Bestov, who knew nothing of being in the spotlight, was so dazzled by the word itself that when the doorbell rang a second time, Maxie's face dissolved in its blinding glare. At last Frau Bestov was able to overcome her terror and hurried to the door. Yanking it open, she froze once more. Standing there on the landing, all smiles, was a little grey-haired Vietnamese man. Shyly, modestly, he moved to extend his right hand in greeting, while his left one (from the wrist of which dangled a small bag) was clutching a bouquet of red roses. Frau Bestov, similarly, moved to put out her right hand. They both smiled. She accepted the flowers and led him into the hallway, inviting him to take off his shoes and put on a pair of slippers which she had organised for this purpose several weeks ago. She couldn't find a vase, since her mother — whose house and home she had inherited — hadn't ever owned one. Instead, an empty pickle jar had to be used to display the beautiful long-stemmed red blooms. Herr Luck seemed so familiar to her that she wasn't afraid to take him by the shoulder and lead him into the living room, where they sank down into the two heavy old armchairs opposite each other. For a moment Frau Bestov was tempted to continue their conversation of earlier that morning. But Herr Luck couldn't speak German well enough to take part in it. When she noticed this, she slapped her forehead in the instantaneous realisation of this basic fact, then began, in very simple sentences, to ask him about his life. She quickly found out he ran a snack bar in the nearest big town, had come here long ago as the supervisor of a whole gang of young female laundry workers from Vietnam, and had only been able to stay because he had faced off all opposition and married a German woman. When Frau Bestov inquired as to her present whereabouts, Herr Luck's eyes fluttered like startled sparrows, uncomprehending, but she repeated the question slowly and clearly, and the sparrows settled: she left, *gone away*, he said, so he must now look for a new woman. He liked her very much, *yes! yes!* He was nodding emphatically while appearing to cower, as if expecting a blow; and sure enough, in the sudden giddiness brought on by all the embarrassment, Frau Bestov — affecting a cough — reached for the three-month-old newspaper, rolled it up and, with a flirtatious giggle, coquettishly dealt him a whack. Herr Luck's face appeared to be searching for an expression, then slowly, a smile broadened and spread from ear to ear, and finally he threw his head back, over and over, each roar of laughter emerging from deep inside and abruptly exploding. Only after many such eruptions did they manage to calm themselves down.

When Frau Bestov turned her thoughts to her fridge, her feeling of well-being instantly evaporated. She could only bring to mind a small remnant of processed cheese, a half-used pack of Cervelat sausage, and two crumbling, sorry slices of pumpernickel languishing in there. Oh no! She didn't want to make this kind of impression on Herr Luck, not with him being the owner of a fast-food outlet. Cosy dinner scenarios swam in her brain. But Herr Luck, as if he'd seen this coming, pulled out two packets of Asian noodles from his really very tiny bag, along with a little bag of fresh diced vegetables. He quickly made up the noodles in boiling water and fried the vegetables in Frau Bestov's ancient cast-iron pan. A few drops of Maggi sufficed for soy sauce, and when he'd tossed it all together, the aroma within Frau Bestov's old and fusty four walls was so unimaginably delicious that there was no stopping her. She fell on the food with ardour, taking way more than her share until she was holding her tummy. This only made Herr Luck nod in hearty approval.

*   *   *

The finale is quickly told: they liked the double-barrelled name Bestov-Luck so much that within six months they were married. Herr Luck moved into Frau Bestov's flat and devoted the little spare time he had to making her comfortable. To this end he brought home a wall-hanging from the Asian market in town, along with a few artificial potted plants. Right at the outset he had painted the whole flat in gentle pastel hues. Frau Bestov was pleased that her ancient accommodation up in the attic of the building was now more adequately furnished. The two rooms had always been a little too big to heat them both in winter just for herself; further, the fact that she could ask for a helping hand from someone who earned his living with his hands made her joy complete. In the early morning they both commuted into town, where Herr Luck was delighted by Frau

Bestov's cleaning talents, as it meant he no longer needed to fear a hygiene inspection. In the evenings he brought home whatever dishes she wanted. Very rarely, at Christmas or other holiday times, she brought out the moulinette for a beautiful potato soup which they would both thoroughly enjoy. But what she was to celebrate each and every day, right from the very start, was coffee time with the regional newspaper, which Herr Luck had given her as a gift. He had started the subscription for her fifty-sixth birthday, so that when she left the town at noon (while he himself had to stay on into the evening) he knew she was taken care of and had something to keep her busy. She would cut things out, sort and file them, laying out on the table anything she thought was either important, funny, or just worth showing him, and would then present him with a daily press review — whereby he gradually learned more German, because of course she was helping him learn to read.

As for the small ad that had once caught and anchored her randomly wandering eye with its black outline and the emboldened word **Stop!** and ensuing three lines, she glued a border onto it then inserted it into a little pine frame that she kept in her bedside drawer. And every night, before falling asleep, she would clutch this to her heart. The glass in the frame would be cold, and only when that was no longer the case — when she had warmed it through — would she remove it from her bosom and stick it back in the drawer. She had written the ad's publication date on it in red pen. When she considered how many daily papers had fluttered by her since the start of her wretched unemployment, her soul rejoiced that, of all days, she had walked past the refuse bin in front of the post office with her new moulinette on that particular day.

The whiner in the diner

ONE MONDAY IN MAY A THUNDERSTORM TOOK ME BY SURPRISE. My black brolly activated itself, shooting up into the air. The storm came raging in, jolting me out of my thoughts so that suddenly I no longer even knew what I'd been thinking about. Instead I was struggling with the umbrella, trying to close it. The rain was driving between my hood and my hair. Having managed with some effort to stuff the thing in my rucksack I was just getting my bearings again, wearily casting my eyes around, when I saw them: two pillars, stomping along. And an instant later, a body, then a face. They were the legs of Sophie Klomp. The ankles hardly any different in circumference from the calves. As in, barely recognizeable as ankles. *Nomen est omen* came to mind. It's all in the name. I had seen Sophie Klomp every day, but never her legs. She always wore maxi-skirts, and in a flash it now came to me what her legs had been up to under there. Hiding, that's what.

I grinned.

She grinned back.

We chatted. About the weather, the state of the roads, motorists, the long walk to the bus stop. This all took some time, during which we started walking. Reaching the stop, we couldn't think what to say. I took a surreptitious sideways look at Sophie Klomp, which, due to my hood, went unnoticed. I was really impressed. What a lovely-looking woman. The rain had tamed her grey unkempt curls, and thankfully she wasn't made up. Since those gusts of wind, the maxi-skirt had now settled back down to ground level. She was of slender form. Petite was the word. I had in fact always clocked her as 'petite'. But now that I'd seen her legs I felt I knew her better. Having arrived at the bus stop we were silent. I knew where she was heading, and she knew I knew.

I sat next to her on the bus. Catching the smell of her triggered an urge for a cigarette. At such close quarters she would surely get a whiff of my own smell. Engine oil.

I had been working since the mid-1990s in the garage that was part of the Ridbacher Street petrol station. My doctor had called me in that day, which is why my commute was delayed till noon. My neighbour Sophie Klomp was heading for the same place. Not the garage but the diner that's also part of the petrol station. She had her midday meal there. Every day.

When we arrived I wished her a nice lunch and we went our separate ways.

I'm certain our acquaintance would have continued in this desultory way if I hadn't seen her legs. From that time on they haunted me. Many a bakery's floor-tiles must be set a-tremble, I mused. As well as that slender footbridge that connects the hospital campus across the river Wuhle with the surrounding area. And the parquet floor of the auditorium at 'The Box' – the little club to which I'd like to take Sophie Klomp some time. Every time I turned round, though, to see who was causing a tremor, it would turn out to be a heavy man. At which I'd usually let out a sigh. I'd imagine how, and where, her legs ended. No storm in the world could have dragged my thoughts away from these images although I'd often have preferred them to disappear.

I opened my own dossier on Sophie Klomp. To this end I asked Frau Trollop round for a cuppa. Frau Trollop lived above me. On the day of the formal opening of this block of flats, she was the first person to move in. That was more than twenty years ago. Frau Trollop was my age; as in, just into her fifties. She wore her peroxide blond hair in the sort of bun which, thinking about it, would have been just the thing in her mother's generation. Leastways my own mother had done her hair like that in the 'sixties, though not dyed blond – that wouldn't have conformed to her idea of the 'natural' look – but back-combed with the same vigour. Frau Trollop perched herself on my sofa in her much-too-skimpy skirt and waited. I poured her tea and, more importantly, added a plentiful shot of rum. We blethered for three or four cups before I mentioned, as if quite randomly, Sophie Klomp. Unnervingly Trollop hunched closer to me, and told of how Sophie had previously been married to a Herr Klomp, who'd seemingly blown in on the wind. One sunny summer morning back in the mid 'eighties, he'd been lying fast asleep in the doorway of Sophie's flat. Black leather jacket, dark beard, old-fashioned canvas holdall, no shoes. She herself had been the first to see him and rang the doorbell to get Sophie, who'd come to the door all sleepy. Between them they'd given him a 'right good flannelling down' in the flat (the turn of phrase allowed me to hazard a guess at where Frau Trollop hailed from – probably today's Saxony Anhalt.) Well, what had gone on after that she couldn't say, but anyway about three weeks later Sophie and Herr Klomp got wed. She'd found it really odd because Sophie was a graduate, a strict type, an expert in Art who worked at the Bode Museum, and before that at the Museum of Prints and Drawings in Dresden. Always modest; always in those floor-length skirts, hair scraped back. It was so unconventional, all done without guests or ta ra, just like that, one Wednesday in May (she knew it'd been a Wednesday because her children who lived with their father would come on Wednesdays). The pair of them had just rung her doorbell giggling like teenagers and announced they were Sophie and Peter Klomp. Then three weeks later, Klomp disappeared.

Blimey! What a story!

I got rid of Trollop quicker than she was expecting and for the rest of the evening sat in my armchair. Outside, the traffic tailed off. It got quieter. The headlights which at the start of the evening had been strobing the living room in quick succession were now only occasional. I went to bed late: I'd been unable to just keep to the rum, and had drunk half a bottle of red wine on top. Obviously in my fantasies Sophie Klomp had drunk the other half, so first thing next morning saw me frowning like an idiot at the still half-full bottle.

In the following weeks I took every opportunity to find out all I could about her. The neighbours were surprised by my sudden talkativeness, which didn't fit with their image of me (nor indeed with my own of myself). I learned from old man Weidler that after Sophie's husband had disappeared she'd had a miscarriage. He'd got that from his wife who was a nurse at the hospital back then. Herr Kormann talked about the unemployment she'd brought down on her own head because, after Reunification, she'd used her savings to criss-cross the whole of the reunited Germany looking for her husband. She'd resigned from her job, having no idea of course that two years later, walking back into her profession would be completely out of the question. The reuniting of the two Germanys was, in the end, effectively a revolution. Frau von Donnersmarck, who was normally too snooty to talk to people, gossiped to me that every Wednesday, Sophie would have a whine. Her living room was, after all, next to Sophie's, and back under the former regime no-one had ever (of course) done anything about sound-proofing.

At my questioning look, she flushed and emitted a high-pitched laugh: not a *glass of* wine, obviously! A *whine*, meaning, a yowly crying fit. Every Wednesday from ten till eleven thirty in the evening. She'd come to know Sophie's exact timing. And if I didn't wish to take her word for it – well, if I brought another lady with me for reasons of propriety, I would be welcome to come to her living room next Wednesday and listen.

I did actually go and ask the girl who worked the Sunday shift on the till at the petrol station if she'd accompany me.

On Wednesday, the pair of us stood in good time at the door of Frau von Donnersmarck's flat. We knocked softly so as not to give Sophie any inkling of our visit to her neighbour, and were let in. We sat down. Frau von Donnersmarck had even prepared a fancy little buffet for the evening and had arranged bottles of beer, fruit-juice and Selters, a pricy sparkling mineral water, on a side-table. We got stuck in. I'd taken the top off a beer and was about to partake of a finger-roll laden with traditional Berlin-style onion-garnished mince, when sure enough, it started. What we could hear reminded me distinctly of the noise a moorhen makes: a high-pitched, grating whine interrupted by a kind of low chuckle. No way could a concrete wall stop that coming through. I asked Frau von Donnersmarck if she'd ever brought this up with Sophie, but she said absolutely not: other people's quirky habits were no concern of hers, and furthermore if one turned on the television one could barely hear it. To prove her point she switched on the late talk-show.

I was flummoxed. I pleaded with the girl not to tell anyone, and handed over twenty Euros for her assistance.

Sophie's legs were ever-present. They came to me if I closed my eyes, and on re-opening them the image wouldn't just go away. I heard her whines all over the place, in the starting up and idling of an engine, or in my armchair in the evenings, as the frequency of the passing headlights slowed. Other than this I would always notice her from the garage's high-up windows at lunchtime, strolling to the diner, then an hour or so later, back to the bus stop.

Till one day I'd had it. (Or hadn't had it, more like.)

Two weeks ago on Thursday, I didn't eat my packed lunch but went round to the diner. They didn't like us going in wearing our overalls so I'd made myself look nice and presentable. I sat down at Sophie's table, facing her.

What is it that makes you cry every Wednesday?

She just looked at me, then cracked out laughing. And it was exactly the same noise as on that Wednesday, except there was now no concrete wall between us. She couldn't get her words out for snorting, but gasped, at last, that she was a member of a laughing club and every Wednesday night, when hopefully everyone else in the block had gone to bed, she'd do her homework exercises. By doing courses and various other things to break up the monotony, her life on the dole was now something she could just laugh about, which was better than how it had been before, when the mystery of her husband's fate was only one thing among a whole lot of things that had made her incapable of laughing. By now, tears of mirth were streaming from her eyes.

Four hours later my shift ended. I rang the doorbell of her flat. She let me in. Above her wrap-around maxi-skirt she was wearing a black camisole top, which for a moment focused my entire attention on her lovely delicate arms. She asked me to come through, took the roses I'd bought at the petrol station and was still holding in my hand wrapped in paper, removed the wrapping and put them in water. Edging round me to get past in the narrowness of her little hallway, she came very close.

So close that I unwrapped the skirt from her hips, and when I saw her legs, I knew where she wanted to go.

And she knew I knew.

A little bit of 'lerv'

LUCIE WOULD ALWAYS have made it down at least three steps before his words got her between the shoulder-blades, like a volley fired from an old gun in need of a service. Although Mr Wiklam gave her the same order (for liver) every Wednesday without fail, his voice filled her with dread every time. Each week she'd be in haste to hang the plastic bag containing what he wanted – a meagre few pieces of liver, brown and bloody, weighing barely a pound – on the door-handle of his flat. The feel of it through the packaging made her queasy. Not once had Mr Wiklam reimbursed her for one of these portions of liver. And as Lucie fearfully closed the door of her flat, her neighbour across the landing would silently take the bag inside, using only his left hand and without revealing more than twenty centimeters of his arm. What he then did with it, the devil only knew. Lucie had been familiar since childhood with the reek of liver being cooked, whether stewed with apple and onion, or the smell of a simmering ragout. But she never smelled a thing. And the guy didn't even have a cat or some old mutt that he might have been feeding it to. He was by no means old; more like forty, same as she was, Lucie speculated on this particular Wednesday as she unloaded her shopping into the fridge. Something compelled her to unquestioningly obey him, this man who'd been her neighbour for eight months. Prior to that, his flat had stood empty. Since she'd moved in three years ago there'd been occasional viewings, but clearly no-one till Wiklam had liked the place. Then one day Lucie had been greatly intrigued to hear high-velocity pissing coming from next-door's bathroom, and by the time the flush ensued, had deduced it to be a personage in the order of Mr Wiklam. Only a bloke could piss that loud.

In the first few weeks of Wiklam being her next-door neighbour there had been no sign of anything untoward. The residents in that building had hardly anything to do with each other, so Lucie was always pleased to discern what she thought was a slight incline of Wiklam's head, as though he might be nodding a greeting. And she was even more pleased that day in August when, locking her flat before sprinting down the stairs to ensure she caught her train to work, Wiklam's first 'liver' utterance had skewered her right through, driving between her shoulder blades and ribs and into her heart which, in her momentary swoon, skipped several beats. But she'd never forget Wiklam's face when she had timidly knocked on his door, not having returned till evening and feeling guilty about the late hour and therefore intending to deliver the paltry pound of fresh pig's liver into his hands – and had dropped it on the floor. The thin paper packaging had split, exposing the bloody glob. Wiklam had visibly recoiled, his expression almost unspeakably pained. You could practically hear his pupils shrinking as his eyes drew together in a scowl that within seconds made him look frankly terrifying, and Lucie had begun to scream. At this he'd slapped her in the face – in quite a practical manner, as though to 'release' her – and she'd been able to stop panicking and shut up. At least for the time being. Back in her flat later, door safely locked, she'd been sick on her mint-green carpet, and as a non-meat-eater was flummoxed by the greasy brown hotpot she'd vomited up.

This business with Wiklam had gone on for several months. To avoid any repeat of that first hiccup, Lucie had from then on got the assistant at the meat counter to put the liver in a plastic bag. She had also given up her morning cleaning job, so that fulfilling Wiklam's order didn't have to be left till the evening. Her afternoon job as a teacher for a well-reputed private tutoring agency was sufficient for her needs. She earned enough to give her security, and the weekly outlay for her neighbour was neither here nor there. She was actually very happy to jack in the cleaning. After being out of work for a number of years she was proud to have got back into teaching. Under the former regime she had not just tutored individual kids but taught proper big classes, Russian and history, confidently taking them through to their school-leaving examinations. She used to slip reports to her then head-teacher (no record of which would be kept), detailing who was or wasn't a good pupil, and which parents could be relied on for their loyalty (or not). She passed these judgements according to the criteria she'd been taught, though nowadays she couldn't even remember what those criteria had been. Pupils would then sometimes get a shiny little medal in assembly, or a cloth-bound edition of one of the *Stories of our People* books. She'd always been really uplifted by that part. Her two daughters, having been brought up by her, had subsequently gone and sought out their fathers. This had rather upset Lucie. She hadn't kept the two gentlemen a secret from her children, but neither man had ever shown any interest. But then once their respective daughters had come of age, it evidently gave the fathers great pleasure to take the young ladies out, and introduce them to their families. In fact the younger one was now living effectively right on top of her father. Having never contributed a single penny towards her upkeep, he had swiftly installed her as the tenant of his villa's little attic flat. Lucie sighed, putting the milk in the fridge door.

Sitting by herself in the evening, as she nearly always did, she found herself dwelling less on her two daughters than on a certain Mister Wiklam and his one solitary desire. She had to confess she'd been checking the dustbins behind the building every now and then. He had to be disposing of the weekly pound of pig's liver somewhere. Did he eat it raw, or what? And what was it that compelled her to submit without question to his lust for liver, and to tremble even when safely inside her own front door? Today she'd actually bought liver for herself, going on the theory that dealing with blood should nip her phobia in the bud. She set about cutting the liver into little pieces, frying it in oil, and adding apples and onions. Almost with wonder she caught the familiar waft, as though from her childhood, though she'd have preferred it to be wafting from Wiklam's flat.

With her thoughts miles away, she dissolved stock in boiling water, added it to the pan and put the lid on, then began the wait for the end result, a ragout. Once this was achieved, she disposed of the food in the kitchen bin where, for a long while, it carried on steaming.

At about half past two in the morning Lucie woke up, which was not normal. The noise that had roused her was unmistakably that of a male engaged in sexual activity. Lucie had lived in the building long enough to know it could only be coming from Wiklam's flat. The longer she listened, the more certain she was that he was his own lover, so to speak. Or maybe hater. He masturbated on and on, moaning out loud, emitting groans and grunts, in among which he seemed to be begging for help, even saying names. 'Saddo, wanking over porn mags,' said Lucie's head, but immediately she told herself off, considering that she too was starting to moan *I hear you* or some such thing. Unable to contain herself any longer, she got out of bed, and her feet, blue with cold, found their way across the dark landing. There, and indeed throughout the stairwell, liver and onion stew cooked with apples hung in the air, turgid, all-pervasive. Lucie had simply intended to put her ear to the glazed part of his door, but it swung open, having only been put to. The smell permeating his flat was the same as on the landing and over in her own place. Her blood was pounding fit to burst as she crept in the direction of the noise, feeling thrilled now, aware of her transgression. When at last she saw Wiklam in the glow of the TV's test card she leapt onto his torso and, quite matter-of-factly, like the way he'd slapped her terrified screaming to a halt, rode him to his climax. She wasn't at all surprised when Wiklam then promptly fell asleep. She herself was soon nestled deep into his shoulder, where she finally escaped the stench of cooked liver that she'd sent over to get his attention.

Friday saw Wiklam and Lucie having breakfast together for the second time. It was only when the elder of her daughters had dropped by with a scholarship application and Lucie had greeted her with *sdrastwujtje* instead of 'hello', and patted her daughter good-humouredly on the bum with a cheerful *nu pagadi!* that it struck her: she was speaking Russian. These last two nights that she'd spent pandering to his every desire – massaging his balls, her parted lips and tongue gliding up and down his spine – had she really been making love to him entirely in Russian? As though to confirm this for her, Wiklam, seeing her bemusement, was now playing games, uttering heavily rolled 'r's and sultry, deep-throated 'wo's and tricky little 'i' sounds, his sibilants long and languid. Lucie's responses came lilting unerringly back, though she herself could hardly believe how well her tongue was fluting and cooing. With all this going on, the daughter beat a hasty retreat, after which Lucie spread-eagled herself below Wiklam's chair and started a question-and-answer game. As this progressed, Wiklam plumbed Lucie's depths ever deeper, while on her part, the first real spark now flared, as she discovered what he'd really meant by 'liver'. It transpired that *A little bit of love would be lovely* was the only sentence he could speak in the language of his new country of residence without worrying about his terrible accent. This didn't mean he spoke it with no accent at all: he'd actually been saying it with a distinct regional twang, which had made it doubly credible: Lucie had assumed it was Swabish, maybe Frankenwald, even though she didn't know exactly how people talked there. *A li'l bit of liver'd be lervly* is how she'd always (slightly mistakenly) heard it. Turned out that in his former life in Ukraine, Wiklam had been a meat curer in a market-hall in Kiev, selling charcuterie to those who could afford it. Quite possibly at around the same time as Lucie had been passing the unofficial reports to her head-teacher, which, following Germany's reunification, was to be the grounds for 'discharging' her of any further employment in schools. Wiklam, too, had been 'discharged'; in his case, of his Russian citizenship, owing to his application to duly follow his sister (then still alive) to the German-speaking world in which she had already gained residency as a migrant a few years previously. Having been held up by interminable bureaucracy, he eventually arrived to find not his sister but her death certificate. His brother-in-law, a native of Kazalot, and his two nephews had immediately made their way back home; her ashes, caught up in bureaucracy, would follow behind. Their trains quite possibly crossed paths at Brest Station, going in opposite directions, if Wiklam were to believe the one and only letter he received from his brother-in-law. Wiklam's German wasn't actually all that limited, but he was enormously shy about using it. Until, that is, it had come back to him – how the words of that nice, expensively-tailored gentleman at the market in Kiev had unfailingly elicited the eager submission of the women on the meat counters: *A li'l bit of lerv'd be lervly, if one of you ladies moight obloige?* The man's utterance of this sentence had made the women go all giddy. Far from offering him an item from their reeking stall (such as a portion of liver), his words had got them hoiking their blood-stained white coats right up, and 'accidentally' dislodging their chef's hats to show off their nice hairdos and also show they were up for it. And right then and there, the nice gentleman – a shoe manufacturer over on business – had always had a little appointment with one or the other, backing her into a corner to sample her wares… Wiklam had heard on the grapevine that the man would pay a princely sum for this delight.

Arkady Wiklam, grandson of Emilie and Hugo Schwamberger on one side and Galja Borisovna and Viktor Wiklam on the other, his mother being Regina Schwamberger and his father Sinoviy Wiklam, had hoped, by means of those words, to ease a loneliness that Lucie had never once suspected when, time and again, she hung those little Wednesday packages on his door. Wiklam now carried Lucie across to his flat – literally. Once over the threshold he set her down with great care, closed the door behind them, and led her into the kitchen, where he nodded towards the freezer. On lifting its lid, the untouched packages of liver were all in there, frozen in their own blood, their price tags still on. At the sight of them, it wasn't only the smile on Lucie's lips that froze; so too did the Russian on her tongue, which made Wiklam laugh, just like her students had sometimes laughed at the way she spoke – with such zeal.

Pussyfooting

He'd often see her when he looked up from his desk and across the street. The girl would sometimes be standing in front of the pizzeria smoking, or else she'd be sweeping the pavement with a twiggy broomstick that looked like a prop from that Russian film *Queen of the Gypsies*, swishing the cigarette butts into the gutter with a practised stroke then depositing the broom upside-down in a tin bucket hanging to the left of the door. To the right was another bucket which, similarly, held an upside-down broomstick. He had sometimes wondered why she never used the right-hand broom, but on his trips to the café to pick up a pizza or a chilled Coke he'd always forget to take a closer look. Inside, the girl would be standing behind the counter washing glasses, or else pouring pints, the foam blooming over. She wasn't particularly slim. Fat-rolls spilled over the top of her low-cut jeans, and his ogling eyes would always be drawn to those ten fabulous centimetres exposed below her sweater, seeking his now familiar friend: a large and prominent brown birth-mark. Situated a hand-width below her belly button, it was only visible when the girl reached up and made her belly slip a bit further out of her jeans. When she stretched, the fat roll disappeared and the birthmark came out to say hello. It gave him a thrill every time.

Was it a feeling of yearning? Spread before him was the editing job for the small publishing house that was only able to pay him a pittance. Though it wasn't even half-done, a hunger pang shot through him with such suddenness that he literally flung down his pen, ran into the hall for his shoes, threw on his jacket and donned his tartan deerstalker. Out on the landing he remembered his money was still in yesterday's pants and doubtless, like his pants, in the laundry basket. So he had to go back in. It was when he had closed the door once more and turned to go downstairs that he saw the cat. It was sitting on the windowsill in the stairwell. As far as he knew, no-one in the house owned a pet, which he'd always been glad about. When he'd lived in shared student houses with dogs and cats, his allergy had played havoc with him. He had trailed to see a doctor many a time with swollen, crusty eyes and asthma attacks before finally, one came up with a possible explanation. A test confirmed it: animal hair and pollen were like poison to him – though he couldn't fathom why there'd been no sign of this in his childhood, when his parents had cared not only for their four children but also dogs, guinea-pigs and gerbils. But that was just how it was. It started right after he turned eighteen. He clearly remembered the first incidence. His favourite cat (which he'd called Feisty after her mother, who lived in a village near Anklam) had caught something nasty and was lying listlessly on the rug. There was no question of it just being old age: Feisty was barely two. So they had to find a vet, a task for which he had naturally assumed responsibility. Since they hadn't been living in that flat for very long he'd asked the neighbours if they knew of one locally. Herr Fackelmann on the third floor had given him directions: just go round our block and it's across the road. When he got there he had to chuckle at the vet's surname: Feist. A tall, wiry, affable bloke with those round nickel-framed glasses, and what you'd call a shy smile. Straight off he'd asked for the pet's name. A tenderly uttered 'Feisty' was not manageable due to the convulsive laugh that was threatening to explode out of him any second now. Instead a mumbled 'Fanny Fackel' came out. For a fleeting moment the vet had looked slightly taken aback, but then duly recorded the name, and shortly thereafter diagnosed a poisoning, shaved one of Fanny Fackel's front legs, and put her on a drip. Maybe the sight of that bare, skinny, bluish-grey leg lying there on the white paper towel with a needle stuck in it had been too much; at any rate, his allergy flared up for the first time that same morning.

Keeping as much distance as possible he tried diving past it, but the cat jumped from the windowsill and landed right between his feet. He had to grab the banister to stop himself being flung down the stairs. The cat purred, extended its tail and arched its back around his calves while rubbing its head against his legs. He couldn't help himself – he dropped down on his knees and looked her in the eye. She seemed so plump and so familiar, the way she nuzzled up to him in that confident way of cats. He sighed, thinking of the state he'd be in shortly. Nonetheless he ran his hand through her soft fur, fingering her feline bulges. Then he placed the tigress back on the windowsill, assuming someone in the block had recently acquired her and that she'd escaped when they opened their door. Unsure whether she'd stay put, he kept his eye on her until the next landing, but she made no effort either to follow him or slope off anywhere else.

Outside it was unusually cold for the time of year. Surprised, he did up his jacket, turned up his collar and let down his deerstalker's earmuffs even though he was only crossing the road. Today he remembered to check out the brooms. While the one on the left definitely looked more used than the other, he realized that actually the brooms had not been placed there for doing the sweeping up but as decorations.

As he entered the pizzeria he was smiling. It was empty. The girl was perched behind the counter, book in hand. Till now he'd never seen her reading. She was evidently so engrossed that she hadn't noticed him. At first he wasn't sure whether he should clear his throat or make a bit of a noise. In the end he just sat down quietly at the nearest table. As he gazed at her she seemed familiar in some strange way that had nothing to do with his scant actual knowledge of her as a person. As though his fingers knew what she felt like; a familiar plumpness. Furtively and with puzzlement he looked down at his hands with their apparent memories, turning them over as though they didn't belong to him. At that moment she noticed him, perhaps having registered the movement from the corner of her eye. Calmly and, he thought, in a deliberate manner, she set the book on a shelf above the counter, then gave herself a shake, clearly struggling to return to the reality of an ordinary pizzeria in an ordinary German city.

Beer?

No, a beer wasn't what he was after. Even his hunger seemed to have passed off. What did he want here? The girl was eyeing him with curiosity, standing there waiting with folded arms, but not one word came out. Instead, he was intensely aware of the tap dripping into the sink; the gentle trickle of music from the CD player; his own heartbeat. The latter instantly embarrassed him: he felt a blush coming up his neck towards his face. Luckily his collar was still turned up – he hadn't even removed his deerstalker. With an apologetic gesture he backed out of the café and out of sight. Once outdoors he drew some deep breaths, then set off on a long walk that took him over the Kraemer Bridge and across the square in front of the cathedral to his former abode on Mittel Strasse where they'd had an abundance of cats. He only remembered this when he was standing in front of his building – number nine. In those days there'd been mildew creeping up the walls of the ground floor rooms; it had even been visible from the outside, going up the dirty grey rendering. Today, in the twilight, the building's facade was a terracotta shade, and a built-on steel structure as high as the house supported balconies that opened off the living rooms. The immaculateness of it all put him off wanting to go in, which anyway wouldn't be possible without buzzing one of the residents and requesting entry. In the old days, cats had scampered in and out of the block's permanently open front door. Once, one had actually given birth in among some coats and anoraks in a cardboard box that was kept under the stairs for the charity shop. He needed to cough and, guessing it was the first sign of his allergy, turned away and walked on.

Later he had no idea how he'd got home. He only came out of his daydreams when, back in the stairway, he saw the cat still perched on the windowsill as though the last two or three hours had never happened. She blinked, unconcerned, which surprised him, as he could remember cats jumping, startled, when a light went on. Could she be blind? Something like pity was stirring in him, and this certainly didn't abate when, to test his theory, he watched her as he continued up the stairs and saw how her eyes listlessly followed him, as though she wasn't really with it.

Later still, seated in front of the telly, he wondered in passing why his allergy hadn't flared up. Eyes neither swollen nor watering, no runny nose, no fits of sneezing. It would actually have suited him down to the ground, that day, if he could have had this sound reason to take himself off to bed and not work; it was after all only work… After the news he heaved himself up with a sigh and shambled over to his desk. The essay on Pier Paolo Pasolini did actually interest him; he'd even bought a box-set of DVDs and been on the edge of his seat, watching the movies. But his thoughts were adrift, and he now found Passolini a difficult subject to lose himself in, which he really needed to do in order to achieve the high standard he set himself as a proof-reader. It suddenly came to him that in a month, he would turn forty, and just as suddenly came the idea of inviting friends and relatives to the pizzeria across the road, which would surely be delighted to have a big party in for an evening... A glance across oddly made him catch his breath: the girl was standing smoking in the shade of the left-hand bucket, and as she gazed out into the blue under the street-light he fancied he could see cats' eyes. And wasn't that a tail, rising from her tight-fitting hipsters, its wavering shadow distinctly visible on the pavement? For a moment, he closed his eyes.

Next morning there was a list of more than fifty invitees beside his bed. Something was going on with him: he felt a great sense of contentment. When he thought about it the sensation was clearly coming from his stomach. He let out a belch and was astonished to discern traces of Gorgonzola, walnuts and chicory, with which his favourite pizza, Gorizia, was always generously topped – but it was three or four weeks since he'd last had one. Weird. He'd eaten nothing else that would leave behind quite that taste. He went to grab a quick coffee from the automatic machine in his kitchen. He liked it best with brown cane sugar. He poured himself a large cup and, finally returning to his desk, cup in hand, looked across the street. Shutters down. A grill over the pizzeria's entrance. It was still early. He sipped, slipping his left hand into his back pocket. Between each little sip his taste-buds kept on sending him walnut alerts, like notifications to stay on track with his birthday plans, so at last, he sat himself down at his laptop to design an invite. The text itself he quickly dashed off, but as well as signing them he also intended to handwrite a greeting to all fifty-two to give each an extra, personalised promise of the joys in store. Before he could insert the date he'd have to wait till he'd discussed it with the pizzeria. Happening to glance across again, he saw the girl bending down to reach the grill's bottom lock. Snap! The same bowed back as the cat's on the staircase yesterday. When she stood up again and turned, the way she moved was so similar to the tigress that he felt dizzy, his fingers instantly recalling the feel of the cat's feline bulges. And then he was so overwhelmed by an impulse to squeeze those womanly bulges that he had to sit down, contemplating his hands in disbelief. He felt wonderful, which instantly terrified him, and he thrust his arms into his jacket's sleeves and his feet into his shoes, intent on fleeing from his confusion – though his shoes had no other intent than to take him to the pizzeria by the fastest possible route. In the stairway he took pains to look straight past the window, not at it. In his mind the cat was now an irrelevance. After all, the allergy hadn't flared up again.

The girl had apparently been expecting him. At least that's how it seemed when the moment he stepped inside, she herself deliberately stepped over to the dining area and started lifting down chairs, the opposite of yesterday when she'd put them up so she could sweep and mop. The way she moved was extraordinarily supple, which amazed him considering she was so plump.

Like the cat in my staircase, was writ large in his mind.

You guessed right, he said aloud. *I'm hungry.*

The girl looked at him, totally at ease, studying him for a long moment as though deciding what he might like, then went into the kitchen and set about cracking two eggs into a pan. She took a freshly baked loaf from her bag, cut some slices and arranged the eggs on them.

I've been waiting for the One for so long, she said softly, *that I didn't realise you were he.*

He understood everything and nothing, but put his arms around her waist and kissed her. He spent the whole day in the dining area, on a couple of occasions helping to wash the glasses. More was not possible because the cook forbade it, refusing him entry into the kitchen. When she had time for a breather he stood with her beside the upside-down brooms and smoked, which was totally against his principles. It was then that they discussed his fortieth birthday party. He knew he wasn't being his usual self, and yet he was more himself than he had ever been in his life, which led him to conclude that not-being-himself was perhaps his truest nature. Late in the evening, after he'd put the chairs up onto the tables and she'd mopped the floor, the girl quietly pulled down the entrance grill.

She was carrying a large bag that she hadn't arrived with that morning but rather, that she had kept in her locker for this day. The bag contained everything she thought she'd need for survival in case anything happened. He took it from her. It wasn't heavy. They crossed the street together. In the staircase he put on the light, and in that split-second of their entry, he thought he saw a tiger-striped grey cat shoot between his legs and run outside.

Tadeusz. Full stop.

SINCE HE'D LIVED IN GERMANY he'd called himself Taddius. But to him the name felt awkward, not slipping easily over head and shoulders but always snagging round his neck and getting stuck there, suspended, like a social pleasantry or insincere *How are you* or trite remark. He'd had to practise for ages to eliminate the fizz on the tongue which comes at the end of *Tadeusz*, and had fully expected that his achievement of this would give his self-confidence a boost, but it had no effect. Instead, he went on living a limited, timid sort of life with his wife, whose surname *Geissler* he had adopted when they got married. In the long stretches of free time that the days offered him, Tadeusz Geissler would imitate birds – *Erithacus Rubecula, Troglodytes Troglodytes, Emberiza Citrinella* – puckering his lips and sucking in his cheeks, giving off trills and whistles that were spot on. Or else he crocheted, making his wife ever more crazy hats that she could never get enough of. The pleasure she took in wearing them was his greatest reward. Her joy would show itself first in her face when, in donning the hat, she'd lower her elfin chin in a way that seemed to give even greater breadth to her dazzling smile. But then once she'd actually tried it on in front of the mirror and done a couple of twirls, she would fling herself on Tadeusz, kiss him exuberantly and set about unbuttoning his jacket, shirt and trousers. He loved that. Though a strict Catholic he'd been unable to control himself when she'd first made a move on him. She had travelled by bus from Gotha to Kielce with her women's choir to sing at the Church of the Holy Trinity. After the morning concert he had been one of the men tasked with showing the women round the town, but only she had gone exploring with him, the rest preferring to celebrate their boss's birthday in the hotel. He'd taken her to the Krakow bishops' palace and the famous Paradise Cave before they came to a halt for a coffee-break on the historic Sienkiewicza Street, both of them trying to brush up their Russian to get a little more intimate. As she would later confide, the angular, sinewy shoulder of his left arm had somehow happened to brush her hand when he was bending down to pick up a dropped match. In that instant she was done for, and came up with a pretext for taking him to her hotel room where, without further ado and to her own astonishment, she'd fallen all over him. That was seven years ago and today they were both into their fifties. Pia Geissler continued to love her husband as much as when they'd first met. The fact that he hadn't exactly been taken to heart by her family no longer upset her. She was an independent woman, PA to the director of the former automobile manufacturing plant that had just about struggled on through the revolutionary years of Germany's reunification, and she earned enough money to cover the small flat, her Polish husband and a regular bottoming with good old *General Bergfrühling* 'alpine spring' cleaning fluid. Since coming from Poland he had learned to speak good German. For his fiftieth she'd given him a course of driving lessons, and now they took turns at the wheel when they explored their local area at weekends or drove out of the region for holidays. Two of her girlfriends sometimes came with them, Berit and Silvia, whose lust for him was virtually on a level with Pia's, although – as they had to keep reminding themselves – they had husbands. Being unemployed like Tadeusz, they hung out at home with beer and movies, but unlike him would never dream of becoming experts in crochet hook specifications or in imitating birdcalls. Bergit's grey-eyed gaze met Silvia's green one and they sighed in unison, then mostly they stared out of the car's windows, each on their own side.

For this particular Saturday Pia Geissler had suggested a jaunt by the Famous Four (as she liked to call them) to Johanngeorgenstadt. After breakfast she cut some sliced bread into heart-shapes and piled them up so amply with salad, salami, ham and slices of egg that it was going to be tricky taking a bite out of such a sandwich. All the while, Pia was popping the cut-off crusts into her mouth, but not before naughtily balancing a little bit of ham on them, or a sliver of salami. Eight sandwiches, each made of two bread slices, amounted to sixteen thick crusts with hearts cut out of their middles. Pia burped happily, wrapping the final sandwich in paper. Her husband was warm and cozy under the duvet and emerged only slowly. While he was in the shower Pia glanced round the door, which he never closed, and felt a frisson of happiness.

Berit and Silvia had, as always, tarted themselves up to the nines. Berit's newly re-dyed red hair was down today, not up in her normal sixties-style bun. Why she usually wore it like that was a mystery to Pia, considering she otherwise dressed in quite a modern style, without being ultra-trendy; the sort of look you'd typically find in catalogues for the fuller figure. Silvia was wearing a three-stringed coral necklace and lipstick of exactly the same shade. They had rung the bell and so Pia had opened the door to them, but since they were now hovering in the hallway she had to take her husband's clothes to him in the shower – otherwise he'd have had to come out naked in front of the ladies!

For the moment the three of them sat in the kitchen. Pia had brewed a big pot of coffee and she poured some for her girlfriends before putting the rest into a big fat thermos. A few giggles, some titbits of gossip – five minutes had soon passed and Tadeusz now appeared, hair gelled, in a well-tailored suit, white shirt and bow-tie and black leather shoes, inviting the ladies to please accompany him. Berit and Silvia were clearly as turned on as Pia, but as always they had to take deep breaths and keep a lid on it.

Once on the motorway they drove up to Boxberg, despite it being the opposite direction to their destination, because this route would take them through Sundhausen and Leina, and Pia knew how much her friends liked these two little villages. Later they stopped at the petrol station in Muehlberg to get some bottles of water they'd forgotten to buy, then bowled on. Tadeusz was at the wheel. As Berit, lost in thought, let her gaze wander around inside the car, she was suddenly struck: his hair looked darker than before. Yes – his grey hairs had definitely gone. She had to smile, imagining a sweet young hairdresser taking him in hand; how she would have applied the dye after a long, lingering hair-wash inclusive of scalp-massage. (Or had he just done a wash-and-tint at home?) She herself would have loved to be that girl whose job it was to wash hair etcetera, but she was, let's face it, too old now to find work in one of the many salons that had mushroomed everywhere, and anyway her hairdressing apprenticeship was far too long ago. She wouldn't have the confidence to return to hairdressing after the many years she'd spent first as a library assistant in the State Rubber Processing Combine and later, after the winds of change had blown, as a Public Relations bimbo for the local authority. As for Silvia… Berit looked at her. She too was ogling Tadeusz, though her main focus was his rugged jaw. To feed this fantasy she always kept a pack of Daydent mouth freshener with her.

Pia told them about the previous week at work, when Tadeusz had stepped in as a translator and been paid a substantial fee by her boss, and now hoped to be called on more often for this type of thing. Their town encouraged commercial relationships with Kielce, there was even an office for it in Gotha, and how many people could speak Polish?! (Obviously the whole thing was better for the Poles: on the Kielce side they had no problem finding people who spoke German.) Pia Geissler couldn't stop endlessly raving on about Tadeusz, all the while constantly readjusting her top and her hair and re-touching her eyeliner. Although it was his skill as an *interpreter* she was extolling, Silvia secretly swapped that word for *lover*.

They left the motorway at the Meerane exit. In Zwickau they allowed themselves a toilet stop and sat in a little ice-cream parlour. Berit noted they'd got little tubs of Swedish ice-cream *just like the old days,* and ordered one. The others of course followed suit, and the four tubs arrived. Revisiting the joys of the vanilla ice-cream with its apple sauce, egg liqueur and lashings of sweet cream, they were completely transported from the present into reminiscences about former times. Tadeusz excused himself to go to the toilet. The previous fifteen years of recession were forgotten. Instead the women were reliving the forty years before that, competing with each other to launch off on a tale, cackling with laughter about the days when Berit was eternally embarrassed about her fat thighs; going to the picture-house in the market square; the massive numbers of grilled sausages they'd get through at the carnival in the city hall. Those long, skinny Turkey bratwursts with that good mustard from Born & Co in Erfurt. Till Berit suddenly said, *We didn't suffer back then, did we. Not really*. And in that instant, an awkwardness descended like a shroud, chasing the smiles from their lips, making them concentrate on their ice-cream tubs. And it was not to be shifted.

The awkwardness continued when they got back into the car and drove the last fifty kilometres to Johanngeorgenstadt. The stubborn silence now gripping them had seen off their former high spirits as swiftly as they'd seen off those turkey bratwursts. Pia Geissler was giving the contents of her handbag a thorough sort-out as if no-one else were there. Berit fiddled obsessively with one of the strings of her hooded anorak, winding it round her finger, unwinding, winding it round again, while staring hard out of the car window. For Silvia this sudden uneasiness reminded her of her mother's habit of speaking out against the tide of opinion. Her mother had found it entirely in order to have a State Security Service of some sort to keep an eye on anti-social weirdos. And nowadays she went round saying she'd been able to go on better holidays under the former regime than she could now – so what, if it had only been in the east? At least she'd been able to afford it, whereas today *ordinary working folk* such as herself had to scrimp and save and watch every penny, and even then would be left wondering where it had all gone... The three women were sighing again, but this time it was not over Tadeusz, who had noticed from his place at the wheel how quiet the ladies suddenly were, but had no idea why. Thinking to perk them up, he started to whistle.

They reached the destination of their Famous Four jaunt four hours after leaving Gotha – thank God, as Pia said (though Tadeusz was the only real believer among them).

A festival was underway in the market square which they of course hadn't known about but which seemed highly opportune, providing them with a needed distraction. The immensely popular *Randfichten* were playing, a band hailing from the Ore Mountain border region who sang in the local Saxon dialect. The current song had been a big nationwide hit, a tub-thumping, rabble-rousing ditty extolling Saxony's famous potato dumplings and mushroom gravy and those jolly holidays to the Czech Republic of former times. Pia absolutely wasn't into this kind of music, but she let herself be drawn in, stamping and clapping along as if her life depended on it. Berit and Silvia followed her lead. Tadeusz, who (due to the dialect) couldn't understand a great deal, was the one now left sighing. He went off in search of another beer.

All three of them were dwelling on former times. Pia, on her time as an 'informer', which was over before it had really started because she'd let on to Berit about it. At that time Berit had the library job at the Rubber Processing Combine. She'd been specially picked out for it, and saying no to the Powers That Be would not have been a good idea. Which meant that, when Pia had divulged her secret role, Berit had had to hot-foot it to her workplace's Stasi official to report an 'Act of Disclosure'. Acting *in good faith,* as she'd told Pia later; after all a person like Pia wasn't really cut out for that type of work anyway. From then on the Stasi made no further contact with Pia, which had made her wonder a bit, but over time the whole thing had passed from her mind. Silvia, meanwhile, had for that whole era been quietly stuck in a demeaning role serving the local chapter of the Party, because after she'd moved here from Jena to be with her husband she'd had first one, then two and ultimately three little children at home, thus missing out on the social life that belonging to a workplace would have brought. She certainly hadn't been happy about the duties she held, but they had taken over her life with such natural progression that she eventually abandoned all thoughts of another career. First came the Party's district training college, then the regional college for cadres, and ultimately the Party Academy, but she left this when diagnosed with cancer, thereafter drawing a pension. That was more than twenty years ago. The trigger that had made the three of them dwell on all this had been the implicit question, *Did we make others suffer?* in that remark by Berit. The question edged itself in amidst all the clapping; amid the roaring in Saxon dialect of a thousand people around the square, the thunder of the bass guitar. It resounded ever louder in their ears until it was finally embedded and could no longer be ignored, and as the music took over their senses they knew the answer was *Yes!* which they began to roar, along with the crowd, at first hesitantly, then louder and louder... At last, completely exhausted, they linked arms, and exchanged a look of mutual understanding that no outsider like Tadeusz could ever fathom. The *Randfichten* had not yet finished their set but the women had had enough. When they saw Tadeusz standing over by a beer tent, they felt so painfully embarrassed that they looked away. He gestured at them and, to get their attention across the considerable distance, called something out. He should not have done this, because he outed himself as a foreigner – one with a Slav accent, to boot – and at a beer tent in the market square of Johanngeorgenstadt, this was dangerous. Two drunken yobs jumped on him, pushing him and knocking the beer out of his hand, and before he knew what had happened, had floored him with a punch in the face. The three women got there so fast that Pia was able to fling herself between Tadeusz and an approaching foot, which she not only stopped but grabbed hold of, while the other of the two bewildered attackers got belted by Berit's leather handbag. Before the cancer, Silvia had done judo, and though it was a very, very long time ago, the memory of a simple *Osoto Otoshi* throwing

- 142 -

technique flooded back effortlessly. They soon had the two young yobs in arm-locks and pinned to the ground. They had handled it as a team, with Silvia and Berit now continuing to hold the men down while Pia took care of Tadeusz and got the bar-man to call the police, for whom they didn't have long to wait. Tadeusz was back on his feet when the policewoman asked him his name. He should have answered, as always, *Taddius Geissler*, but a tooth had become dislodged. In a gush of blood he spat it out. He could enunciate neither *Taddius* nor *Geissler*; instead it hissed from his mouth, sounding ugly (or that's how he heard it at first). He uttered it a few times with what Pia had always described as a 'broken accent' when he first started learning German, hissing *Geishh-ler, Geishh-ler* and *Taj, Tajashh...* But as he spoke, it sounded more and more like the Polish pronunciation –

Tadeusz, he said loudly. *Tadeusz. Tadeusz!*

Pia looked at him in surprise. *Full stop!* she added emphatically. And arm in arm, with Tadeusz in the middle, the three girlfriends departed from the town square with their heads held high.

The police were staring after them in such bafflement that the yobs, seeing their chance, scarpered into the crowd.

Under wraps

On Monday I brought down a bolt of calico from the loft. I always keep in a good supply of this for the spontaneous sewing of things, like curtains or dresses or bags. I wondered why my heart was thudding so hard, but decided it was just my age. Inevitably there'll be a first time when clambering up the steep fold-down ladder makes you breathless. I thought about re-starting my daily jog; maybe that would hold off my inexorable decline a while longer.

I put the bolt on the table and unrolled a few metres of the fine, unbleached white cloth. What to make? Before I'd really thought, I'd already cut off some arm-length strips. These I folded neatly and set in a pile on my bedside table. I then put the bolt back in the loft, pushed the folding stairs up and closed the hatch. Done. The machine was brewing fresh coffee. I sat behind the house in the shade of the birch tree sipping coffee, dwelling no further on the matter.

On Tuesday I re-potted my houseplants. The dragon tree, the hibiscus and the sansevieria. The crassula ovata had become so big I was unable to extract its roots from the rotund pot. Shame, as I really liked the bulbous shape of that pot. It was decorated with braided sisal and looked very attractive. Never mind! I smashed it with my husband's carpenter's hammer and gave the jade tree a bigger, but straight-sided, pot. I'd just have to get used to the look of it. The pot's braiding was surprisingly easy to separate into individual strings. I gathered them up, tied them in a bundle. So many of the perennials in my garden needed holding up all year round. I could re-use the sisal to attach them to rods. And the climbers to the fence, too. It would feel like a good thing to do. Supporting nature with something natural.

Happily, I placed the strings next to the pile of calico strips on my bedside table.

From the moment I got up on Wednesday I noticed my heart was thumping. Funny. I slipped on my housecoat. My body was acting like it was going to explode, which was a bit of a nuisance because Wednesday is my shopping day. After husband and children were out of the house I didn't get dressed, but lay down on the kitchen floor. And waited. My heart didn't. It thundered inside my chest till everything went black. Dazed, I crawled through to the bedroom and got myself one of the strips of calico. Then another and another. With a dexterity that astonished me I managed to wrap the fabric right round my chest and tie it in place with the sisal. My heart was playing games with me now, I thought. I felt it hammering with redoubled force against the binding of cloth and string, but I felt sure that by this method I could stop it from making me explode. I got dressed, choosing a loose tee-shirt, and went shopping as normal.

On Thursday I intended to cook the mince I'd bought on Wednesday. I wasn't feeling the slightest bit uncomfortable, being 'under wraps', so to speak. It had gone on giving me a feeling of reassurance, actually. Fortunately it's been the case for quite some time now that, when my husband looks at me, he doesn't really look. Under my housecoat I was wearing the loose tee-shirt. I hadn't taken it off overnight. I waited for husband and children to disappear before I began slicing onions, soaking the bread-rolls, and making a nice meaty dough. It took me no longer than usual. Eventually, being lost in thought, I sliced not only the onion but also the index finger of my left hand. I sat down on a kitchen chair. It didn't hurt, which puzzled me, but the blood was really gushing out; like, my thundering heart was pumping it torrentially out of my body. After a while my heart did calm down a bit. Was it my blood that had put it under such excessive pressure? My heart got my sympathy. I monitored its beat, which was now calmer. I can't say how long I went on sitting like that. And no-one came to see if I was alright. The notion that I shouldn't let further blood flow into my left hand must have been what made me wrap up my left arm, using the calico and sisal, meaning my blood could no longer get out of me, which was in my interest.

Friday was my People Free Day. For about two years my husband and I have had one day a week when the other is responsible for doing all the chores and family stuff. The people-free person does what he or she wants. I had mostly gone to see a man I had met through a small ad. Now, though, with my upper body and left arm wrapped up, I didn't really think I dared visit him. He knew neither my phone number nor my name, so I didn't need to worry that he'd call me. Instead I lay in the deckchair on the balcony. I had stripped down to my calico wrappings, and was marvelling at the warmth of the March sun. After half an hour I realized my lower stomach and legs were starting to burn. For how many years now had I not let a single ray of sunshine onto my skin? The children had still been small; I had played with them on the beach on the Baltic, bathing in the waves. That was way more than a decade ago. To protect my belly that was no longer used to the sun, I jumped up and ran down to the bedroom. There were seven remaining strips of calico. I carefully wrapped it round every body-part on which a ray of sunshine might have fallen, leaving only a narrow slit free for my eyes. Funnily enough, the sisal strings from that decorative pot were exactly the number I needed, as though I had counted them. Wrapped up like a mummy, I slipped back into my deckchair. People Free Day.

On Saturday my husband missed me at breakfast. No, he missed his breakfast first, before he missed me, who should have been putting it on the table after my People Free Day. But I had spent the night on the balcony, having fetched myself a blanket and then, because the fresh air was doing me so much good, slept right through. My husband found me still half-asleep in the deckchair and looked surprised. I didn't immediately get why he was so astonished, but when I tried asking, I realized I'd wrapped up my mouth too. Obviously, anyone would be astonished. From beneath my wrappings I suddenly felt like pulling a face at whatever he was going to come out with. A *lewd* face. That's how safe I felt, under there. Disappointingly my husband said very little, just telling me to cut it out and come down to the kitchen. My daughter had already laid the table. As I sat down she dropped the saltcellar in terror. It smashed on the tiled floor.

On Sunday I noticed how I had started to stink under my wrappings. I hadn't washed for days. The previous day my husband hadn't spoken to me all day. It did me good not to have to hear his voice, and I couldn't have responded to him anyway from beneath the fabric. Moreover, straight after breakfast my son and daughter had disappeared, so I had all day long to ponder my own thoughts. I had lain awake all night, on the balcony once again. Due to my stinkiness I now went to the bathroom where, locking the door, I ran water into the tub and – adding a big glug of my daughter's bath oil – unwrapped myself. The bath was hot and felt good. I washed my hair. Getting dried I felt the silkiness of my skin from the oil. I brushed my teeth and slipped into the housecoat, then scooped up the calico strips, sisal strings and my toothbrush, and brought them all into the kitchen. Eventually the whole lot stood wrapped up on the table. As in, wrapped in tissue paper and tied with a red bow. Gift-wrapped. I then wrapped myself in my clothes. My husband wasn't there, and I knew he'd never really be back. Or, if at all, only to keep on collecting more of his belongings.

I yawned, stretched.

By and by my children, already in their late teens, tapped on the door and put their heads round, asking where he was. I didn't answer.

I just thought – under wraps.

The longer I stared at the gift-wrapped thing on the table that Sunday, the stronger was my impression that its red tongue was sucking away at my husband. Eventually, when he'd clearly been sucked down to nothing, I could safely assume he was now inside the gift-wrap itself, along with the calico and sisal. And with enormous pleasure I threw the whole lot in the dustbin. The end.

On thin ice

SHE OFTEN THOUGHT, ONCE SHE WAS OLD ENOUGH TO THINK, that her brother was probably to thank for one of the first times her mother had ever been in a state of cork-popping euphoria (that she could remember, anyway). Her brother, who'd picked and packed his chromosomes from the gene warehouse with such care not to miss any good ones – and yet, in the nine months of uterine ensconcement, had evolved into (at first sight) a plucked chicken. His skinny, yellowish, naked-chicken body didn't go with his big chubby head. Had their mother felt any reservation whatsoever about the hybrid creature she'd brought into the world? If so, it must have lasted a mere nano-second. In the little girl's memory, the flood of mother-love into the woman had been instantaneous and had engulfed her baby brother and fulfilled his every infant need. Apart from breastfeeding. In her mother's view this was *not* the way to help build up the baby's body to fit with its head. No – a milk formula of two thirds milk to one third water was the order of the day.

Being only his sister she was kept completely out of it when, at two weeks old, the squealing little thing got pneumonia and had a mustard wrap applied each day by a black-clad nun, which made Little Squealer scream, his skin beneath it glowing red. The doctor who attended daily to administer an injection was unable to guarantee a happy ending. Since Mother and Father were completely helpless with worry over their plucked chicken, she'd had to bring about that happy ending herself. Climbing onto a chair below the skylight in the loft of their building, she beseeched the Lord Jesus to appear, and lo and behold, the Lord sent his emissary unto the loft in the form of the boy from the neighbouring flat, Kuno Bause, and bade them sing in one voice and at top volume in that hidey-hole under their families' shared rafters, *O sacred head, now wounded...* She knew the hymn from the Sunday services held in the small chapel in the garden behind their building. No one else had a real church in their garden. She regularly dragged child-visitors in from the street to impress them with it. Despite being forbidden of course, from going inside (they had nothing to do with all that. No connection to that place. *Ignore it*) she nonetheless spent her Sunday mornings round the back of the little chapel playing, whether with the sledge among the washing lines in January or amid the ripening strawberries in June, and her parents were unaware of the chapel's back window, which was usually open so the worshippers didn't smother, and had no inkling of the wide range of devotional hymns and liturgical words their little girl was taking in. When she knew her parents were in bed or had gone out, she would go and crouch directly below the loft's open skylight and imagine she had a ticket for the German State Railway. Surely she'd be able to get to the Kingdom of God with that! But best of all were her fantasies in bed at night, when she'd spend many an hour wide awake, gazing up through a hole in the floorboards into Heaven (which she accepted as a fact). Like in the fairytale of poor little Goldmarie with the wicked stepmother, her fate on being cast down the well was not to land at the bottom, but instead to be carried upwards. To Heaven. And when, through that inch-wide hole, she spied the Lord Jesus in all his glory awaiting her, she would let out a rapturous sigh, her hands raised up in prayer and her face transfigured, and then fall asleep, feeling safe.

Squealer was clearly getting better, which meant she got back some of her parents' attention. One day, against the instructions of her great-grandmother who had taken over minding the children, she took her little brother for a walk, sneakily pushing the great bulbous pram containing the sleeping chicken (who had put on some weight) out of the garden. But once on the downhill street she was incapable of bringing the pram to a stop. Herr Wehnert being in the vicinity was sheer good luck. Without a second's consideration of whether he should stand in the pram's way and stop it, in a flash he flung aside his bag and submitted his substantial male form to the hands of Fate. Fate dealt with him kindly. He returned the pram to their garden gate with a slumbering creature inside it and a tearful one hanging onto its handle, then with a grin of encouragement, stole away. She sniffed noisily a few more times, then wiped away the snot with her sleeves, and to avoid any suspicion, quickly ran past the windows of their ground floor flat to the sandpit round the back.

From that day on, Squealie was her darling. As she bound around the yard like a little chimp, she'd have an even littler chimp hanging onto her. When their mother was attending to the stove, she would half-chew his little bread soldiers for him and pop them in his mouth. Later she would dress him in the pants her friend Annegret's brother had grown out of, and ply him with pennies from her scant pocket money. She would surreptitiously slip him capers she'd picked out of the fish sauce on her plate (though it should be added, she herself found capers absolutely repulsive). She would bundle him along to choir practice, where he was the smallest boy but also everyone's favourite – literally, the blue-eyed boy. She organized garden Olympics and poetry-reciting contests with him, did his German homework and, in her brother's thirteenth year, was kind enough to go tell a girl on his behalf that he fancied her, though without result. She'd been rather pleased that the girl wanted nothing to do with Squealie, since her own adoration of him had by no means dissipated during thirteen long years at his side. Their parents didn't see anything amiss in the intensity of their relationship; to them it looked normal. The siblings were now into the final months of their daily companionship, since she was preparing to study medicine in the capital.

The yawning hole of her brother's absence healed badly. She nursed it daily. By the third year of her studies, however, she had got as far as not noticing it every day. Her own outstanding grades on leaving school had blocked the opportunity for any further members of their *intelligentsia* family to stay on and do the highers required for university entrance, and so on the very day she sat for her preliminary medical certificate, Squealie left school. While her parents apparently acquiesced without protest to the government's ban on children of the *intelligentsia* staying on for highers 'except in justifiable cases', she herself felt profoundly guilty. Squealie became an electrician, and their father would quip that he was the low-brow side of the family. One good thing was that the electrical wiring in their parents' apartment had yet to be channelled beneath the plaster, and Squealie was keen to be allowed to carry this out. The day after his apprenticeship ended he got to work, and within three days had managed to re-wire their parents' and great-grandmother's huge five-room apartment. For this he got heaped with praise. It was only his great-grandmother who'd noticed that his beer requirements were greater than the household's supply could keep up with, but she kept this to herself.

The little girl was to give birth to three children. After each one, she had to work hard to lose weight. Though her muscle cells were ready to conform to their statutory duty (i.e. define a slim and toned shape), her fat cells unceasingly kicked against the system. She'd had excess fat cells since childhood, and during each pregnancy a padding of blubber would amass under her skin. She called it lard, a word usually spoken with a curl of the lip. Squealie, meanwhile, was stuck back in their hometown. He never came up to Berlin to do healthy walks with her or maybe introduce one of his girlfriends. She mourned for him. If she went on holiday with her children, Squealie did use her flat (with or without a woman), but when she got back he was always gone. Admittedly when she finally decided to get married he travelled quite a distance to be there, but only, she felt afterwards, to upstage their modest celebration with the announcement of his own engagement. From that time onwards the little girl suffered from a swallowing disorder.

She hadn't known Squealie was a drinker. It was only when her mother phoned her in far-away Berlin to demand she force him to go into rehab, then broke down in tears, that she found out what had been going on. His fiancée had bid him farewell due to the alcohol, which only served to make him lose yet another tooth on yet another bender. (To be accurate he'd only lost one tooth previously – he'd got totally wasted seeing off a pal to the army and his face had smashed onto the kerb – but that's not particularly relevant right now.) Obviously she'd never dream of *forcing* her brother to do anything. As she was telling her husband all this, he was for some strange reason packing his things, and when she asked him (as a by the way) what he was doing, he availed of the moment to tell her he was going back to his first wife. Just like that. And closed the door as he went out.

She spent the following weeks on sick leave until her mother came to take her and the children to Thuringia for the holidays. She wept for the duration of the long train ride, ignoring her children. When they got off the train her father and brother were there to pick them up. She immediately noticed their broad grins and that they were bursting to say something, which she found hard to reconcile with her own state of mind. She'd expected sympathy and condolences on the demise of her marriage, but the men were wearing these happy smiles and could barely restrain themselves from proclaiming the Good News with a look in their eyes like missionary zeal, which she found surprising to say the very least, given the atheism of their household when she was growing up and which prevailed to this day. All seven of them squeezed into the Trabant, one child perched on each of her legs, the third in Squealie's lap. Once home their father brought out a bottle of expensive Greek cognac, leaving hanging in the air the question of how on earth he had come by it, and then announced the Good News: Squealie had done the Lotto on the State TV channel and landed a row of fives – the highest possible score – enabling him to claim fifty-five thousand marks from the German Democratic Republic. After his cognac their father stroked his belly contentedly; however it was suddenly obvious that her brother intended to spend the rest of his day getting out of it, wasted, totalled. Sure enough he'd soon had a sufficient skinful to be cheerfully arseholed, and was whooping it up.

In secret, the little girl sobbed.

Weeks later, when she returned to Berlin, he bought her a piano.

She loved playing the piano and was good at it. As a student and in the years since, she hadn't been able to. A good piano would have been far too expensive, and she wasn't prepared to play any old donkey. Much of her free time was now spent wallowing in Rachmaninov, Kabalewski or Prokofiev. The Russians affected her. Made her dwell on him. Their parents were expecting Squealie to buy the apartment building in which they lived. They said the old woman who owned it, Frau Blauwald, didn't have any children or probably any relatives at all and would surely let him have it cheap. He wouldn't be permitted to live there himself, as the Municipal Housing Office most definitely wouldn't allocate him one of those big flats, regardless of whether he owned the building. On the downside he'd have all the nuisance of trying to save the old wreck from collapse, with all the leaks coming through the holes in its roof, the perished seals round its windows and the huge areas where the rendering had fallen off. The whole thing was just waiting for a take-over, with no-one really paying much regard. Since he was in that line of work himself he'd probably have no problem finding craftsmen, but paying them a fair wage would surely mean his (unearned) wealth would get prised out of his hands faster than he would wish... She decided to advise her brother against it, and since in those days neither had a telephone in their own home, meaning they could only converse on the phone belonging to old Frau Blauwald who lived in the flat above her parents and who'd avidly eavesdrop any private calls made on her landing, she wrote him a letter instead. He showed this to their parents, who ranted and raved about what an absolute stab in the back it was, considering everything they'd done to help *their lad* get this far... But *their lad* did indeed turn his back on house and home, and serendipitously – or so she thought back then – built himself a twin turntable deck with the most expensive kit he could lay his hands on, and became a DJ. He got a qualification through the

Area Office for Cultural Development and after a while was taken on at 'Kulture Kamp', a newly-built provincial youth centre. Though the job was caretaking, his DJ's licence got him many a night's gig doing the disco, which provided both a showcase for his not inconsiderable talent and a place where he could discreetly drink. Until, that is, he very nearly lost his hearing. During his army days, his *malleus*, *incus* and *stapes* – middle ear components – had been removed from one ear, having disintegrated, and it now seemed those same components in his other ear had failed to withstand the onslaughts of his sound system.

Just as he was about to sell his disco deck, the revolutionary changes in the country due to the process of reunifying with West Germany effectively rendered worthless every single piece of equipment he owned, so he was stuck with it. Furthermore, his unspent winnings totalled more than the newly decreed maximum sum of eleven thousand East German marks that individuals were permitted to exchange 1:1 for so-called 'German' marks. For him, the exchange rate was instead 2:1.

It was time he got married.

He had not been looking for the woman he found. Luckily his mother managed to prevent old Frau Blauwald from dying on their actual wedding day by taking her an ample serving from the reception. She only died a good day or so later, having devoured every last thing on the plate. Then, unexpectedly, a great-niece of hers came out of the woodwork, who admitted frankly that before the 'revolution' she'd never have acknowledged her kinship with Frau Blauwald and, had they managed to trace her, would have turned the inheritance down. In these new times, however, she was extremely glad to be inheriting a residential building with solvent tenants in it as well as Frau Blauwald's own wonderfully spacious flat, into which she moved at once. This caused her no disruption whatever, either work-wise or domestically, since she'd become unemployed six months previously. The building was transformed: insulation, new rendering, new plumbing, new bathrooms for each flat. The increased rents were just enough to cover the repayments of the loan that had financed all this and provide the owner with a modest income.

So that was that.

Squealie didn't let himself think too much. His money had taken a walk. He regularly did this with his wife these days, though she always wanted to walk back to her previous tiny flat in a "period" tenement which was now as pristine as a new-build. Soon they had two little boys, who brought their own challenges. Having reached his forties he'd have loved at this stage to build a house for them all, or at the very least rent them a little allotment with a summer-house. The loss of his caretaking job dated back to the day the youth club was shut down. Later his wife, too, had lost her job in a bank, which she'd thought was secure. He applied to be a newsreader at the regional TV station. On his return from the audition he never told a soul what had gone on. He recovered from his attempted suicide only slowly. Though his sister had by now had a telephone for a few years, she once again tried writing, telling him he was still her dearest darling, he knew that didn't he? *Dear little Squealie,* she wrote, *can you remember us sitting in the little handcart and riding right into the middle of the raspberries with Grandma? And blueberries and blackberries? And going to that place where we found the larch boletes and those great big orange oak boletes? Remember? Slicing mushrooms and coating them in breadcrumbs and frying them to make schnitzel… Or those winters when us two went skating, and that wonderful crunching noise the ice made under our blades…* She conjured up the past as though it were, rather, a wonderful future on the horizon – a future they were approaching as one, gliding over thin, ever-shifting ice with one holding the other firm, being a support. It was quite obvious where she wanted him to be. But he read the letter without a single recollection, and on reaching the end, poked it in among his books.

Her children were now grown up and their lives were constantly changing. One moved to Sweden, another to Thuringia. Only the third, a boy of eighteen, still lived with her. When she thought about The Future, she worried. It was as if she had already lived through everything that was yet to come; as if the mirror of mid-life was reflecting the past and it was now recurring. As if the scene that was currently rolling had already been performed, though in a different setting and with different actors, and was coming to the end of the loop, whereby it would, for her too, start over. She went over the past more and more, searching for clues, but all she found was Squealie making a rumpus in short *lederhosen* with his short hair and short attention-span. The leather trousers he wore nowadays were full-length and black and he wore his hair in a pigtail (he didn't exactly have a lot of hair to play with, his head being graced with a bald patch that was creeping inexorably down the back towards his plait). But his attention span had continued to be short, and she had finally accepted she couldn't go on fretting over this. She wished him luck in the job he'd got through a temping agency. He was now away from his wife all week, travelling throughout Germany, and when he came home he'd be in a relaxed enough mood for this to last the weekend. Sometimes, if he was working in Berlin, he stayed over with his sister. Every visit, including this week's, he got littler, bounding around like a chimp inside her head. When she'd bought him a child's cutlery set and, one suppertime, had put them out beside the Little Red Riding Hood plate, he hadn't even blinked. With a normal face he now ate the little bread soldiers she'd cut up for him. He was so tired that he dropped off while he was still sitting there chewing. She lay him down on the bench, took off his slippers, tucked him up under a woolly blanket and sang, softly so as not to wake him, *O sacred head, now wounded…*

Shack's last laugh

HERR SHACK OWNED THREE RESIDENTIAL PROPERTIES: Ridinghood Cottages, Haricot House, and a 'chalet'. It so happened that their relative positions around the town of W. in Thuringia ("the green heart of Germany") formed an isosceles triangle. He'd seen for himself that this was more or less the case when he'd treated himself to the helicopter tour on the occasion of the town's five hundredth anniversary.

Ridinghood Cottages was to the east of the town on the attractive Ziegenberg ridge of hills, a property consisting of two semi-detached residences, their shared dark green roof sloping steeply down at the back. Herr Shack had bought it from his savings for his sixtieth birthday ten years ago.

The 'chalet' was a wooden barracks big enough for one family, in what was known as the 'Bamboo Grove', a camp on the town's western outskirts built to house the foreign workers in the former socialist Republic. It was where Herr Shack himself had lived as a child.

He had also latterly inherited Haricot House from Edeltraud Lysi, who in her later years had chosen him as her companion. Haricot House was the only house on Haricot Road, which ran out into open country to the south of W, not far from the station. No-one else had chosen to settle on the road, which had been built for those wanting to better themselves in the boom years of the late nineteenth century, and so, over the decades, it had become heavily potholed, all the way to its dead end. Though the years had robbed the fine mill-owner's mansion of its Art Nouveau details, leaving it with a flattened, grey look, no passage of years could ever have robbed it of its doughty proprietor, Frau Lysi.

Herr Shack managed his properties from a small rented flat off the market square. If you drew three lines on the isosceles triangle, one from each point, crossing to the exact halfway mark along the side opposite, it was clear that his rented flat was roughly where the three intersected; in other words, at the triangle's heart.

In the last few years, Herr Shack had no longer ventured any further than this triangle.

He was content, living in rented accommodation. He was equally content to manage his properties from the armchair of his flat, which was positioned close to the window overlooking the market square, and from the armrest of which dangled the TV's remote control.

One morning in early April Herr Shack's attention was caught by a documentary about the life of one Mr Kaunadodo. He hailed from Namibia. While he was speaking, Mr Kaunadodo's wide-brimmed hat completely disguised his face, due to the dappling of his brown skin by shimmering sunbeams filtering through its loose-woven straw. The effect made Herr Shack think of reflected light; how moving waters could throw reflections onto the beach if the sun caught it the right way. The smell of the suntan oil of his early childhood came flooding back. Dark brown, walnutty. He started to listen more intently. Mr Kaunadodo was speaking German, but with absolutely no trace of a foreign accent. Not only that, he sounded Saxonian! It was exactly the way Ute Schöller had talked (an early love from his student days who'd come from that godforsaken hole Gänsefurth)... Herr Shack pulled himself round on his armchair and turned up the TV. Mr Kaunadodo was talking about his childhood. About surviving the Massacre of Kassinga aged three, though his parents did not. Then, as a six-year-old, ending up in Bellin in Mecklenburg; that was 1981. His good, secure life there. To be perfectly honest he'd felt blessed, after the stressful conditions of the Kwanza Sul refugee camp. Herr Shack had no idea about any of this. The commentator explained that the South-West Africa People's Organization had asked the government of the German Democratic Republic if it could, in solidarity, take in, look after, educate and train some of the children who'd been orphaned or abandoned, and so Bellin's historic manor house had been deployed to this end. The official line was, the children would eventually belong to Namibia's elite class. Their education was officially carried out in compliance with strict rules and conventions, recounted Mr Kaunadodo, but unofficially, emotional attachments between themselves and their German carers had developed. His teacher, the caretaker, the gardeners, cooks and housekeeper had attended to him with what he could only call love. Though he went on to add, he wasn't sure what the word 'love' meant.

He then spent his final school years in Stassfurt, until 1990 when the German Democratic Republic was absorbed into the Federal Republic of Germany. That year, out of the blue, he and all the other young Namibians were put on a flight home. Back then he hadn't really understood what was going on, he said, but he remembered his return to Namibia with horror. Although in both Bellin and Stassfurt he'd been tutored by Namibian women to ensure he wouldn't completely forget his mother tongue *Oshivambo*, he had nonetheless grown up in Germany, so life in the Namibian reception centre had simply terrified him, and he'd run away. Not wanting to live for ever after as a goat-herd or casual labourer, he had searched for fellow East Germans – *Ossis*, as they called themselves – and succeeded in finding one: Patrick H, his best friend during that period. Patrick had put him in touch with an aid scheme, with the support of which he was permitted to re-enter the new Germany to pursue an apprenticeship. He thus became a Business Manager in Baden-Württemberg. Despite this, his German residence permit got terminated. With legal support he reapplied, having been advised that in cases of exceptional adversity the authorities could waive the stipulation that renewal applications be made within five years of initial entry and before the applicant's twenty-first birthday. But it was still turned down. So he decided to go under the radar, and with the help of various church ministers, and to be honest various women too (he smiled), he has till now managed to stay in the Federal Republic.

Herr Shack now understood the function of Mr Kaunadodo's wide-brimmed hat. He was imagining being in his situation.

He was thrown into turmoil.

His own family had been expelled from the Sudetenland. The day they were admitted to the barracks in the so-called 'Bamboo Grove' his older sister had gone and lain down, no more to rise. He himself, after a few halting steps into this place that was now 'home', had messed his pants, he'd been so terrified. And he had been the one to find her, in the common dormitory. He'd been struck dumb for a whole year.

He seated himself at his desk and wrote a letter to the Association of Public Broadcasters of the Federal Republic of Germany asking to be put in touch with Detlef B. and Annalisa G., having got the names of the two filmmakers from the TV supplement. After six weeks he was informed of Annalisa G.'s address, and he wrote to suggest his plan, saying for the last decade his financial situation had been very comfortable, which surely gave him the right to facilitate the granting of official residential status to an undocumented Namibian by paying his maintenance costs and National Insurance contributions. Further, he would be able in due course to offer the young man a flat since he was the owner of three residential properties in the county town of W. in Thuringia. He described Ridinghood Cottages, the chalet and Haricot House in meticulous detail, and implored her to put him in contact with Mr Kaunadodo. He finished off his letter with "Venceremos!", even though he was vaguely conscious of this word having originated in a former era and rather different circumstances.

Now came the wait.

In early June, he received a call.

A woman's voice, that of Annalisa G, thanked him with what he felt was a hint of amusement for his eagerness to help Mr Kaunadodo. This was however out of the question as he had by now been caught and deported. As to his whereabouts in Namibia or what he was now doing, she had absolutely no knowledge.

Such a shame, said Annalisa G.

It is indeed, said Herr Shack.

He thought long and hard.

And very slowly, the realisation dawned that the door to a world beyond his triangle stood open. If Mr Kaunadodo wasn't allowed to come to him, they certainly couldn't stop him going to Mr Kaunadodo. As time went on, this subversive idea began to exhilarate him so much that sometimes, while attending to his business or personal affairs, he'd let out an involuntary guffaw. At Winkler's travel agent's behind the school he bought a self-drive package holiday to Namibia. He wrote the address of the *Allgemeine Zeitung,* the German-language newspaper in Windhoek, in his address book, and duly contacted them. An editor promised to put him in touch with the 'Ossi Club', where he would find either Mr Kaunadodo himself or someone who knew him. This part was definite. The grey area was how Herr Shack might otherwise spend his time in Namibia. But this felt secondary, given the possibilities his money offered. He visited a notary and had a document made; this was, however, to be kept in his bank's safe, discreetly sealed in an envelope.

Finally he appointed Frau Gehlenhardt, at fifty-five the youngest of the Ridinghood Cottages tenants, to manage his finances for a decent remuneration.

On the twenty-fifth of June he transformed his plan into a reality. He locked up his flat, handed Mrs Gehlenhardt a key, took a taxi to the railway station of the little county town, boarded the train for Berlin, then flew with Air France via Paris and Johannesburg to Windhoek, where he is at this very moment leaving the airport.

He told the neighbours he was off to stay in a shack in the sun.

His guffaw is still echoing in their ears.

Gustav Brendel's journey to Molauken

GUSTAV BRENDEL, THE GRIZZLY OLD BEAR, was back on the road, his coat a billowing sail, his ears' ragged rims stinging in the wind, the swollen bladder of his rucksack giving him grief. His body's hull of chapped flesh bore several areas of inflammation, some superficial, others deep and festering and giving off a smell. Brendel loved the stink of his body: it made him aware of himself. Aside of that, he was aware of very little, as he journeyed back to Molauken. The few solitary, abandoned thoughts in his head mourned their lonely state or else scurried out of his sight. Now and then he would slow his pace, and on a few occasions he turned right the way round.

He chose his direction of progress with closed eyes, which saw him zigzagging straight through ditches, muddy puddles, bushes and cow-muck. Fences would stop him, as would (when he drifted through villages or towns) front doors. Brendel was only on the road at night. For weeks he'd slept through the days in abandoned cars, or just in a ditch somewhere.

He thought he'd come a long way. In the summer a young lad had moved into the flat below his, and had started visiting him, occasionally bringing him food. About twenty he must have been, working as a driver for a transport company. Brendel knew he had single-handedly shot this lad dead, way back. Out of nowhere, he recalled the face (so he thought) precisely. Brendel was still unsure what the boy's motive had been, doing him all the little favours. It seemed conceivable it was all meant as a thank you for making his death, back then, so short and sweet. Brendel didn't want any thanks. Brendel liked a quiet life, which is how it had been in the half-century that had slipped by between him and that boy. If the latter hadn't been standing in front of his door one day with a pot of soup and a bottle of wine that he'd *just thought he'd share with his new neighbour to celebrate moving in*, Brendel wouldn't have had to take to the road. But he had swallowed the soup. And soon after, left his flat. In the direction of Molauken, so he'd thought. And henceforward had lost all sense of direction. Brendel shivered.

At dawn, while he was poking about in the dirt for fag-ends and running his flashlight through his rucksack and the four or five bags he still had after the loss of the big brown cardboard suitcase, he laid his hands again on Irmintraut's last ID. What a stunner. Even in the black and white of the small photograph, he saw how her hair spilled vivid red over her shoulders then down and down for ever. Brendel knew full well that the day this snap was taken, it had fallen right the way down to Irmintraut's hips. He had driven her to the Wilfroth Studio in Anklam. She had put on her best clothes: the saffron-yellow dress, with a coral hairclip over her left ear so as to have a clear view of the lens. Brendel lay down in the roadside ditch and slipped the ID (having replaced between its pages the memories of Irmintraut's beauty) under the belt of his mud-caked trousers, into the little bit of body-warmth he still had. She'd be well looked after alright, with him. As he fell asleep he felt waves of her red hair around his waist: she was warming him up. Brendel did not hear the three noisy young men staggering through the field over the other side of the road, evidently heading for him.

The boy had his music on loud and was in the middle of a

smoke when the doorbell rang. It was a scrawny old woman, her feet in shiny child-sized boots, her small form wrapped up in a well-cut little cashmere coat. She apologized, before asking him about Brendel, from whom she hadn't heard for weeks, hence had made this long journey from Glauchau to look for him. The last few kilometres from Anklam to this godforsaken dump had been particularly dreadful, the bus connection so bad she'd had to stand half a day at the bus-stop. The boy was not in the habit of letting strangers see his mess, but he nonetheless asked her in. He took the little coat from her shoulders and said she was welcome to keep her boots on. But no – to boost her sluggish circulation, which comes to us all with age, she needed to give her feet a stretch and her calves a massage to make sure her legs wouldn't just finally pack up one day as her doctor said would happen if she went on being inactive; the train ride was exhausting and she hadn't dared to take her shoes off in the compartment to do her gymnastic exercises for collapsed veins. As the boy poured her the requested glass of water in the kitchen, he was amazed at both his own courteous hospitality and the uninhibited behaviour of the old lady, who had cleared a spot in the chaos of his living room to make a space to exercise in. When he came back with the water he nearly tripped over her legs which, from her prostrate position on the floor, she was lifting and lowering with a cheerful expression and a determination, as evinced by her furrowed brow, to ward off the ageing process – *Brendel could have done with me around, that grizzly old bear*. Ah – was that what all this was about? *He's gone off somewhere,* the boy readily responded, and he told of how Brendel had left one day without a word of goodbye. A neighbour and the sales girl at the village baker's had seen him with his brown cardboard suitcase going past the bus stop towards the forest. That must have been about eight, maybe nine weeks ago. He tried to recall, and dredged up from his memory a couple of fruitless occasions of ringing the doorbell of Brendel's flat, and a conversation with the volunteer who looks after senior citizens, but the main thing he'd reported to this lady was, Brendel had posted him the key to his mailbox, in an envelope with far too many stamps on it, along with a message that rent, electricity and water had all been paid for until his return, and that his plants had been shared around some ladies in the village to be looked after. *Until his return.* The boy grabbed the box from the bookcase where he kept mail addressed to Brendel. Since leaving, Brendel had received a lot of post; any rate, more than the boy would get in a whole year. He hadn't bothered to check the envelopes for their senders. The old lady quickly and efficiently fished out of the pile her own cards and letters posted to Brendel in recent times, then without any ado, started reading them aloud. Before it could occur to the boy to protest against this un-negotiated demand on his time and the disturbance to the normal soundtrack of his life, the narrator had hooked him in.

Bad Sülze, 31ˢᵗ August, 19 ...

Dear Gustav,

my heart has gone on yearning for you but to no avail. What a joy, after all these years, a letter at last, I can't believe it. Will answer when I get home from rehab. Guess what - in June I had a stroke. I dearly wish to hear more from you

Your Reni

Glauchau, 18ᵗʰ October, 19 ...

Dear Gustav,

Well, I'm home from the clinic, no post from you there, and none here either. What's going on??? After all those years, you got round to writing to me, but with no contact come of it yet. Your letter felt so full of promise. Oh Gustav. Pick up a pen!

Am sending you my reply from my last few weeks in rehab, I wrote it when I was bored. Was often bored, so has turned into long letter.

14th September

It is lovely to hear from you again after so many years. I haven't moved house since 1955, when Irmintraut's last letter came. I'm still here in Glauchau on Ruhlandt Street, in a property that's seen better days. What made you think of writing a few lines to your old Reni again? Round about now would have been Irmi's seventy-fifth birthday, I still remember how we always drove over to Molauken at the end of October from our place in Bischkehnen, and there'd usually still be a few asters in the gardens for Irmi to enjoy. I could never have known, back then, that you'd swap me for my best friend. We were actually already engaged by then, you and me. Despite that I've always held Irmi dear in my thoughts, believe me. And I always thought very highly of her that when we fled west, she took me with her, when I could hardly walk for that trapped nerve that was down to our Gustav, little Gustav, already in there. You put me and Irmi in the family way at almost the same time, Gustav, and both babies died. I know you know, mine died in the womb. Irmi will have told you, I didn't get the chance to name little Gustav 'Alfred' like we had agreed. We packed him in a box and buried him at the side of the road. Irmi's boy lived a couple of weeks with us two women, he was named properly, Gustav Alfred, we so loved him, yet we had to lay him to rest. We were in Glauchau by then, and half the town walked behind his coffin because Irmi this red-haired beauty had all the men under her spell, and all the wives up in arms, all of them watching out to see who she'd turn to next, after little Gustav's death. But Irmi only ever had eyes for you, so therefore, seeing as nobody would declare you dead, straight off I put in for our divorce. The man I married after Ellinor's birth had actually wanted to go with Irmintraut, but took me because Alfred was the only name Irmi would call out in her dreams, then one day there was news that you were still alive, so I was glad that the divorce had since come through and I was already someone else's wife. I can still see your face as you came up that Saxon country lane and just clumps of rags round your feet, and how you hugged me and my husband and baby Ellinor, and how you then went to Irmi and the two of you went all round Anklam, united in heart and soul, and how everybody wept when you left. It was wonderful. What I liked about us was, we were able to part on good terms, and then come together again on a different understanding. But then sadly, you hardly ever got in touch, Gustav, you were so completely under the spell of Irmintraut's beautiful face and flowing locks. I can understand it. Sometimes, when I was upset, even I'd go bury my face in that flame-red silkiness, and we'd both be thinking about you, Gustav, with me fingering her curls, and about what you might have got up to in Molauken, back then, when we could already hear the Russians coming and, being women, we had to head off, go west. Maybe you wanted to save Molauken for the sake of Irmi and me and the two future Gustavs, you were hardly blinking twenty-three! and had given each of us a baby, my God, you were already a fine man at that age. It's a good job me and her were friends.

And now with Irmi long dead you're getting in touch again. I'd gone on writing regularly to you folks and did get a couple of replies from Irmi, saying there were no more children, and you were always faithful to her, Unto Eternity. My husband has gone to Eternity as well, he is laid to rest here in Glauchau. Maybe we could spend our days of old age together Unto Eternity and have some more nice times in this life, what do you think, Gustav, wouldn't that be a good thing, for both of us? And go back to Molauken. I've always wanted to. Irmi

didn't. She told me herself. I think she'd completely cut off from
everything to do with our old home, frankly. But let's go, us two, and
see what we left behind. It must all be completely straightforward
now, to go. Where our little Gussy is laid is on the Polish side. Oh
my, I'm all in a state now with telling all this. Having to dwell on
Irmintraut such a lot, and thinking of that long journey. She'll have
told you everything so many times herself anyway. Irmi was so sad
when her Gustav followed my Gustav into the grave. Didn't we have
bad luck, all three of us. At least back then. I've had two more little
lasses though who are grown up now and have made me a Grandma.
You know Ellinor from when she was a baby, she was in my arms
when you came back. Then three days after "Your Wedding" Helga
came along. Irmi will have told you. I'm just going to get myself my
buttermilk now for my digestion, I'll be back in touch soon, with Love
–

16th September
Got a bit of time again. More to say!
Dearest Gustav, you ask whether I still have feelings for you. Yes I
do. In all those years there was never a cross word between us, thank
God. I was sometimes sad that the whole of me amounted to only one
eighth of Irmintraut's attractions, it's just how it had to be, you
wanted her and I never got you back after your convalescent leave. At
least our Time gave us little Gussy, even though he never lived...

The old woman, the boy had noticed by now, was reading
out more to herself than to him what she had written to Brendel
some weeks ago. His thoughts ran away with him. He had
never experienced anything as insane as this skinny creature
who, devoid of inhibition, had drawn him into a mad vortex of
long-ago love stories, all the while bobbing up and down to
exercise her ludicrous little shins, or tottering stick-legged

round his room, with interludes spent sitting on the floor or lying on the rug, during all of which she was reading aloud, in a constant, regular tone and rhythm. The latter brought to the boy's mind the little gold watch his mother wore. That amazing watch was as old as his grandmother, whose mother had received the precious item from her husband upon the birth of their first child. The boy suspected that the steady pulse of Time beating in that metal capsule on his mother's wrist would continue long after the throb of her actual pulse had faltered. Though the watch did need winding up each night. The boy's thoughts meandered to whose pleasure it might have been to wind up this old woman's voice-box for this performance.

Listening to her he remembered that evening in Brendel's kitchen when, being a new neighbour, he had introduced himself with wine and soup. The old man had reluctantly, so the boy thought, asked him in and offered him a seat on the kitchen bench. At the time he had put Brendel's off-putting silence down to what was presumably his long-term state of solitude, and had reciprocated with silence. A day or two after this first encounter, Brendel had asked the boy to take one of the valuable old cabinets from his living room to an antique dealer in Schwerin. Brendel had sat beside him in the driver's seat and for the whole of the long journey had again been silent, when, to the boy's mind, it could have been a journey towards better acquaintance. After all, he'd spent ages begging his boss to loan him the van for a private trip. He got especially annoyed when he happened to notice how much money Brendel was getting for the cabinet, carefully counting the notes into his money-belt – and then only paying him for petrol.

Old geezers had never been his thing.

The boy only went and visited him, that quiet, cool, late summer evening, because it was customary. It'd be expected. He did not live here entirely from choice; he had moved to be out of close range of his parents, who were in one of the nearby villages, counting the years until retirement. Their years of drawing a pension would differ from the years preceding them insofar as the couple wouldn't have to suffer any further badly-paid employment schemes. This suffering was a great bond uniting husband and wife – at least in the evenings, when they'd sit there on the brown corduroy couch, after days spent watching each other and silently endeavouring to humiliate each other amid the rickety rabbit-runs and quagmires of chicken-shit and the broken-down barn. There they sat, awaiting the homecomings of grown-up children, not facing up to the stark fact that before too long they'd have nothing else to suffer except each other. That's just how it was, and the boy, who could scarcely find adequate words for his parents' condition, had felt a very acute sense of foreboding. It had made him flee from his ageing parents on their brown corduroy couch; they who, despite sitting so close as to be within a beer-glass's radius from each other, were incapable of *closeness*. While he was still growing up it hadn't bothered him. By now, however, being long past the age when he'd had to buy shoes due to outgrowing the old ones, it felt like his life was trickling out of a leak in his body, and he was afraid that if he didn't act soon, little of him would be left, other than a small trace on his parents' cheap living-room carpet.

It was good that Brendel had no expectations of him whatsoever. This made it easier to go up a few more times after that, and bring him something to eat, or a newspaper he'd bought while out. The third time, Brendel had started talking, but their conversations had not turned out to be particularly fruitful, simply because the boy had barely any knowledge of the things that had shaped Brendel's opinions, and so couldn't fill in the gaps that yawned ever wider in the stale air with each word from Brendel's mouth. Brendel, himself irritated by this ever-increasing gulf, would after a while ask the boy to come back another day and leave him in peace for now.

Obviously the boy had no idea that Brendel recognized him.

Meanwhile the old woman was arranging things so she could sleep on the settee in the boy's living-room. He was actually okay with it: just closed the door, and sat in the kitchen. The television was there and he switched it on. Every so often he marvelled once again at the familiarity with which the old woman, starting from zero, had more or less bridged the gulf between the two of them, with her funny little legs and her fanciful romantic propositions that kept her trailing after Brendel to this day, a man she'd been married to so long ago, before he was born. The boy, too, had made a girl pregnant, while still at school, and he remembered with relief the early miscarriage. Seven or eight years ago it was practically *de rigeur* to have a child when very young, and get married as soon as you reached the age of consent. His parents had wanted that for him too, but his connection to that girl was no more than a dull, unpleasant memory, so he just didn't get it: what was behind them, this old woman's letters to Brendel? A man who got two women pregnant simultaneously and left the one he had just married straight after the wedding to go off with someone else – in his view that wasn't exactly a reason to mourn him for life. Though the old dear hadn't exactly lived in mourning; she'd gone and had other children with another man, for whom she to this day didn't have a bad word. And the women on whom Brendel had bestowed two Gustavs who'd both died – they'd remained friends, hadn't they? He was confronted with puzzles. He wished things in this story could have had clearly drawn battle-lines, like in his normal life going back as long as he could remember. He was now having another smoke, the sun's reflection on his watch sending a purplish ray across the kitchen wall. For the first time, the boy felt he'd got hopelessly left behind; that the four walls of his parents' house were not the real boundary he ought to have crossed; rather, the narrow, beige pettiness of the corduroy couch had invaded his parents' house from somewhere beyond, but where that might be, he no longer had any idea. As ever, he felt himself stuck in a bubble: the air currently in his nostrils had been breathed countless times; stale, stagnant, shut-in air whose regeneration was confined within the limits of narrow-minded pettiness. And as he stood at the open window looking out onto the freshly rendered manor house that had opened as a hotel two or three years ago, he started to cry.

Brendel was freezing. It was the last sensation he could still identify before the blow that knocked his head deep into a muddy puddle. One of the three young men gave him three or four more kicks in the belly and to his legs and feet, which luckily caused Brendel's head to loll back onto dry ground. He lay there like that, and the three moved on. One who had got up close to Brendel, having fallen into the dirt himself whilst kicking, had retched due to the repulsive smell. The other two retched shortly after. In fact they'd already been feeling sick due to the Goldbrand, a cheap and cheerful socialist era brandy they'd consumed as breakfast in a long-disused bus stop outside the nearby village. When Brendel came round he could still hear the sound of them vomiting their guts up. He was trembling, biting his lip till blood came so as not to let out a moan, despite his distress. He groped in his trousers for Irmintraut, pulling her clear of the mud that seemed to have completely saturated him, and dabbed the picture until it seemed more or less dry, but he couldn't tell through the veil of blood all down his face whether there was anything still to be seen of Irmi's loveliness. Only when he thought the men were a safe distance away did he try to get up. It would be light for a while yet. Autumn had thus far had the decency not to send any frosts to cull people like him. Weighing things up, it might be preferable to die right here on the spot, thus rendering the search for a washing facility unnecessary. The best thing would probably be to go back to the petrol station whose owner had treated him fairly the day before yesterday, even taking him into his office for a sleep on an air mattress, under a woolly cover which, after all the past weeks of roaming, he'd compulsively pressed to his nose, over and over. The fresh smell of detergent it gave off had actually made him decide to just go home and confront the boy. But then he moved on again because the petrol station's proprietor had kindly got a lady from the welfare onto his case who wished to take him straight to a doss-house. He had already been privileged to encounter some of these sorry establishments; they were mostly closed when he wanted to go to sleep, and only opened again after he was already on his way. So they were no good to him.

Brendel knew, moreover, that Molauken was definitely not in the same place as it used to be. Often he would sense it to be just nearby, feeling it was showing him signposts, then suddenly it would disappear behind the lumpen mass of lowering November clouds. Brendel's zigzagging trek was like the game of a little child who hadn't yet learned to gauge the speed of the grown-up's pace in relation to the distances to potential hiding places: in his befuddled determination to hide, seek and find, he was flung from one emotional extreme to the other. When it had first come to Brendel that it was time for him to make his Grand Return, when he still had enough money in his pockets to buy tickets, he had travelled lengthy distances by train. Reaching Berlin and finding out that he'd been travelling in the wrong direction, he'd hung around the East Central Station for days on end before setting off back to the northeast of the country. His further explorations had then been limited to the territories of northern Uckermark, the island of Usedom and the Oder estuary. He had visited these places with Irmintraut in their younger day, when they had gone on many a hike, but he now no longer recognized them and could barely manage to remember where he'd been only yesterday. Only when he was asleep did he reach his destination and recognize everything once more: the long approach to the village on the tarred road with fruit trees growing either side offering their fruits for free; the church, and from its gateway, the street splitting into two lanes that came together as one again behind the cemetery. In his dream he even lay the naked Irmintraut down in the middle of the street, her head towards the gateway, parting her flaming hair and lashing it around the church and the cemetery before tying it in a knot in the nape of the churchyard's neck. Having blocked the street leading out of Molauken with Irmi's hair, he crawled deep inside the knot of it, and from this hiding place, created more fantasies for himself. He saw the milk shop and the vegetable stall in front of Wernicke's farm. There was a broad strip of turf between the street and the houses on either side. Children had trampled the grass into the earth where they played. Brendel saw their bare feet flying up to kick the ball; he heard the geese in makeshift pens in front of the houses, their cackles chopping into the hot air. He often saw Reni approaching in the distance and, at this, would pull himself deeper into his den of hair. When Reni had passed by and was no longer to be seen, he would crawl out of hiding and run into Irmi's flowing locks. In front of the church gate he made love, slippery with sweat, to his sleepy lover, her eyes only half-open, and when he helped her to her feet he sensed in the dream that Reni had been watching them; that she'd been hiding behind a bush or a fence. When Brendel woke up he sometimes thought he saw the flutter of a skirt, far away; a skirt that always flashed with the colour of the dress Reni wore the day after her wedding. When Brendel woke up, the smell of Molauken lingered for a long time in his nose, and for a good while longer his ragged-rimmed ears were filled with Irmi's sleepy sighs and the sound of bare female feet on the street's tar, running off.

Brendel felt that to be able to breathe freely again he'd have to swallow the blood in his throat, though the feeling that blood was already upsetting his stomach made the prospect disgusting. He felt rage soaking into him from his wet, stinking pants; consuming him. He knew he didn't wish this to happen, and began laboriously taking off his clothes. From one of the bags he took out another pair of stinking trousers, and a plaid shirt - the only one he'd still got saved up for his arrival in

Molauken. He gave himself a cursory wipe down with his filth-impregnated vest then put on the dry clothes, and on top of those his coat, and set off walking. All was still. He moved with all the strength he could muster. The fragile sail of his old coat surrendered him to the wind, and from a distance he looked like a boat buffeted by the waves. It had been an effort to throw the sail over his shoulders and fasten it securely across his chest with a paper clip. Where once buttons had shined on the dark fabric, frayed holes yawned, and Brendel had un-bent the clip and pushed it through one of these holes, then through the corresponding buttonhole on the left-hand lapel, then twisted together the two ends of the wire. It suddenly seemed to Brendel that the easiest way to get somewhere was to just let fate take over. He was still wondering why he hadn't thought of it earlier, on the road he'd taken yesterday when he was actually being blown the other way. And every step back confirmed his belief that he was closer to Molauken than ever before. He hadn't been on the road in daytime for a long while. The sun, even though not at its height and still cloud-covered, was imprinting bright, painful spots on his retina, and now and then Brendel was forced to stop and press his fists deep into his eye sockets. This would momentarily make him feel better, but when he lowered his hands again the pain would intensify. Brendel was now stopping more and more often because the pressure of his knuckles created black spots that blocked his vision. Hours passed before he reached Anklam from the west. Anklam, where no amount of commercial activity, of afternoon hustle and bustle – the shoppers, the browsers in the aisles, the beer-drinkers around the fast-food stalls and arcades, not even the crazy traffic – could hide it; where this new urban buzz was at best a thin veneer, hiding the region's complacency and indifference; where Brendel couldn't hide from the fact that he had – yes – shot the boy, back then. In the summer of forty-four, while on convalescent leave from the front, he had put Reni in the family way and married her. Weeks later, a bolt of lightning had struck the young Brendel – lightning which he'd already for some years noticed passing him by, while he was on Reni's arm. This was Irmintraut, with whom he fell so deeply in love that he was compelled to spend the rest of his convalescent leave unrolling sturdy rush matting across a bubbling, gurgling, dangerous swamp; the matting being divided into two lengths, then thrown alternately across the unstable terrain. The first part of his leave was completely focused on Reni; the second part was then Irmintraut's, and it was his sheer good fortune that it ended with the two women taking turns to support him through a time when he was struggling to survive. Together they had hidden him in the barn of a hurriedly abandoned farmhouse that was falling derelict. As a deserter's wife, Reni had been interrogated and threatened a few times, and then when the visible fact of her pregnancy could have given her some protection, it was no longer of any use: everything was unravelling and people were heading westwards in a mad scramble. They'd been unable to take Brendel, not only because he was a wanted deserter, but because he'd simply disappeared. A long time after, Irmintraut told him that at dawn on the day she was to flee, she had run to the barn to check on him one more time, and that, as she was taking the ladder out of its hiding place to climb up to Brendel, a dead boy had fallen at her feet, and how she had screamed, then looked into the boy's face. In her frenzy of fleeing, she was still able to see he was a good boy who didn't know what he'd done to deserve his murderer's bullet; his face therefore having, even in death, a completely astonished expression which didn't leave him, reported Irmintraut, even when she stroked his eyelids closed and put the weapon lying a few meters away into his hand.

No – there had been no battle in his soul, as Brendel recollected it now, between the appeals of Reni, Irmi, his superior officers, comrades, Hitler himself, and his beckoning Adulthood, each wanting to pull him in their direction. Rather, one single entity made up of all of them had – with an inchoate and resounding roar of machismo – taken a slug at his brain and pummelled it down like a warmed and risen dough, then left it to rise again. And it was when this dough in Brendel's head was about to splurge from his eyes, nose and mouth, the boy soldier had turned up, out of nowhere. After a short scuffle Brendel, being the stronger man, had got the pistol off the boy and shot him in the head, putting the barrel of the gun onto the boy's pulsating temple that had once attracted his mother's gentle kisses. Shooting the boy – not even a man yet – had been like shooting his own reflection. Seeing his adversary's face, blanched with fear, as if it were his own, had torn him up inside. In the sudden silence in his own head, mirroring the deathly silence – how could it be other – in his adversary's head, he had fallen asleep, and when he'd woken up and realised what he'd done, he had fled from his deed. From that day forward, every step he'd taken was towards Irmi and the Adulthood he wanted to spend with her. He had succeeded in picking up her trail, and had followed her without revealing himself, because Reni and Irmi's feelings for him were too similar. He had gone under a different name for a while, and it was only after Reni got married again that he'd dared to announce Gustav Brendel's Return, and had at last walked up that Saxon country lane, at the far end of which Reni had introduced him to her newborn daughter, while Irmi had flung herself on his neck, and later he and Irmi had moved up north. Brendel knew all this full well; this moment of truth he was having on the station forecourt at Anklam was quite unnecessary. As for his downstairs neighbour, he could now see plain as day that his encounter with that boy, who was in utter despair over his future, had somehow mirrored Brendel's encounter with his victim, fifty years before. And feeling his body up and down through his clean shirt, Brendel knew where he was.

Fish dish

VIKTORIA KNEW, OBVIOUSLY, that it was a trooper who'd fathered her; quite an old one to boot. This fact carried more weight than the fact that she'd been conceived in her mother's love for that trooper (by whom she was then to be widowed). Viktoria had been battling all her life. Even her farts, as a baby born at the end of the war, had thundered like cannons. Throughout her school years she fought all who had been Otherwise Conceived, slapping them; jabbing them with her elbows. She developed the physique of a storm-trooper yet still loved tight little blouses, flounces and lacy collars. Her face shone like a buffed-up medal awarded for exceptional bravery in the face of the enemy, the sort of medal she'd been desperately trying to obtain for her father shortly before his death. Victoria learned to fillet fish, and by this means earned her keep, interrupted only by a single maternity leave. The one luxury she afforded herself was expensive bottles of imported scent which she wore every day.

She left her first short marriage due to suffering chronic bouts of not feeling anything, though over the course of her life this would give her a strategic advantage on quite a few occasions. For example, if she'd had proper feelings, she'd have been unable to enter a second marriage. But this she did, and once married, was able to embark on her ultimate offensive. She campaigned for, and won, a gallant little trooper whom she kitted out in cute sailor suits of increasing size over the years, while at the same time gradually increasing the no-man's-land between herself and his father. By her son's eighteenth birthday she had completely expelled his father from her terrain. During one of her bouts of not feeling anything she did once try to make herself fancy him again. The effort not only failed, it made her give up on men entirely. Today, with the dawn of her fifty-fourth birthday, Viktoria felt victorious, convinced she'd at last been granted an indefinite furlow from sex. She reprimanded herself for having agreed to put on a spread for her lady and gentleman colleagues. It was Sunday and she had wanted to go over to her son's, but his lack of gallantry increasingly upset her: he would visit her four times a year at most. So she had heeded her workmates' suggestion that they might, for once, come over to her place for a nice cup of coffee and to see her collection of scent bottles and also peruse the old Record Book of what had formerly been their workers' collective. Up until a decade before, Viktoria had collated this with conscientious accuracy. She'd always been especially taken with their visits to the 'parent unit' – the Red Army station to which their collective was assigned. The young men's hollow grins captured by her *Pouva Start* bakelight camera had left her cold, aside of being marginally turned on by their somewhat shabby uniforms.

Viktoria put a record of military band music on the ancient gramophone. Then, as every year on her birthday, she struck up a conversation with her father. The old trooper was entirely at home in his daughter's head. Since his responses came out of her mouth, their exchanges were fluent and lively, with Viktoria sometimes formally clicking her heels to put his question, or smoothing down her skirt as she answered him. She loved these conversations with her father. They brought up emotions that were otherwise completely missing from her life. On finishing school, her son had immediately acquired long frizzy hair and a preference for baggy jumpers and the kind of trousers that flap wide and loose around the leg, along with a preference for wide and loose women, one of whom he had married ten years ago and had somewhat pulled in by the drawstrings through giving her half a dozen children to contend with. Viktoria had a hard time playing grandmother to this chaotic, frizzy-haired flock. She didn't love her grandchildren and indeed her love for their father had waned. She pulled two frozen desserts from the freezer compartment: an egg liqueur tart and a Black Forest gateau, and put them to thaw in the little room that had once been her son's. Viktoria used to borrow him encyclopaedias from the local library and would snip out pictures of the army uniforms and rank insignia of the Warsaw Pact countries and attach them to a big board she'd hung above his bed. Her son didn't like these pictures and pinned animal posters, photos of girls and the front covers of popular magazines on top of them, which would routinely earn him a slap. But none of this was in Viktoria's mind right now, as she placed the cherry brandy to hand beside the frozen desserts and got out the Record Book in readiness. She might have noticed, as she went past the front door, that a photograph had slipped from between the book's thick leaves and was slowly sailing to the floor.

Next, she dusted her bottle collection in the bathroom. The display of these had necessitated the purchase of fifteen glass shelves by mail order. She undid the top of her nighty and sloshed DEMIRELLE into her cleavage. As the perfume reached her privates she happily felt the anticipated fiery sensation. She could now get dressed, but first rubbed the last of the rivulet into her belly. Glancing in the mirror she was sure she saw a glint of vinegar in her eye. When Viktoria bent over the bathtub to decide in which order she should kill the three enormous carp, they remained absolutely still, as if playing dead might put off their actual death, and as if oblivious to the disgrace of big fish like themselves living in a bathtub. Viktoria named the creatures after three of the workmates who were due at her place that afternoon, and checked that none were showing any signs of the dropsy that commonly afflicted *Cyprinus carpio.* Manfred, Gundel and Heiner were rehearsing their eventual *rigor mortis* in tiptop physical condition. Viktoria was surprised to be dithering over the order in which the handsome fish with their fine scales should go under the knife. Manfred was watching her with yellow eyes like plucked marigolds. Gundel's stare reminded her of her son's, back in the days when he was still wearing those sailor suits; meanwhile the curiously doe-eyed Heiner was, she noticed, giving her a come-on look. She looked from one to the other, indecisive.

She quickly regretted her decision to leave the order to chance. Her strategy of closing her eyes to grab one of the creatures trapped in the tub's murky waters failed woefully, but Viktoria never submitted to defeat. She wiped her hands on the waterproof barbecue apron that the canning factory had bestowed on her and all the other fish women one Women's Day. Her body, which while being heavy was toned and angular, sprang with agility into the lounge where the sewing machine in the bottom of the oak sideboard was on standby for one of its rare deployments. At the slightly-too-low table Viktoria cut some strips of Velcro and sewed them onto the inner surfaces of two odd gloves she'd kept for years, then pulled these on and tried her luck once more. Gundel turned out to be the first one she caught. The creature's eyes reminded her once again of the looks she used to get from her sailor-suited son; nonetheless she had no problem with smashing and cutting off the carp's head with the meat cleaver and, with expert hand, slitting open his belly, making bladder and intestines slide into the basin. A similar fate befell Manfred and

Heiner. Viktoria boiled up the fins, bones and heads, making a magisterial soup, the aroma of which carried through the whole building; meanwhile the salted and marinaded carp fillets were laid to rest on a bed of steamed vegetables. Thereafter they were kept warm in the oven while a saucepan of coconut oil was placed on the stove ready to fry the freshly chipped potatoes that Viktoria had had delivered from the supermarket yesterday along with a box of sweet Hungarian wine. She noted happily that there was still a little time before the guests were due to arrive. Time which she thought she might pass with a not too modestly poured glass of schnaps. She removed the stopper of a bottle her son had brought her one summer from the Czech Republic where he and his family had taken a cheap break, he said. A farmer had had the moonshine on special offer at the holiday lets. Viktoria's tongue savoured the lingering taste of plum, and it briefly crossed her mind, she should offer her father a glass. The old trooper had liked to drink spirits, and had told of how they'd get themselves hammered, and a good thing too, before the final battles on the Eastern Front. She saluted her father with a glass, and he proceeded to tip it down the hatch in one. Viktoria gasped, contented. A second toast followed, this one being the old trooper's call, obviously. Soon, father and daughter were bending each other's ears just as they'd always done.

The guests were annoyingly late. Viktoria was displeased, and took the fish out of the oven. She picked a piece of fillet out of the tinfoil and popped it in her mouth. Put the fish back in. Turned off the gas. Decided to sit at the window so she could start heating the oil as soon as she saw her colleagues coming up the street. Her father demanded schnaps. She obeyed without further ado, and downed another glass before leaving her look-out post – fidgety now – to go slice the desserts.

Thus, for a while, she teetered about within her flat's four walls, going back into her son's room to fetch the cigarettes she kept in a wooden box for special occasions, lifting the plate covering the bowl of chipped potatoes a few times, not knowing quite what to do, for the moment, with her slap-happy hands – until she heard, loud and distinct, the old trooper's command for a third glass of schnaps. Her father's roar, coming out of her own temples, felt like punches to her skull, so before knocking back the old geezer's shot of a classic plum schnaps – Sliwowitz – Viktoria dissolved a sedative into it.

It was starting to feel warm. Viktoria began to undo the clothing she'd changed into ready for the visit, starting with pulling up the waistband of her button-through skirt because it was very tight and felt better if the top button was positioned above her stomach bulge. Then she undid her glitzy yellow blouse to a good way down and, with her left hand, endeavoured to reach the old-fashioned clasp of her old-fashioned brassiere. At last she sat herself in the armchair in front of the window, stockings down, knees blue and shiny, ankles crossed, and sang. Her colleagues arrived shortly after to see a somewhat dissolute Viktoria leaning a long way out of her open window and belting out *Lili Marleen* till it was bouncing off the walls of the building opposite. They were bemused. Viktoria had always been regarded as odd and dour, while at the same time very controlled and precise. No one would ever have thought her capable of bellowing out ditties into the Sunday streets with such abandon. Beset with embarrassment Manfred and Heiner grabbed each other's arms and hastily made their entry through the main door which was already ajar, uncomfortably scanning the windows of the other flats to see if anyone was looking.

It was a while till, between two verses, Viktoria heard her

doorbell ringing and attempted a brisk goose-step to her front door. Peering through the spy-hole she'd had installed four or five years ago to protect her from surprise visitors, she at first saw three carp, and needed a further moment before realising it was Gundel, Manfred and Heiner. Greeting the men with gusto she let them in, slammed the door behind them and led them into the lounge, one of her stockings all the while wriggling further and further off till it trailed along behind her fat blue leg like a train. Her guests, seated on the settee behind the slightly-too-low table, cleared their throats nervously, clearly not daring to confer on how to deal with this. Meanwhile Viktoria, now in the kitchen, was battling with turning on the gas to fry the chips.

The next ring brought into her flat the four women who stood day-long beside Viktoria at the conveyor belt extracting intestines. On seeing Victoria practically undressed, standing at the stove, the youngest couldn't stop giggling; the others however saw danger, and took themselves and the cook to the safety of her bedroom where they put her clothes back on properly, pulling up her stockings and making her hairdo nice again. Victoria promptly regained her dignity and, drawing herself up, went through to the men, where the look in Gundel's eyes made her remember the tray of fish in the oven. The old trooper (of whom, needless to say, her colleagues were unaware) roared for a schnaps. From being his sharp-elbowed little fighter with her ready slaps all those years ago, Viktoria had gone on wanting to please him, and so poured him a fourth glass and drank it. The women got busy in the kitchen and, unsure of which of the prepared dishes to take through first, decided by tossing a coin that they'd start by frying the potatoes. Manfred uncorked the first bottle of wine which, due to their urgent need for relaxation, was polished off in a quick succession of servings. Viktoria kept up, which was no mean feat. Luckily the oily fish made her settle down into more like a daze, and she managed to reach for the Record Book. A bout of not feeling anything had come on, so that she almost couldn't be bothered to show them it and talk through the old days, page after page. But an innocuous inquiry about her son jolted her back to her usual form, including a mouth sealed in what was nowadays a very firm silence on the subject of The Past. They sank ever more comfortably into the settee, extolling the merits of the wine and filling any potential gaps in the conversation with cake. And thus, all slipped into a hazy glow that made it perfectly alright to make up tales about the Red Army soldiers immortalised by Victoria's *Pouva Start*: how the German city had been seeded with their romantic love affairs; how the deserters among them had roamed through the nearby forests before their inevitable deaths. So warm and tender was the glow that Viktoria's womanhood became aroused, and when Heiner looked over with his doe-eyes, she very obviously tilted her chin at him, coquettish. All had lost track of the time when (on Heiner's insistence) the guests headed off into the night. Viktoria closed the door behind them. She felt elated. In a return to her usual meticulousness, she put on the door chain, then, out of a desire to surrender to this unfamiliar feeling of happiness, she lifted one of her blue legs in order to do a little twirl on the other, as though starting to dance. At this, the photograph which had sailed out of the Record Book that morning inserted itself between the sole of her slipper and her fifty-fourth birthday's peaceful end. She went down with a whack. Late in the night, after Viktoria's breathing had already stopped (though the old trooper was still bleeding from a head wound), the son whom she had not been expecting today came by.

The Death Wish

MUTHILD SHANK IS LYING FLAT ON HER BACK. She has foraged some Slimy Cortinarius, some Velvet Shanks, and some Herald-of-winter. The basket of mushrooms is on the floor beside the head end of her bed. She is deep in thought, mulling over their suggestive names. Muthild Shank is especially taken with *velvet shank*. She pushes the mushroom's soft shank into her tummy button, wraps its little hat round her earlobe, then eats it raw and awaits the high. But it won't happen with this mushroom – a harmless, velvety-shanked sort of chap who's eager to be popped in a casserole or a frying pan, the end result of which definitely won't be hallucinatory. So Muthild Shank tries the slimy one typical of the Brandenburg heathlands. When she rubs it dry on her pubic mound, the slime has the fateful effect of stirring up the Reason For Her Death Wish. One by one she squeezes the mushrooms beneath her armpit till a little pile of mush has accumulated, from which liquid is seeping. She slurps this up, then turns onto her stomach and sticks her tongue into the fungal pulp. Not bad: a bit like bread with almond butter. On her back once again, Muthild Shank waits for the high, but it refuses to come because the Cortinarius, like the Velvet Shank, isn't a total villain: he's just an unctuous little slimeball, the sort you come across everywhere. What next? Muthild Shank crushes the Herald-of-winter mushroom firmly between her bare left foot and right calf, smears the mulch over her ankles, then dozes off into two concurrently unfolding dreams. She flips back and forth between the two, swayed by the adventures of one scenario and the disappointments of the other, unsure as to which one she might best develop to a happy ending – and wakes up seven hours later confident in the belief that she is now dead. She gets herself up to make coffee. The morning is no different from any when she was alive, with the sun gracefully rising beyond the window and Muthild Shank scrabbling about for her travel card. In former times she used to work in a hat factory, steaming felt and forming it into head-sized hemispheres, trimming brims and inserting feathers into silk-look acetate bands, sewing rhinestones onto the finer hats, or affixing tulle veils beneath which brides and widows could hide their joys and sorrows. She had qualified as a milliner and paraded through her provincial existence adorned with a variety of hats until the day her factory got incorporated into one of these 'Industrial Park' affairs and she was offered retraining as a saleswoman. She had acquiesced. The days of all those old hats in her cupboard were over. Five days a week she had travelled to the nearest big town for a training course. Which is where she met, one day, the Reason For Her Death Wish, a classic model of middle-aged man: big-boned while somewhat on the short side. Head hunched and in a hurry, he was walking past the bakery just as Muthild Shank was in the middle of buying a sandwich to eat in the training course's lunch break. But now she swiftly grabbed her change and, leaving the baker's wife holding the bagged-up bread-bun, followed the male who was to be the Reason For Her Death Wish to the Job Centre. She sat next to him (which he didn't even register), and bided her time until, looking flushed, he re-emerged from the room into which he'd been sent, stumbled, fell over with a bang, and just lay there. Muthild Shank knew this was her chance. She ran to the toilet, soaked her clean hanky, and within moments was pressing it on the swollen forehead of the eventual Reason For Her Death Wish. The Classic Male came to, having been briefly unawares; a sign, Muthild Shank instantly surmised, of a more profound lack of awareness. He wrapped his short arms around Muthild's shoulders to pull himself to his feet. During this process, his jacket's buttons got tangled with her coat's five buttons so that he was unable to draw back from Muthild's breasts. Disengaging the buttons took a while, so she was obliged to remain in this position for some time. Muthild Shank stared into the heavy-lidded, rather small male eyes and saw, deep within, imprinted on their retinas, delusions and wounds and a lostness, none of which were strangers to her, and which made her take by the hand the eventual cause of her death wish and lead him to the local train, by which means, without a word passing between them, they arrived in Muthild's little town. They raced up the stairs to the flat and fell all over each other, not pausing even then to exchange words. Muthild Shank remembers it to this day, even now when she's dead and gone (as she believes), and busy searching her pockets for her travel pass. She's intent on going to the big town one more time to seek out the now erstwhile Reason For Her Death Wish and see how he'll take the news that, with the help of some little mushrooms from the local heath, she has done away with herself. But she can't find her travel pass. The pockets of her coat and jacket offer Muthild Shank some breadcrumbs and a penknife, two snotty cotton handkerchiefs, a few paper clips with which, when alive, she'd poked out her earwax, five letters written by the Classic Male back in the good times, and some long-since shrivelled mushrooms. She decides to travel without a ticket. After all, she's dead now; no one will notice her (or miss her either, for that matter). Now she's dead she can brazenly travel without a ticket. I can have a field day, Muthild Shank tells herself, but feels so guilty about this she starts to cry. For the first time since being deceased, she is shocked: she is still being brought to tears, though she'd promised herself that death would free her of every trial and tribulation. The greatest of these tribulations had been that the Classic Male refused, month after month, to provide Muthild Shank with grounds for the maternity leave for which she'd longed for many years, yearning for it far more than just any old annual leave with a trip to some exotic country. Muthild starts wailing and screaming – after all, no one can hear her. It had been high time she went on maternity leave. She was already gone forty when she hopelessly fell for the eventual Reason For Her Death Wish, but there might still have been the chance of a child, big-boned while somewhat on the short side, with a nice head on which to place the most exotic of the hats. The eventual Reason For Her Death Wish had never really understood what had aroused Muthild Shank so extremely when they met. He smelled of mouse, the same as his musty flat which he shared with an elderly widow. Sometimes he even smelled of the elderly widow, which only seemed to arouse Muthild more. And he had no money, a fact which was not going to change, however many times he went to the Job Centre. By contrast, Muthild Shank seemed to be settled into a well-ordered life: she was retraining; she sometimes wore really fabulous hats, which certainly took a lot of courage, and she never smelled of mouse or elderly widow. She was certainly a bit younger than him. He could never have imagined she might have such a low opinion of herself. So what did she see in him, wondered the man who Muthild had once (due to his stubborn refusal to converse) referred to as Werner and had then stuck with it. Yet Muthild Shank didn't have Werner down as the Reason For Her Death

Wish for quite a while longer; she was busy contorting her body against, on top of and underneath him in the hope of fulfilling her wish. But it didn't happen. It was only as the evenings and nights went relentlessly by, never bearing fruit, that she became more and more miserable, sometimes not opening her door, and then not opening it as a matter of course. On one of these days, the barren Classic Male broke down in tears, and from then on stayed away. Feeling the onset of the menopause, Muthild Shank took the decision to collect mushrooms. And she is now aware of the basket beside her bed-head, and now aware she's been dead a while, and she'd like to go and give the Reason For Her Death Wish an explanation. Putting on a fragrant feather hat that she never actually dared to wear in her lifetime, she parades to the station and gets onto the nine o'clock train to the nearest big (though not really all that big) town. The Reason For Her Death Wish gets onto the train right on her heels, because for the whole of that long night he has slept, like many other nights too, in the entrance to her building, so he is now in hot pursuit, wanting to get her back. Back to life, thinks Muthild Shank. Back underneath me, thinks the erstwhile Reason For Her Death Wish, and he flings the dead Muthild onto the leatherette bench, the full length of him on top of her, and if she hadn't been dead, Muthild thinks, it might even have happened. Do you have to die first to make a man give a thought to the future? Muthild is bitter. The ticket inspector walks by. He can't see me, thinks Muthild, who is now forced to accept that Werner has come over to her by dying himself. How else could they have been united? She now starts to really enjoy being dead. Some time later, she puzzles a little over why they're not removing her from the flat, into which (at last) the dead Werner also moves. Why isn't she being laid to rest in a cheap coffin beside the erstwhile Reason For Her Death

Wish? Be that as it may, Muthild is soon busy with skirt and trouser alterations, having gone back to the training centre, where everyone behaves as if she is still alive. Evidently that's how she comes across, so she lets it pass. In death she enjoys frying the Slimy Cortinarius and Velvet Shanks in butter, seeing as they now hold no danger whatsoever. And eventually she gives birth to a child, big-boned while somewhat on the short side, and has a wonderful maternity leave, and takes pleasant walks with the erstwhile Reason For Her Death Wish. If I were still alive, she thinks, none of this would have happened. And she reaches to caress a mushroom beside the path, her own head caressed by the bobbing feathers of her fabulous hat.

The key to the Fatherland is on the hook by the door

IT WAS DEFINITELY MAY BECAUSE THE LILY-OF-THE-VALLEY, called 'May bells' round here, were tinkling under the trees in the Burgberg Woods till they almost made me giddy. I was on my way home from my housewifely duty of getting the groceries in and had chosen the path that skirted the town, crossing the Waldplatz into the open country and the herb-scented meadows. The Burgberg Woods that were currently ringing in my ears bordered the meadows to my left; meanwhile the sea of herbs that had sprung from the damp earth to my right was a further sure sign. Definitely spring. Spring was still in my (kind of narrowed, these days) mind when I started this thing of swapping one word for another. I was perturbed; at first, only by how odd the resulting sentence sounded, but then, what with still being quite a way from our garden gate, by the physical reactions that the word-swap seemed to be setting off. I'd got a pain in my eardrum, and my heart was palpitating. My monitoring of these symptoms actually made me forget the sentence that had brought them on. I opened the door of our house, then (as always) locked myself in, dumped on the kitchen table my burgundy faux-leather bag and the wicker basket that had seen better days, and began unpacking and sorting out the shopping. I stowed the four litres of fresh milk in the fridge, put the black pudding and block of plain, mild cheese in the larder and the toilet paper in the cellar cupboard, cleaned out and refilled the encrusted sugar tin, hung a half-metre length of salami on the row of hooks beside the kitchen cupboard, then took both bag and basket into the garage in front of our house, having decided I'd do the next shopping trip by car. I was feeling wobbly. When I returned indoors, the sentence that was causing my wobbles (though I wasn't aware of this, last May) suddenly came back to me: 'The key to the Fatherland is on the hook by the door'. In my these days narrowed mind, I'd swapped the word 'house' for 'Fatherland', probably because I was trying to attune my thinking to that of my husband who back then – last May – had held a respectable position in the German Postal Service. It only came to me now that my husband had always swapped one word for another. He called our son *Harold* even though twelve years previously we had, by mutual agreement, registered the name 'Yan'. And he called our daughter *Rupie* after her weekly Rupert the Bear comic, though in my opinion she wasn't remotely like a teddy. He called his job *Controller*, though all he 'controlled' (to much amusement all round) was the mournful-looking clerks' tits as they went about their rubber stamping and cashiering; or as far as I could tell, anyway, from when I sometimes popped in after buying the groceries to suggest he should come home on time as I was making chips. He habitually called me *Mum*, though I'd never related to him in a way that justified him calling me that. And at first I'd actually been quite annoyed (though not particularly surprised) when, to get me in the mood for sex, he'd called me his *cheeky knave*. It was only last May when I noticed the words he used had a particular leaning.

The previous winter, two families that'd fled from some war or other had moved into a house on our street which had been standing empty. I'd never asked where they came from, not having been interested, until one evening last May – the very same evening of the day when I'd swapped one word for another for the first time; the evening when my husband had brought up the subject at home, calling them *sheep-shaggers* and *stinking Turks*, although in my opinion (having sometimes come across one of the women at the grocer's) there was no way their language was Turkish. As it happened, on that particular May evening the potatoes steaming away on our supper table were sprinkled with curry powder; furthermore, recalling how my husband had gorged down a 'shashlik' mutton kebab at the Festival of Southern Europe in the city hall that time, I'd actually bulked out the meatloaf that was our main course with a bit of mutton. When, after supper and with the children in bed, my husband called me to him, I was astonished to find he wasn't wanting his *cheeky knave*, but more meatloaf. I had to grin when, even with me already laid there, he returned to the kitchen to cut himself another little slice, and came back to bed smacking his lips and raving to *Mum* over it. It got me out of my wifely duties for the night.

That night last May I began to think about how the words in my narrowed mind might be swapped to make them mean something nice. The key by the front door went on being the *Fatherland* key; I was comfortable with this. But I wasn't comfortable with *Harold* and *Rupie*, and even less so with *Controller* and *cheeky knave* and *Mum*. As for *sheep-shagger* and *stinking Turk*, these were absolutely not nice whatsoever, so from then on I called them *jumbo jets* and *hot air balloons*. On that May night, I began to wonder about them: what language *did* they speak? And those long, leisurely meals I saw them having from our kitchen window on hot days: what sort of food was it? I went to sleep with this on my mind.

The next morning I saw off *Harold* and *Rupie* for ever, opening the front door of our *Fatherland* and promising I'd collect them from school at midday. My husband had long since gone off to *pick plums*, as I intended to call his work from now on. The *cheeky knave*, meanwhile, was ensconced deep inside me. I never again wanted to let that creature out. Ever. The only one still taking the floor was *Mum*. The children still needed their *Mum*. Today, from the moment I picked them back up from school, I was going to bring them up as Yan and Sabina. I couldn't therefore entirely eradicate *Mum*. A headache that was plaguing my narrow mind that May morning turned into *Susie*, a friend. Although I did like my friend *Susie*, I couldn't really cope with her behaving like this for very long, and so walked into town to get some painkillers to help get rid of her. I'd known the pharmacist since school. She'd been in the class immediately above me, and she'd done those hard stares even back then. She handed me the pack without comment, which surprised me since I'd never previously demanded pills from her to get rid of my friend *Susie*. Walking out, I realized I'd have liked to tell the pharmacist just what sort of friend *Susie* was, but there were too many people queuing at the counter. In the market square I took a big gulp from the town's drinking fountain, washed down two small white pills, and sat on the steps, waiting for *Susie* to just clear off. Later, back on our street, I stopped one of the jumbo jets and hot air balloons and asked where they came from. The man answered unintelligibly in a language that, going on what I hazily remembered from my distant youth, I ventured to guess was Russian. I nodded at him, gratified that Turkish could thus be completely eliminated, and that I had found this out all by myself.

Yan and Sabina got very boisterous on the way home in my car that afternoon during the three-hour 'adventure' detour through the region's scenic, hilly landscape. So excited were they after their outing that they opened the door of the Fatherland and practically carried Mum over the threshold.

Later on my husband shook his head in denial, affronted, when I asked if the plums had been extra-juicy today since he'd come home so late. I was waiting with curiosity to find out how the cheeky knave, if called upon, would respond, and was almost sorry when my husband fell straight asleep. But that gave me a little more thinking time: we were on the brink of summer, we'd got a holiday in Tunisia booked, and over the winter I'd got fat. Clearly I needed to lose a few pounds, but on the other hand, that would lead to the cheeky knave not getting a minute's peace while we were away. I'd be having to clench my thighs tight shut to keep the creature in. I reflected that my pregnancies had been a safe protection against my husband's advances. The holiday would be easier to endure if I were pregnant. I might even get a break from my housewifely duties of grocery shopping. The jumbo jet came into my mind – the one who masturbated at the open window each day while I was hanging out the washing in the spring sunshine. Till now I hadn't given this much thought, but actually, watching it gave me a pleasurable stirring down there. I went to sleep with this on my mind.

Before the summer was with us I'd fallen pregnant. The young, pale, almost feminine jumbo jet had used me as a landing strip only the once (what a novelty for the cheeky knave!). On the way to the airport I told my family, then proceeded to have a truly relaxing holiday. Yan and Sabina took over all the errands and bought me ice-creams, lemonades, newspapers and crossword puzzles. Over there my husband was constantly spitting out his words for jumbo jets and hot air balloons, adding *son-of-a-bitch, savage, camel shagger*, and *curry-breath*. I was amazed at how my husband could even fit all these folk in his mouth. It didn't strike me at the time, but not one of those names was for a female person. I myself came up with the sexless *helicopter, paraglider, bi-plane, turboprop* – till the sky got so choc-a-bloc I was wondering how we'd manage to fly home. But the flight took place without incident. Over the holiday I'd got even fatter.

My housewifely shopping trips for groceries took my mind off the discomforts of pregnancy, and I sailed safely through autumn and winter. Looking back now, some good things did happen during that time. My husband's plum-picking job ended abruptly – and not at all fruitfully – because one of the clerks decided it was no longer amusing, and reported his assaults. It didn't come to court because I paid the woman hush money out of my savings. My husband was therefore very grateful, and the day I left him, taking Yan, Sabine and my bump, he wasn't particularly surprised. My pale, young, 'feminine' jumbo jet was hankering for me, and offered me refuge at his place. It was warm and welcoming there. The children picked up Russian quickly. I bought my husband a blow-up Mum doll and puffed the cheeky knave out of me and into it. I was so delighted to be totally rid of that knave, who could now be called upon to meet my husband's needs whenever required and was no longer my concern.

My baby was born in March. My new facility for replacing one word with another was rendered entirely superfluous when I was told at the Office for Births Marriages and Deaths that my jumbo jet's mother-tongue was not Russian after all but Serbo-Croatian. This replaced the point of using any words at all. We now had to agree on a name for our daughter. After an hour, she was finally called Liubica. Yan and Sabrina could pronounce it without difficulty. Since I was still married, my husband asked to see the baby, just to make certain it didn't look at all like him. My jumbo jet was perfectly happy with this, so three days ago, it being May, we invited my husband over for a glass of seasonal punch made from the wonderfully-scented tiny white woodruff flowers I'd picked in the Burgberg meadows. My husband didn't come alone; he was accompanied by two people I didn't know – a male and a female. At first they were all being nice, but in the course of the evening I asked my husband if he could let me have my key from the hook beside the door of our Fatherland because there were still some things of mine I urgently needed. Furthermore, once my husband was permitted to go back plum-picking, I could take the opportunity to clean. Fatherlands like that one need a proper bottoming sometimes. Obviously I also wanted to see how the cheeky knave was getting on in its new home. Endeavouring to make more small-talk, I confided in my husband that since a walk I'd taken through the spring meadows in May of last year, my mind, which had got really narrow, had broadened out again, and another great thing – my friend Susie, who'd been a total pain, had never again showed up since I got rid of her with the pills given to me by that dour woman pharmacist. My husband took my pale, beautiful, 'feminine' tiny daughter Liubica in his arms and nodded to the female stranger, who took me by the hand, led me out of my jumbo jet's Fatherland and into the street, and sat me in a car. Shortly after, the male stranger got into the driver's seat and, after an hour's drive, brought us to a rambling, albeit fenced-in, campus on which a scattering of redbrick buildings had mushroomed between the grand, ancient trees. On entering one of the buildings, which I – as an instant reflex – declared to be 'Gudrun', I was given a little room with barred windows that I haven't yet been allowed to leave. Despite not having the slightest urge to call Gudrun 'Fatherland', nor go on about a key on a hook beside the door.

The demise of Herr and Frau Blumner

WHAT A DELIGHTFUL PROSPECT, I SAID RESIGNEDLY into the telephone, feeling rattled. I recall patting at my hair-do as though Herr Wagenauer, on the other end of the line, was already insinuating that I'd turn myself out in a style inappropriate to the occasion. Tomorrow Herr and Frau Blumner were going to be eighty – both on the same day. In outward appearance the old couple looked very like those two digits. Viewed from whatever direction, Blumner himself was nought-shaped, whereas she still had a hint of waist, so looked like an eight. I was tasked with visiting them at home on Wagenauer's behalf, to offer his warmest congratulations and take them a big bouquet of flowers which I was to order from Moller & Partner. Such is the secretary's lot, I reflected. I had just the same issues with Blumner and his wife as Wagenauer did, but he was able to make his excuses and avoid all face-to-face encounters that weren't absolutely essential. I slammed the receiver down, though only because I knew Wagenauer had already hung up. And immediately picked it up again to place the order. Moller's elderly senior partner came to the phone. He inquired as to my preferences, *my dear lady,* in his peculiar carpet-slipperish voice, and offered me five different floral arrangements in the medium price-range that Wagenauer had specified. Suddenly – surprising even myself – I was overtaken by an impulse. Pretending I'd made a mistake, I asked instead for the lower price-range. The cheapest was *Van Gogh*, consisting of three sunflowers along with some blue statice, ferns, angelica leaves, and exotic palms, plus two stems of *bupleurum* that I'd never heard of and couldn't visualise. I was paying close attention to the precise components because I was in fact hoping Moller's elderly partner would include 'asparagus fern' with the sunflowers. Cheap and ubiquitous, I loathed it for symbolising life under the former regime. For a moment I imagined the actual vegetable – literally, some sticks of white asparagus – tied artistically to the bunch of three sunflowers. This made me giggle out loud, causing a moment of distinct irritation in the flower shop. I ordered this arrangement times two, bringing it up to the price Wagenauer was aiming for, with the happy plan of purloining one for myself. Because sunflowers were far too nice for the Blumners.

Their mantel as one of Wagenauer's most lucrative clients had been assumed a number of years ago when, according to the 'right to restitution of family property' following our Reunification with West Germany, they had reclaimed a number of hotels on the Baltic Sea. They had gone on to sell them and since then had been sitting, tight-fisted, on their mountains of dosh. This necessitated the services of a wily tax accountant to help them navigate the rocky channels of the law. Wagenauer had been paying himself well for giving them his guidance. In truth, that Blumner woman would have preferred to wear the money strapped round her body till she looked like a nought herself. In my opinion, anyway. I interpreted her choice to drink greyish, blended rosé wine quite simply as pretending to like cheap stuff so no-one would know she was loaded. Obviously Wagenauer had sworn me to an oath of confidentiality regarding the circumstances of his clients. Despite this I did once unthinkingly rant on at length to my husband about the poor little Blumners who, in reality, were swimming in dough, but he'd carried on reading the paper, responding only with the vague comment that swimming in dough was completely impossible due to its texture. I hadn't mentioned them since.

I had obtained Wagenauer's agreement that I needn't show up for work the next day till after I'd been round to the Blumners', which could not conceivably take place before ten in the morning. He was okay with that because he could then pressure me to stay longer in the evening. So after getting up I spent a good hour playing the beauty queen, painting my finger- and toenails in a lustrous browny-red, putting my hair up and donning the tight little black number that made everyone's tongue hang out, irrespective of gender. (Was that ancient Blumner actually a man? I didn't care to pursue that thought. His wife was a woman – that was certainly beyond dispute.) By this means I managed, a little later, to get the senior partner at Moller's to write down the two bouquets as 'order of flowers' on the receipt, omitting a numerical breakdown. The ambiguity meant I didn't even need to feel dishonest. I packed my own arrangement in the boot while putting the one destined for the birthday celebration on the passenger seat. On arrival I parked my car in a side street and finally tramped up the four flights of stairs to the Blumners', wondering again, as I always did, why they still lived here in rented accommodation, as they had for decades, on the third floor of an old-fashioned building on one of the city's busiest main arteries and on an upper floor that could hardly be described as suitable for the elderly. With all the wondering, I stomped straight past the open door of their flat up to the fourth and last floor, where of course I realized I'd gone wrong. Slapping my forehead I hurried back down, and on the landing ran into a nice middle-aged lady bearing a gift-hamper. She introduced herself as chairwoman of the local People's Solidarity, the social welfare network carried over from the former regime, whose members were still self-evidently taking care of one another. We looked at each other. She knocked tentatively on the wide-open door and called the Blumners by name, but there was no response. Again we looked at each other, then wordlessly entered the unfamiliar flat. It was empty except for a large round oak table in the living room which, having had its leaves pulled out to make it full-sized, took up half the room. On it, on a dark red velvet tablecloth, elegantly attired in black and looking nice and peaceful, lay Herr and Frau Blumner. Propped on the tabletop was a note. It was carefully hand-written in the traditional old German script, which I had some trouble with but managed to decipher.

Welcome!

We greatly appreciate that you have found the time to pay us a visit, on this day at least, and we are taking the opportunity of our joint 80th birthday celebration to say our final farewell. Dear Frau Hardgrafter, please offer our warmest greetings to your good master Herr Wagenauer. Also, dear Fräulein Schmidt, we are sure you will have brought us a wonderful gift hamper, like you did five years ago. May you thoroughly enjoy its contents! We would be deeply thankful if you could make appropriate burial arrangements. A funeral insurance has been taken out, the paperwork being located beneath my wife. Within the last few weeks we have sold the furniture and today have put all remaining contents out with the rubbish, so at least you have no house clearance to do. We are delighted that you have come. If you could see your way to spending a few moments in silence beside

*us at our Table of Rest we would be most grateful, and will remain so
until the day we stand side by side in comradeship once more, Herta
and Hans-Dietrich Blumner*

Only now did it enter my mind that they might be dead. I
realised my eyes were involuntarily scanning for bullet holes, as
I just didn't see how they could have passed away like this,
holding hands and obviously at peace. I'd always imagined the
process of dying being a battle for life, right to the end, but I
could see no hint of this on the Blumners' faces. They must
have taken sleeping pills, then a lethal dose of poison. With
their cash-pile it certainly wouldn't have been hard getting hold
of the stuff. My search for some kind of sign of dementia was
also fruitless. Fräulein Schmidt undoubtedly had a better
training in What To Do in such cases as this, though she did
admit, she had never yet dealt with quite this type of
occurrence. Before the arrival of the doctor, and also the police,
whom she had called just in case, I went to get the second
flower arrangement from the boot. Once upstairs again, I took
each out of its cellophane and positioned them at their feet, as
though this had been their request. The yellow sunflowers
looked fabulous against the black and dark red.

As to their wealth, I was told later by Wagenauer that they
had emptied and closed all their accounts. The money was
never found.

*The landscape
beyond L.*

I FRANKLY HAD TO TAKE MY HAT OFF to that flat landscape beyond the town of L.; how it lay there on its back as though it had let someone overpower it. I'd love to have been that someone. But I'd never overpowered anything; certainly not any landscapes – and *definitely* not the fear I'd have needed to overcome in order to commit a 'premeditated act'; absolutely *no way*, of that I was quite sure. Even though I was fearless when it came to dealing with neighbours complaining about the garden hedge not being trimmed, or about my rubbish bags that got torn open by foxes in the night so that the next morning the street would be littered with squashed beer cans and stinking milk cartons. Which contrasted starkly with how pristine everything looked, once you were beyond L. Today being no exception. I was able to view it in detail from the car window since I wasn't driving but was in the passenger seat, into which I had firmly wedged myself with all the weight at my disposal, namely, a hundred and sixty-eight pounds. Which the male at the wheel self-evidently wasn't put off by. As was his habit, he was taking me for a drive, his left elbow sticking out of the open window into the fresh air, glancing sideways at me now and then. Adoringly, I still believe to this day. I had married him sixteen years previously; a quiet wedding, as weddings go, even though it was my first. He liked fish so we had made the handful of guests choose from the menu at 'The Starfish'. Sadly, out here beyond L. there isn't a restaurant that does anything like that. We couldn't have brought those guests together anymore either: Grandma Gertie had been dead three years; my father had got together with one of my friends after the death of my mother and moved to Italy, from where he got in touch at most once or twice a year. As for my husband's relatives, they shunned any further contact with us after our wedding, because of me. Why? I'm not sure. Least, not exactly. My husband's father knew how fuckable I was; maybe that's what did it. Though it didn't take place *that* often, before the wedding. Mostly it was when my future husband had a couple of things to see to at his parents' house, and his father knew I would be sitting waiting in my flat. That's when he'd come round, in fishing gear, or else overalls. When he was naked his drooping scrotum hung to his knees. Incidentally, that was the decisive factor. Anyhow I'd have forgotten all about him again by the time my husband was finished with his DIY and would phone to say he'd be round shortly. But this is all beside the point. Here, out beyond L., it was of no consequence, since my husband had no clue about any of that. I liked it when he drove without stopping and then instructed me that he'd be pulling into the next available lay-by, where we would get the blanket out of the boot... And after we'd done the deed, I'd be permitted to get the sausages and salad out of the cooler bag.

We haven't got kids, luckily. That wouldn't be so brilliant, right now. Obviously.

I'd always adored that landscape. It was so flat. Flatter than I could ever be in my life. As my husband was stroking my hair from my forehead, I got the urge to chuck our little dog – who was gazing up faithfully from his comfy seat on my knees – out of the window. Do him good – be away from us for once and have to sort out his food for himself; he could do with that, the spoiled thing. Two or three more urges then came over me, such as, grabbing my husband's shandy from the drinks-holder and finishing it off, or tipping the passenger seat down and having a little nap. I didn't trust the dog to leave me alone so I carried on sitting there without moving. Basically it was the usual thing, my lethargy increased inversely with the male's compulsion to accelerate and to blast the music ever louder. I was used to it. My husband was intent on finding a fish restaurant, and kept driving; we'd got nearly as far as Neuruppin before we finally found a small village eatery which offered eel, with fish in aspic as a starter and then a fruit compote with raspberries. Incidentally the landlord immediately caught my attention. In his pigskin apron he was literally sweating like a pig, so that I couldn't help seeing the apron as his actual skin. I couldn't stop myself from touching him a few times when he brought the plates and the wine we'd ordered. It didn't go any further. It's just, that's how quickly I get aroused. My husband paid by Visa; I remember because I was amazed they had a card-reader in such a small establishment out in the sticks. Later, while walking round the pond on the village green, I made eyes at my husband. That I was so turned on was also down to the wine, besides (obviously) the landlord's sweat. My husband didn't need to know that; he was enjoying seeing the gorgeous guy reflected in my eyes, and hearing me describe him as such. Which was fine by me, and anyway it was true. While being in every other way his father's son, he himself only had a short, bulky and therefore completely wrinkle-free scrotum, which I simply couldn't get excited about. At the beginning of our marriage it would still arouse my interest a bit; after all, it might get longer with age, but this hope petered out as the years went by. It was fine anyway to just make eyes at him. Besides, I'd always got a lot to do. Above all, preparing lessons. In that respect my husband had always been a good partner, cleaning the kitchen or hallway. I had nothing whatever to moan about; when it came to household chores, we had a fair division of labour.

Anyways, out here beyond L., from where we were starting our return journey that day, the sun, post-lunch, looked so astonishingly high in the sky that we pulled up, it was just amazing. I put the dog outside on the ground and searched in the glove compartment for sunglasses. With the sun that high, I couldn't possibly see out there without my sunglasses. I was looking for them with my back to my husband, my head right down in the car, when he straddled me, steered me in front of him and coupled with me over the car radiator, wedging his plump scrotum between my bum-cheeks. I continued laughing whilst at the same time (not being the least bit turned on) begging him, giggling, to cut it out. I wasn't even frisky due to the wine any more. Not that I was uncomfortable with what he was doing: if I hadn't been scared that people might see us from the street, I could have let him relieve himself, no problem. His penis would have arrived at that place below my belly where we 'become one flesh', and it definitely wouldn't have taken him long to come. The stupid thing is, I swivelled my head, and saw how he was staring into the sun with his eyes wide open, whereas I'd actually been stopped from finding my sunglasses, and I remember how absolutely furious that made me, that he could blithely stare directly into the sun, while I, from just turning my head, was getting such a pain in my eyeballs and everything around me had gone dark, really extremely dark, though you said later that it was absolutely bright and clear that day, the air so clear it made one want to just stand there breathing it in. However, I didn't only see how my husband was staring at the sun, I also saw his bulging belly at the back of me, the solid ball of it not even slightly jigging with the rhythm; rather, that impenetrable wall of abdomen serving to hide the engine that was driving the thrusts with which he was currently hammering me with ever greater force into the car. In that darkness, what was going on at my back held a suggestion of pigskin leather, and I wished I could conjure up the sweaty smell of the leather-aproned landlord or my father-in-law's long, wrinkled scrotum, but nothing would come.

My husband was laid on the ground with blood running out of his eye. He wasn't screaming; just gasping a bit, if anything, and pressing his left hand into his eye-socket. It didn't feel too nice when you read out the grounds for my arrest down at the station and showed me the fish knife they said I'd used to take his eye out. I'm not actually in the habit of nicking people's cutlery. But for sure the knife can only have come from that village eatery. I must have popped it in my jacket pocket. My husband had whipped my skirt up over my jacket, and the jacket's two fronts with the pockets were splayed out on the hood. As you know, I was distinctly calm going into that little duty room; enough to make you wonder how I could manage to be so composed after such an act; in fact it might well have made you conclude that 'premeditation' had been in my poor little brain! It's so lovely you've brought me here again. As my husband always says, once you're beyond L., there are so many beauty spots.

Cut to shreds

I'D KNOWN DOTZAUER – "little Dotty" – since my childhood in the sleepy village of S., a village of inbreds, which accounted for the higher than normal incidence of mental defectives. People talked about this behind their hands in the neighbouring villages and in W., the nearby town, but of course it was never said openly. Dotty's mother was what you'd call older, while her father was a proper ancient monument – you could hardly tell his age behind his beard and his head of silver-grey wavy hair. He'd been lying on the sofa, paralyzed, since Dotty was seven, with his wife constantly shifting him to make him comfy. Whenever we children hid behind the living room door, daring for a glimpse of his bedsores, they'd shock us half to death, our hands flying to cover our eyes and mouths. Just after Dotty turned twelve she could at last happily announce *he's passed away*. Dotty blossomed, but her mum continued to wilt. She withered so much that at seventeen or eighteen, Dotty went dancing with her a few times out of pity and in the hope that her mother might manage to meet a nice man. Dotty would put on her best suit, shave, knot her tie, polish her black shoes and tuck a lace handkerchief into her breast pocket. She was a good foot taller than her mother and when they were out like that, it was actually only Dotty who was a pleasure to behold, handsome and dapper, stepping out next to a match-stick. On the dance-floors of the local area Dotty would, on a good night, be approached by a few cheeky, giggling women, though a sideways glance at the tight knot of her mother's face would make her put them off. Nothing ever undid that knot, so Dotty finally gave up going dancing with her. She moved to a furnished room in G., the county town, which was only twelve kilometres away but at that time twelve kilometres was sufficient to get far enough away from her mother. It took an hour by rail due to having to change at a small local station, and there was no bus service whatsoever. She attended the College of Banking and Finance and obtained a decent degree in Financial Economics, which brought to her withered mother's cheeks the only slight pinkish frisson of pleasure she could remember. On the thirteenth of May 1976 she married a surgical nurse working at the local hospital in G.

The night before the wedding she'd tried on her wife's floral party dress, which was of course too tight and too short on her. That she did this – along with putting a dash of rouge on her cheeks and a black line on her eyelids – might have caused consternation, but she said her bride-to-be just laughed.

They went on to have three children – triplets. The local mayor was appointed godparent. It caused quite a stir in the town when, after half a year, Dotty was the one who stayed home with the three little ones. She was seen as a devoted father, and since she had the right, according to the then state regulations, to stay home for two further half-years with her salary paid in full, she arranged things so she could spend those twelve months at home, and her career at the local council faded into insignificance. She recounted to me that for a long time she'd been feeling ill at ease; somehow not 'at home' with herself, but had put this down to their not actually having a home. She'd hoped she'd get over this feeling once they'd been allocated their first ever flat – three rooms, kitchen and windowless bathroom. Then one day she was given a sewing machine by one of her colleagues who occasionally dropped by. To start with she made blankets for the little ones. This gave her practice. Then she bought a piece of truly gorgeous artificial silk in her wife's favourite colour, mauve, and in secret, made her a beautiful blouse. Puff sleeves, white pin-tucks, rhinestone buttons. And she told me how, between the children's bedtime and sewing the final seam (her wife being on the late shift at work), she almost couldn't complete the lovely thing, due to a sudden wrenching in her gut – and the realisation that, time and again, she'd blocked this sensation by immersing herself in her sewing machine till the pain went away. At this moment of truth, the wrenching had stopped, and, barely aware of what she was doing, she'd put on the blouse and applied heavy make-up. She'd wondered fleetingly how come it fitted her so perfectly when it was meant for her much smaller wife, but in a second the thought was gone. Resolute, she kept the thing on.

Arriving home late and seeing this sight, her wife's reflexively indulgent attitude was soon brought up short, and somewhere between midnight and the end of the conversation (or at least, that first end), the policy of indulgence was in shreds, never to be repaired.

We were in the Frog, the only cafe-bar still open in our former home village, sitting beside each other like we used to, as she told me all this, her eyes moist, though to this day I've never been sure whether it was tears. In the intervening years (it now being sixteen years since the mauve blouse) her breasts had become the size of small female fists. She dressed unobtrusively, wore her now-grey hair tied in a ponytail, and had given up going round in skirts and court shoes like she used to. Her voice was too deep to be taken for a woman's, and even now that Dotty had a birth certificate and ID card 'proving' her to be the female she'd been all along, they weren't of much use. Mockery and catcalling were normal, and these continual violations of her personhood manifested as livid scratch-marks which had come up on her skin after her 'gender reassignment surgery' (as in, the removal of the superfluous testicles, creation of a false vagina, and remodelling of the penis into the soft protrusion called a clitoris). She said she loved how I called her little Dotty, like in the old days, because that diminutive had been the secret location of the little girl she'd always really been. Moreover, the name Dotzauer, at least as far as her lineage was concerned, was about to die out, since neither the three children nor her ex used it. Even after the divorce (a necessity, as two women couldn't legally be married), they'd tried to go on living together, but after two years had both run out of steam. Since then she'd only seen the children from a distance. She sighed, stroking aside her fringe (which clearly hadn't been cut by a hairdresser) from her forehead. I was in love with her, and moved in.

Dotty always bemoaned that the conditional tense was endangered as a species by the 'real truth' of the present; that it would surely soon be extinct. Hence her determined commitment to its use, so as not to let it get ground down in the jaws of 'reality' quite so fast. An example: *If today I'd had a small plate of chicken done in coconut milk with fresh ginger and sweetcorn, I'd now be standing here replete and contented in the day's final hour.* With this sentence she could distance herself from the underlying reality (*darn, I've had nothing good to eat today, the day is ending badly...*) and endeavour to insulate herself from bad stuff. The reality might come to her once she was in bed, as she'd be tired and lazy by then, and chicken in coconut milk might duly drift past in slow motion, but she'd just watch it go by and fall asleep. Her expectations had definitely become modest…

During her long years of being single and unemployed she'd made countless blouses, skirts and dresses that she never wore and which now languished in her cupboards and on her shelves. It was only the mauve garment that would now and then get brought out: *If I hadn't made her this, I probably wouldn't be alive today.* I heard the sentence many times and always misunderstood what she meant. Shifted into the conditional, it was an expression of her longing for peace and death. While I was away on a spa holiday on the Baltic Sea, this longing was fulfilled. Her old mother told me she'd found her sitting in the armchair with a peaceful smile on her face and the mauve blouse on her lap, cut to shreds.

Line of vision

FACE IT, IRENE MATTASCH, SHE TOLD HERSELF: your day is over. Nowadays Arnold Mattasch's days were all that mattered. These had a start, a midpoint, and an end. Sometimes the start of Arnold Mattasch's day, or indeed the midpoint or the end, would bring him to the brink of a black hole, the terminal pull of which would make Time itself stop – until Irene Mattasch kick-started it again. She needed to stay fit for this, so Irene Mattasch ate a healthy diet. Arnold had to be got up, bathed, fed, and have his diaper changed. In former times Irene Mattasch's day had had equal status with her husband's. But since Arnold Mattasch had – in broad daylight – been run over, his days took priority. He'd been a cycle messenger for a delivery service, a job which at forty he could do at greater speed than some of the younger ones. One day a driver didn't see him. Though fighting fit at the time, Arnold Mattasch had ended up at death's door, a state from which he came round only after a considerable struggle. Six weeks had gone by before they brought him out of the artificially induced coma. The doctors had thought he would most likely die, which fortunately turned out to be a mistake. Nowadays he'd often sit in his chair on the balcony. From up there his eyes would find their way from the city's rooftops down to the street below. His eyes had seldom made that journey in his former life. Down at street level Arnold Mattasch's eyes were still capable of finding their way, as they had in the past, except that his line of vision these days was from his 'mobile throne', as he called his vehicle, and at a much slower speed.

On the days when he came to the brink of the black hole right in the middle of the day, he was usually out and about with Irene, who would be pushing him, and it was usually when they were picking up Caroline. En route to the school they would pass Photo Express, a boutique called Be Happy, the Extra minimarket that was part of the ReWe co-op chain, and Hoffmann's sewing machine shop, both dearly hoping that maybe today the brink of the black hole wouldn't come close enough to make Time stop. But on Arnold Mattasch's return journey on this particular day, passing Hoffmann's, the ReWe Extra minimarket, the Be Happy boutique and Photo Express (with Caroline perched on his knees), Arnold Mattasch could no longer see, for Time had once again filled his tear-ducts to the brim. A torrent suddenly gushed from beneath his eyelids. Once again, Time had stopped. Irene Mattasch did everything in her power to re-start it. For example, re-telling the story of the past-their-sell-by-date chickens that the staff of the mini-market had thrown out in the trash, back in January it must have been, only for them to be salvaged by Stinky Willie and his pals and roasted on a campfire on the wasteland near the Metro train stop. This made Arnold Mattasch try to judge who'd got it worse – him, or Stinky Willie and his pals. The jury remained out. Stinky Willie and his pals actually lived at the Metro station. If on winter nights they cooked chickens thrown out in the trash by the mini-market, it was because they were suffering from cold and hunger. Arnold Mattasch suffered neither from cold nor hunger. Arnold Mattasch was suffering the loss of his body. If man is made up of a soul *and* body, then half of his very self was a wreck, he reflected. But if body and soul were fully merged; as in, a single unit, inseparable from each other, then the wrecked half of him had no purpose that he could see. When Stinky Willie and his pals turned their glazed eyes on Arnold Mattasch, he could well believe they'd lost their souls. And in his opinion, by getting up and staggering into the road, they too would eventually lose their bodies. And even if body and soul were a single unit, surely Stinky Willie and his pals were more a gonner than he was? Arnold Mattasch brooded on this. Irene Mattasch knew nothing of it, but noted that Time had gradually started moving again and taken them home. Which was where their life was lived: on Chestnut Avenue, in an attic flat with a well appointed bathroom equipped with Arnold's hydraulic hoist. They had already lived in the flat for many years. Way back, they had tried to veto the installation of an elevator as part of the building's modernisation, wanting to save money, but now of course they were thankful for it. In the rattle of their shutters, the knocking together of Arnold's ever more knobbly knees, Caroline's clattering of her child's cutlery set, and the gnashing of Irene Mattach's teeth, their life drummed on. The 'wailing and gnashing of teeth' was one of the secrets she kept behind her back, away from Arnold. Even Caroline's skinny little back could be depended on to keep secrets. For this reason Irene Mattasch took extra special care of it, regularly applying a vanilla-scented lotion and massaging it in. The little girl's narrow back was strong and resilient and was Irene Mattasch's greatest pleasure. Or else maybe her second greatest pleasure, her first being the moments of peace she got when the Workers' Welfare Union lady, Mrs Eilert, came to bathe Arnold or take him for a little walk. Irene Mattasch would then reach for the phone and call one of her girlfriends. She liked to chat. Actually she liked meeting up too, but such rendezvous were now rare. Now and then, little islands would loom out of the sea of monotony: "5pm Annegret", or "Tonite!

Mona", but as Irene Mattasch knew, these brief encounters could only take place at home. *Home...* Strange concept. Irene Mattasch's constant companion: she could never shake it off. *Home,* where she cooked, ate, washed, cleaned. In the past (though this would be nine years ago, ending when Caroline was born), she'd been a state employee working in public relations. Each day she would get off the Underground at Stadtmitte in the city centre where she worked for the State Symphony Orchestra, where her earnings had been quite sufficient to afford two hundred marks for new boots each winter. Sadly, shortly after Carrie's birth the orchestra went into liquidation. Obviously when Arnold was at death's door, his job went. In order not to have to claim benefits they were now living off a combination of his pension and her parents. This coming winter those boots would be completely worn out. Her even older boots were also totally shot and needed throwing out. *Home* didn't require boots, obviously. *Home* was a place where she could go on scaling back her own needs indefinitely so that she could afford everything Arnold and Caroline needed.

The day came when she was down to her last pack of long, dark cigarillos which she had been smoking on a ration of one every other day. She weighed the pack in her hand; took out the remaining cigarillo. The very last one. Caroline was asleep. Arnold was having his first four-hour sleep of the night, the talk show having finished, and Irene Mattasch was at last free to lean over the balcony-rail with her long, dark cigarillo and blow smoke rings into the still-dusky sky. Her eyes were following the smoke rings when suddenly, off to one side of her line of vision, in one of the flats opposite but down below the level of their own, she registered a naked man. She hesitated over whether she should look, but ended up having a good stare. He was just standing there, then he moved a few paces, picked up a thong from a pile of washing, put it on, posed in front of the mirror flexing his muscles, then gave up and disappeared from sight. He must be in a room that gives onto the other side of the building. Irene Mattasch now saw a naked woman enter the room and take a thong from a pile of washing, put it on, twirl in front of the mirror then bring her face right up to the glass and inspect it, turning her head each way. The man came back with two cups and hovered near her. Coffee? Tea? They drank, kissed, drank again, chatted. Irene Mattasch speculated idly about what they might be planning to do next. She strained her head a little over the balcony's edge, trying to keep sight of them when they were almost completely hidden by the wall between the room's two windows. They were getting dressed. Now they'd disappeared. The long, dark cigarillo was by this time down to its butt. The woman came back into the room with a light coat round her shoulders, which Irene Mattasch took as a sign that they were about to go out, and sure enough the couple emerged from the building into the street, hand in hand, all lovey dovey. They set off towards Zeller Avenue. Perhaps they had a destination in mind, or maybe they just wanted to go for a random evening wander. Irene Mattasch remembered the pleasure of going for random evening wanders; something she'd long since forgotten. She stared after them for a long time.

Shortly after, she herself was out there. At this time of day the street was bustling. Irene Mattasch passed Photo Express, the 'Be Happy' boutique, the Extra mini-market and Hoffmann's sewing machine shop and kept on walking. The people she came across were strolling along, ambling in and out of café-bars, dating, hanging out. Then suddenly she noticed that the whole way down the street, she was moving through threads as fine as a spider's web that strayed off in every direction, criss-crossing, interweaving, spiralling into ringlets. And the further she looked along Chestnut Avenue, the lighter the evening seemed to become, owing to all this trailing gossamer reflecting in the streetlights. Young men and women were moving along quickly and easily, as if unaware that they were enmeshing themselves in a web. In contrast, people a little older were finding the delicate filaments something of a hindrance, having less strength for pushing along through it all. Irene Mattasch, who had always eaten a healthy diet to keep up her strength in order to push Time along, had no sensation of the threads at all... Wherever she looked, people were getting caught up in the web's yielding centre, which encompassed them all! There was room for everyone. Even Stinky Willie and his pals had got drawn into the fine gossamer, she noticed at the Metro train stop. She was going to love telling Arnie that! She walked home smiling, the same straight route as always, past Hoffmann's sewing machine shop, the Extra mini-market, the 'Be Happy' boutique and Photo Express. When she was in sight of home her pace slowed. She stood still. Phew! Walked on again, entered the stairwell and took the elevator up to the attic...

Over on the other side of the street the light went on in the flat of the previously naked couple, meaning they were home. Irene Mattasch saw this between the balcony's rails, and it all came back to her now: how fatigue had overcome her so suddenly that she'd quite simply sunk to the floor. Across the way the blinds were being lowered. She slowly raised herself. She needed to shower, brush her teeth.

Lying in bed later, having brought Arnold another night-time tea and told him all about her dream, she already had the feeling that the midpoint of this night, when the old day stopped and the new day started, was going to be out of the ordinary. The net those people were getting caught by, said Arnold – he'd been seeing it for ages. Fluttering. Ever since his eyes had first found their way from the city's rooftops down to the street below, it had been in his line of vision. He said he'd sometimes thought of letting himself just fall down into it. The net would hold him for eternity, he was sure, and then he'd be at peace, no longer brooding over who was the furthest gone, him or Stinky Willie. The only problem was, he couldn't damn well heave himself over the balcony rail.

Irene Mattasch swallowed. It was exactly midnight, and the black hole was looming, and Time had stopped. Clearly Irene Mattasch's husband had known for ages about this gossamer web she had just seen. The difference was, he saw it as a net. Shaking like a leaf, she determined that the next morning she would buy herself a new pack of long, dark cigarillos. Considering the effort she had to put in, even just to push Time along, goddamit the day ought to be hers, too.

Hark! What cometh forth…

It's just a fact: to say certain things, you need a nice voice. The hollow wooden sound of his own made it a complete non-starter when it came to saying anything meaningful. Every utterance, whether an expression of Lust or of Disgust, would stick equally in his gullet. By now the two had become inextricably tangled back there, meaning neither could come out – not even for one second – without the other coming out right alongside it. So the minute he started talking, alarm bells rang. Obviously, women ran a mile.

He'd got used to it. It was only to be expected. Instead, he'd resorted to offering his services to men. Could be worse. He would accompany them to their variously dark and cold, warm and sunlit, minimalist, or flamboyantly fabulous apartments, and once in their bed would turn himself to the wall. When they were done they'd hand over the agreed fee and he'd get dressed again and leave. He'd got his own flat but never took anyone there. Not even the woman whose scent made him swoon: his sister. He was round at her place easily three times a week. What with her living just two blocks away. To play with the children. For supper. To breathe in the air she herself had just breathed out... He'd appear there out of the blue, and once he'd wolfed down his meal, disappear back into it. A couple of times her son and daughter had asked him where he'd just come from. Not getting an answer, they'd let it go. Just as his sister had given up asking him where he'd been and what he'd been up to. Sometimes, walking the dog late at night, she'd pause under his window and peer up. It never crossed her mind to mount the stairs. She'd mount her husband, more likely, when she got home.

That was their life. The only downside being his voice.

Monday. A gorgeous autumn day. His forty-second birthday. Two men speedily dealt with. Enough money thereby to last all week: a satisfying thought. Ensconced, now, in the first decent café along the street, looking out of the window. A café au lait, a double vodka. Sipping each. Pleasurable. Contemplating 'pleasure', and that he didn't really know what it meant. While he was dwelling on this, his hands were looking after each other in a fraternal kind of way, the one rubbing the other to warm it. This felt pleasing. But was it pleasure? As always at this point, his sister came to mind. He wanted her. To hold her in his arms. He dared not think further; dared not put words to the images in his head and thereby turn them into something real. He didn't immediately register the change – how his hands were suddenly behaving more sort of sisterly: stroking, caressing each other. He put a firm stop to it: sat on them. Clamped them beneath his thighs. Looked out of the window.

And saw her approaching. She was walking slowly, strolling, holding her little boy's hand. He recollected the daughter had ballet lessons on Mondays. She crossed the street no less than three times, drawn by the various shop windows. The ice-cream parlour over the other side, the lingerie boutique, the store specialising in exotic pets. She kept a bird-spider in her living room that would regularly shed its skin. Presumably there were a few crickets or grasshoppers in the bag she was holding when she came back out. Her hair was flying about. The boy had waited out front with his ice cream. She took his hand. Crossed the street yet again. Finished up right by the window behind which he was sitting. Maybe three meters away, licking up the melted dribbles of the child's ice-cream. He watched her tongue, how it came out, curled, lapped up the white cream, went back in again. His heart stopped. Since childhood he had suffered from these momentary fainting fits. Occasionally there'd be several in one day. At such times, if he wasn't already seated or lying down, he'd hold onto something solid: a wall, a tree. After a few seconds the faintness would pass off. Having come back to full consciousness of what he had just seen, it was as if he'd tasted the ice-cream with his own tongue. The flavour of coconut permeated his senses. It was probably a good thing he hadn't followed doctor's orders and had a pacemaker fitted, or he surely couldn't have had an experience quite like this, of fleeting departure then coming back. He remembered that the café's windows were mirror-glass on the outside. He shut his eyes, suppressing the urge to turn, watch her go.

It was all getting a bit too much now because her tongue really was demanding to be let into his mouth, so much so that he was using his brotherly or were they sisterly hands to clamp his lips shut. Where she had appeared from was a mystery: his sister's scent, the surest sign of her presence, was completely absent, just as she herself was completely absent. There was just her tongue, trying to force his fingers apart so that he was constantly having to swap over his hands that were squeezing his lips tight shut. With his sister being an architect and him having only trained as a carpenter, he felt obliged to give way to her in light of her superior status, though a part of him had begun to balk at this. When another hand was again forced off his lips, the invasion of his sister's tongue made him start uttering little shrills of protest. At some point his hands gave up the battle and let go, upon which a cry broke forth, rising to a piercing scream. Shuddering as he screamed. Screaming until his sister's startled tongue, after a baffled halt in activity, was definitely gone. When he opened his eyes, the staff of the café had gathered at his table along with the handful of other customers. Only the manager was standing away to one side, where he was replacing the phone's receiver.

Time to pay and be off.

The church bell was already tolling six o'clock. While wandering the streets at a sedate pace, a fact he'd picked up suddenly came to him: that during today, the entirety of his body's cells had probably been completely renewed six times over. He was fascinated by this idea. Some weeks ago he had pulled a few articles on the subject off the internet and pored over them. According to the experts, a full renewal took seven years. He knew this was not precisely true: skin cells got renewed within only nineteen days, bone cells only after twenty-five to thirty years. But statistically, if you dismissed as insignificant a few non-renewable brain cells, it could be considered true. And then and there, he dismissed All Things Insignificant. His birthday, for example. Each time he'd momentarily remembered it, it had only served to spoil his day. But now that he'd multiplied six by seven and was in possession of the knowledge that, on entering the seventh cycle of life's seven-year cycles, a kind of re-jigging of his life could occur, he didn't mind being forty-two today. He went on to dismiss as insignificant (marvelling at how easy it was) his morning ablutions, money, his sister, the bird-spider and its skin-shedding capacity, café au lait, vodka, ice-cream, and his sister's tongue. In short, the events of today were no longer important. Only the scream was writ large in his mind. It was as if (he thought) Lust and Disgust had been given notice to quit their shared lodgings in his gullet, then forcibly evicted by the scream. He tried out his voice with caution, starting with a few notes sung at the same pitch. The position of his lips stayed practically the same, the tones being created, rather, through the different ways of using his throat and mouth muscles. Then he went for a song. He had to rummage in his memory for ages. *Hark what cometh in from yon.* When (in an utterly relaxed state) he first sang it as *Hark what cometh forth from within,* he spent a minute wondering why the lyrics didn't fit the tune the way he thought they should. When his mistake dawned on him, he laughed. Then the whole song at full length. Then again, even louder. And when the bell tolled seven, his hands were no longer clasped but were conducting his resounding anthem. Two women, then another, then three, who were walking by slowed their pace, listened, walked on. He thought he'd glimpsed, on one of their faces, a dreamy expression.

Lust and Disgust had returned to his gullet, of this he was certain, but they'd lodged themselves in separate nooks of his larynx and would no longer act in unison.

At eight he rang the bell of his sister's flat. He barely spoke, as his sister was immediately wishing him many happy returns of the day and saying, as a sister, it was her job to help him out if he ever found himself in a mess. The children were already in bed and her husband wasn't yet home. He gave her a big hug. Without wanting her. She extricated herself and led him in. By the age of seventy, he'll have lived through a further ten years' worth of Mondays, but there was definitely never going to be another Monday like this. He smiled. Wolfed down his meal.

Her scent was lovely.

And now it's December.

Outdoors it is cold, and musing about the joys of blackberries at this time of year might seem as perverse as sprinkling salt on one's custard. But his musings are being aired aloud, his rich voice pouring like syrup over sour berries till all who are around his table are drooling. He is in a café, and a male voice beside him is whispering a suggestion in his ear. Which he likes the sound of. Which makes him think he won't, tonight, turn himself to the wall.

Norwegian Formula

MY LIPS ARE CRACKING. I need to find a chemist and get some ointment. Or better, a chapstick. *Norwegian Formula* by Neutrogena – that's always worked well. Screaming makes your lips crack. I'm living proof. I was screaming at my child earlier on when it wouldn't leave me alone. I'd carted it off to the playground so I could quietly sort out and file the articles. I'd got myself a folder specially, and had packed the hole-punch into my rucksack along with the newspapers, put the child into the bike basket and taken myself off to this distant playground so that I wouldn't (yet again) instantly bump into a thousand acquaintances. But somehow I got it wrong. It was same as always: my child instantly attracted the other kids away from their own mothers and over to us so that within minutes, they were noisily jostling and jumping around my feet. Unobtrusively I tried shooing them away, but they were quite simply not shoo-able. Meanwhile the mothers were sitting in peace on their benches reading, knitting or just chilling out, eyes closed, their faces turned up to the August sun. Whereas my own face felt like it was icing over. I was frightened by this chill, out of nowhere. I pulled the cigarette packet from my trouser pocket. *Nails in your coffin*, Joss had called its contents. At this I felt an impulse to smile. I fumbled for the lighter; lit myself one. But the smile never made it to my face. Even closing my mouth round the filter was hard, so frozen were my cheek muscles. Give it a moment. Breathe deeply. Collect your thoughts. The first one I collected was, if this child didn't leave me in peace I'd end up killing it. Obviously this thought terrified me and I wanted to cancel it immediately. So I called my child over and started hugging and kissing it, but it was distressed by this and struggled to get away. I was still tightly hugging it when the first yell came out. *Bastard! What IS it with you, you little git? Let me get on with my own stuff JUST ONCE you cunt, you little fucker, you stupid, stupid piece of shit... bleeding little arsehole...* I raged on. Shocked, the other mothers immediately jumped up and indignantly hustled their children away. One came towards me, opening her mouth to speak, but my look was enough to make her close it again and dismiss me with a wave of her hand.

Me and the child were now by ourselves. The other mums had banded together and formed themselves into a silent cordon, fencing in their children, wordlessly taking up defensive positions at a safe distance, and digging in the sand with little spades to have something to do. My child had begun sobbing, seated desolately beside one of the two posts between which the swings were suspended. It wouldn't be hard to bash its head in with the swing's heavy metal seat. I could say its skull had got smashed by accident, but then I'd be obliged to wail and cry. I wouldn't be capable of that. So I had to let that idea go. I had wailed and cried so much in recent weeks that there was simply none of that left for the child. On the seventeenth of July Joss had been putting on his shoes. All I said was, *Why shoes, on a day like this? It's gorgeous out there; it's summer – your sandals would be more appropriate!* But he'd pulled firmly on the laces, tied them in bows, packed his breakfast into his bag and set off to work on his bicycle. The car hit him at about seven a.m. if the papers are to be believed. He didn't die immediately; an emergency doctor revived him and got him taken to casualty for treatment, but at around eleven forty a.m. his heart finally stopped. That's what the death certificate says. They gave me it the day after, but I certainly didn't give it a proper look. My mother took me in. The main thing she fussed about was making me drink enough.

My mother must also have taken over looking after the child. I ignored it. I neither got it up from its little bed in the morning nor put it back there in the evening. All I was aware of was Joss: how he'd tied his shoelaces… and hearing myself saying *Why shoes, on a day like this? It's gorgeous out there; it's summer – your sandals would be more appropriate!* I just couldn't get my head round the fact that something as inane as that was the last thing I said to him – he'd been my husband, damn it! Whenever I'd been at the bank or the council offices asking for a form for *my husband* I'd always be grinning, hardly able to utter it, because it didn't come naturally to say *I am your wife,* or *you are my husband.* Because I didn't belong to you. And you didn't belong to me. Hence I couldn't help but grin when those words loomed like an elephant in the room (– once I'd controlled the grin, the elephant would thankfully dissolve and be gone).

I haven't grinned for a long time, but have smoked too many *nails in my coffin.* When I pick up the child or hang out the washing, my lungs groan. As for cycling – they groan so much I sometimes have to stop and take a break.

To be honest, they're groaning at this very minute.

My child has fallen asleep, thank goodness.

When I cycle I pedal as fast as I can, which, even if you haven't smoked too many coffin-nails, can strain your lungs to bursting point. Joss was big on cycling. On Sundays we'd always go on long cycle-rides with the child on one or other of our bikes. We had a basket each: lovely old-style ones attached to the front of the handlebars so we could more easily take turns transporting the child. On that day – the seventeenth of July – Joss had actually wanted to take the child to nursery. But it slept longer than usual, so I said I'd take it later; there was enough time before my lecture. I've bought all the newspapers that reported the accident. I had for a long time hoped I might magically read that *both my husband and* the child were fatally injured. Then I'd have known better what to do. But that report was nowhere to be found. Instead, the child gradually reappeared, peering out from behind my mother's skirt, for instance, asking for a drink. My mother would then always push it a bit further in front of her and towards me, until finally it stood very close, gazing up with that look of curiosity that Joss had so adored. I hated the child for that. I never used to hate it. I would always carry it around, playing with it; talking to it. But why did it have to sleep for so long on that particular morning? If it were dead, like Joss, I'd have been able to just die. But like this, it has held me fast, not letting me go to him, *my husband.* I have to keep it clean and rub cream in and give it food and take it to the playground – where I still can't be free of it of course; not even for ten minutes in which to do my filing in peace. I can't leave the filing to the evening, because now that my mother has gone back to sleeping at her own house, I'll be in bed with the baby when it is asleep. Holding it tight in my arms. I have to attend to it, see; not just abandon it. Looking at it now, asleep in the bike basket, I have to check its head is supported, not flopping about like a big heavy flower on a too-flimsy stalk. I spend a moment carefully shifting the child into a curled-up shape so its little head is safely positioned, chin-on-chest. So that its skull won't accidentally get wrenched off. Joss would've done the exact same. Joss would probably have pushed the bike around for a while to get the child to sleep. Well, I'll push the bike around too. There's a chemist across the way, I'll go buy myself a Neutrogena chapstick. *Norwegian Formula*. I'll be careful not to wake the child up when I take it out of the basket. I mean, it really oughtn't to be left by itself on my bike. After all, someone could easily take a fancy to a child as cute as mine.

Vaspersky's 'Flattriols'

VASPERSKY WAS SWEATING. This was nothing unusual, here in the south, at this time of year. Everyone who did not hail from here had been sweating since at least April; the locals since a little later in the year. But as Vaspersky knew, sweat ran down his body in January as well as in November or December, no matter where in the world he was. When he had been to his family doctor about a year ago for his sensitive stomach, the doctor had noticed his sweating and wanted to send him for a range of tests. Vaspersky successfully stopped him, claiming it had all been looked into previously and no cause had been found, which was of course not true. He knew full well when he had started sweating. His doctor who didn't know just shrugged and prescribed him an anti-cholinergic. The prescription had sunk deep down in Vaspersky's trouser pocket and disintegrated in the next wash.

Since Vaspersky had been living alone down here on a six-month stipendium from the Foundation for New Music, he'd had a lot of time to reflect. He gave no time to this when at home. Reflection was entirely lacking from his life. Just as well, as far as he was concerned. He made himself a black tea. His Professor of Sinology would always say that hot drinks are good for you on hot days like this. Vaspersky seated himself at his apartment's kitchen table. Outside his window was a terrace. A giant palm lily was growing there. He had the same plant at home. No way would it ever have survived even a mild Berlin winter outdoors, whereas this one had grown about five times as tall as her German little sister who was kept inside, and had no doubt grown just as deep into the ground. Vaspersky realised he'd never given a thought as to whether the temperatures would be anything like wintry at this latitude...

Now though, tea in hand, he made himself get on with the *Flattriols* he'd been planning to compose here and which the scholarship's sponsors would surely regard as the pièce de résistance of his composition. He had yet to find the right thing for the *ostinato* fluttery sound – during the flowing-on of which an oboe, or even a flute, maybe, would add a sense of consternation. Using a musical box felt too conventional; recordings of birds flying off, much too obvious. His gaze fell on the bowl of lemons from the local orchard. One still had a tuft of leaves at the end of its stalk. He was about to reach across and give it a shake – get a sound out of it – when just for a second, above the boundary wall between terrace and street, there appeared a boy's head. Bright eyed, with black curly hair. Vaspersky froze, and even when the boy was long gone, still didn't move. He had looked very different from Raphael, his sister's blond, green-eyed child, but he must have been about his age. Five year-old Raphael. Vaspersky had adored him, and had tried as far as possible to act as a male role-model after the boy's father had gone back to France with no conscience whatsoever about abandoning this role. When his sister was tussling with her doctorate, or rather with her (male) supervisor, and it was far from clear which of them would come out on top, Vaspersky had taken the boy to and from kindergarten. Thinking of this he couldn't help a smile – and then swiftly suppressed his mouth's slight upturn, applying a vice-like grip to his jaw and those woefully disobedient lips. Because when he thought of his sister, he did not want to smile; she who had suffered so much from the loss of her boy; who for a long time now had been incapable of sleep; whose lips nowadays were set in a thin line on her pale, hardened face.

Vaspersky got up and chewed the last two aspirin. The pressure in his head got worse. He wanted to avert the pain and the images that would now inevitably start passing before his eyes. He'd start sweating even more profusely than he was already, and his legs would begin to tremble, then his body, and for the rest of the day he'd be laid out with the shakes. Something like resignation was affecting his limbs, weakening them and making their movements random: sure enough, they were slowly starting to tremble uncontrollably. He lay on the floor curled into a foetal position, seeing himself on the way home with Raphael on the last Wednesday of December two years ago. They'd been on a little shopping trip. The child had been treated to a small felt purse, and while he was happily imagining filling it with coins, Vaspersky was obsessively imagining its jingle, and this jingling in his head took on a life of its own and carried him off into the parallel universe of his internal sound-studio, into which he normally only ever retreated when the boy wasn't around. The child was off in his own happy little world and completely unaware of all this, and to Vaspersky's increasing irritation, chattered on incessantly. Vaspersky realised how annoyed he was becoming and wanted to escape the sound-studio, but he was captive to it. It would not let him go. His body became the sound, and when yet another silly little question came near to destroying the soundscape, his sound-body could no longer handle it, and out of the blue he hit the boy in the face, and with a yell the boy tore away and tumbled into the street. Vaspersky had been incapable of telling his sister, later, that he'd slapped the boy's face. He just left it that he'd broken away, which was true, but which Vaspersky knew was only part of the real truth, and this is what had plagued him ever since. The only memory Vaspersky had of the hours after the accident was of locking himself into his apartment and writing his *Automobiles Indosinfonietta for chamber orchestra, tabla and mridangam*. It was to be his breakthrough as a composer.

When he'd accompanied his sister home from the cemetery a month after Raphael's death she'd begged him to stay over. She had cooked vegetable soup and not salted it, saying her tears while she ate would suffice. She had been in such despair he didn't know what else he could do but get in bed with her, and she had pressed herself against him, which he still thought was not to be taken the wrong way – she'd been far too wrapped up in her feelings for Raphael – although since parting that day, she had never again looked him in the eye.

It was late evening before Vaspersky felt able to get up. He just needed a little walk. To the lemon tree. Or the drinking fountain.

He was sweating.

On the point
of a knife

THE WEATHER WAS THE FARTHEST THING FROM MY MIND. In that first instant when I stepped out of the house, it was therefore a shock: the sheer violence of the rain's stabbing rods. My open-toed sandals began squelching after only a few paces, however it was warm, and I wasn't deterred. Schenke Street with its beautiful old town houses, where I had managed to nab a small flat for Martin and me two months previously, was a long way from any traffic; there was no chance of getting a soaking from a passing car. Anyway that wouldn't have deterred me either, since I had just killed my mother. In normal circumstances it's usual to know precisely where you are. What I knew precisely was that I had rammed a long sharp knife into my mother's chest. Maybe I was unconsciously aware of the street signs, the letterbox on the corner and the slogan of the primary school that promotes 'creativity', because after ten minutes I was exactly where I wanted to be – the Metro-train station. My mother was the only thing I was conscious of. I saw her eyes opening and closing; I saw her mouth opening and closing and the opening and closing of her hands, the latter image inevitably segueing to one of her chopping up a roast duck's brown carcass with poultry shears. After all, she had been the *Queen of Roast Duck*. Also the *Roast Beef Queen, Queen of Steak*

Marinade (Saxony-style), *Queen of Blue Carp in White Wine & Vinegar*, and the *Goulash Queen*. As for Thuringian dumplings, *Empress thereof*, of course. When it came to cooking, my father had held my mother in esteem, but otherwise looked down on her. I never held it against my mother, that my father looked down on her. Since he'd died, some four years ago now, I didn't even hold anything against my father any more. I fixed a vase on his grave so that my mother and I could take turns to leave flowers. We had never visited the cemetery together.

I got on the train going in the direction of Erkner. My boyfriend's parents lived there in their own house. My parents had lived in various rented flats. I suppose I was wanting to tell Martin's mother about how I killed my mother. Things like that, you've got to tell someone. I'd rather have had Martin's mother than mine, but that way, Martin and I would have been siblings and wouldn't have been allowed to fall in love. I always got rid of my disappointment by thinking that. When I first told Martin this thought, he came up with the idea of simply swapping our mothers. Virtually, so to speak. He evidently liked the Queen of Roast Duck. If ever there was duck at Christmas in his parental home it would be black on the outside and still frozen on the inside. We never went to eat at his parents' house without having had a massive breakfast. Martin wouldn't be able to have breakfast today when he found my dead mother pinned on the kitchen table where I had just left her with the knife in her chest. It had all happened in peace and quiet. When, at around five-ish, I went into the kitchen to get a glass of water, I found her – as ever – busy-bodying in the fridge. When I furiously demanded to know what she was doing in my fridge, she responded with a serene face, the know-all smile not even faltering when I grabbed and brandished the knife. I yanked her away from the fridge and up against the table, and stabbed.

I'd never felt furious with Martin's mother. Martin certainly had. That was a further reason why we'd done the virtual swap, some years ago. Martin chose gifts for my mother for birthdays and Christmas. He called her regularly to ask how she was. He visited her far more often than I did and came back replete and contented every time. Last Sunday, however, he had brought her back with him, and was of the opinion that she should stay at our place for at least a little while; she wasn't doing so well; she was hardly even cooking anymore. Who knows how long till she'd be joining my father in his grave? I should give my heart a prod and learn to put up with her; after all, *he* put up with *his* mother. Obviously, in view of her state, I had no right to refuse to let her stay. Carrying on as if she wasn't there was impossible because I was at home myself, having once again lost my admin job. When I came into the kitchen and felt her eyes trained on me, I sometimes felt myself starting to shrivel. So I'd always leave the room at speed, mostly just grabbing myself a plain bread roll or an apple. I hated turning into a child under her gaze. At first I thought that by leaving the house I'd be able to put her out of my mind for a while. But right from moving in, she took me over. No matter how far I went from home, she didn't let go.

What did she ever actually do to me? The more I thought about it, the less I knew. Even then, on the train to Erkner, I was trying to remember. My earliest memories seemed to date back to around my fourth birthday. My mother was wearing a dress with green stripes which one year and one child later she could no longer wear. A full skirt swung in tiers from her narrow waist. My mother and I were running – no, bouncing – along, side by side, our arms crossed over our fronts to have hold of both of each other's hands. We were singing. I couldn't bring to mind what song it was, but at the end of each verse we would turn without letting go hands and bounce back again, my mother's breasts and the long loops of my Bavarian-style plaits bouncing too. I remembered how lovely it had been to bounce to and fro holding Mother's hands without any foresight of the fun coming to an end. Just like I'd had no foresight of Mother's end. Leastways, not how it was going to happen. My characteristic lack of foresight had evidently not changed much... But the images of bouncing were layered on top of other memories. Events that had occurred later were surfacing through the murk, but before I could extract and examine them, we'd bounced across them, over and over till they vanished. We'd been a dynamic duo. I was starting to get upset. Why I was suddenly feeling guilty for leaving Martin alone with her, I've no idea. The alarm would go off in a few minutes. Martin probably wouldn't go into the kitchen straight off, but would take a shower in the bathroom, and get his clothes from the wardrobe in the bedroom. But then he'd find her and, no doubt in shock, would want to get her off the table. I pictured him pulling the knife out of the wood and propping my mother up against the fridge again. He might for instance use his fingernail to smooth the cut on her chest back down flat. Plus he'd be wondering where I was. Where was I? That was probably the moment when I fully realised what I'd done. I whipped out my phone and called him.

Salad days

FLUNKER IS LYING IN THE LETTUCE. This hadn't been his intention when he'd set out on his mission to meet Carmen Schnaps, but to have ended up here is good. He can feel their green heads in his back, while alongside his eyes there are ones to the left and right, as he gazes contentedly skywards, watching the buzzard glide, almost motionless, on the hot, silent air, and the swallows, which are swooping lower than usual. Might there be a thunderstorm on the way? His suit (raw linen, beige, summery) is streaked with green – not from the lettuce but from the grass through which Flunker crawled to get here. So long as he's lying here it doesn't matter, he thinks; and if he goes home late enough – after dark – folk won't notice. 'Folk' had, until now, loomed large in Flunker's life. When he strolled through the streets of the little town or visited the baker's or the butcher's, 'folk' would be watching him from their windows. 'Folk' were in the council office that doled out his money, or waiting in long rows outside it. Their combined effect had been to bring him down to a 'hair shirt' way of relating. He'd wear it when yet more 'folk' – the ones in his block of flats – held the door open for him, or brought him any mail he'd accumulated during his occasional absences. In his humbled state he'd do just about anything to please all these folk. Before that

Thursday two weeks ago, he hadn't even looked folk in the eye, whether man or woman. Until, that is, he met Carmen Schnaps. It was midday. He had popped into the haberdasher's to buy a needle and thread and darning wool: he had buttons to sew on, hems to mend, socks to darn. Having worked out the money that was to be at his disposal in the next year or so, it felt wasteful to throw out socks with holes in them, or ripped trousers. So he was standing in Jurgens' store, unsure where to turn, when someone stumbled in behind him and fell over. Her ankle was sprained, as he learned half a day later. At that moment, however, he just heard a suppressed *"damn!"* and, startled, spun around. And what loveliness he beheld. He could do no more than stare at length, bewitched, into her silver-green eyes which were wincing with pain. His gaze passed over her shoulders and breasts and down to her legs. Finally he offered his hand, which she seized gratefully, pulling herself up. She was in no uncertain terms Female. For a few moments they stood side by side, he holding her bag while she smoothed down her skirt and fixed her dishevelled hair back into a ponytail with a clasp. It was clear her mind was no longer on shopping. Rather, her fern-green eyes were asking whether he could accompany her a little way; offer his support. Though he couldn't say what triggered it, the term *a force to be reckoned with* ricocheted in his head. It was just (she was saying), she had to get back to work. The gallant knight in him, of whose ongoing existence he had no longer been aware, was instantly alerted and took control. An incredible electricity was fizzing between them: when their bodies touched he felt heat and a strange, barely perceptible prickling. The kind that could wait. It didn't need instant relief.

After they'd crossed the marketplace she thanked him and said goodbye for the time being. Before she disappeared into the town hall, however, she asked him to call her in the evening on a number hastily scribbled on a scrap of paper. Because of the electricity, is all he could think.

He went to the underground public toilet. The area that had been touching her was fiery red and covered with a rash. He could now give himself a good scratch. When he came back out a quarter of an hour later his dazed eyes held a look of wondrous incredulity. Instead of needle and thread he bought bread and potatoes.

Until the evening he was busy making a potato soup. It was ready on the table at precisely six. He ate it with a hotdog sausage out of a jar and a slice of bread. The table was cleared and the waxed cloth wiped off when he finally sat down to call her.

Carmen Schnaps, who's calling please?

Carmen! His heart leapt like a bullock before the Torero's red rag. For some moments, speech deserted him.

Yes? Hello! You're through to Schnaps!

Slowly, words crept back. At first only a few roamed free: off the leash, yet halting. But after half an hour Flunker's speech had adapted to the circumstances and he was able to chat naturally with the vision of loveliness he was currently unable to view. About what? After the conversation, he couldn't say, but he had registered that she was about to go on a training course for two weeks. She told him when she'd be back, and that she'd be very happy if he picked her up from the station.

Two weeks.

From that moment on he tried to eat a protein-rich diet to increase his muscle mass, painted his small living-room mint green, bought a new bathroom shelf and a light linen suit. Overall he spent nearly a third of his scant savings on preparations. Unsure as to what such lovely creatures might eat, he considered going to a restaurant on picking her up, if Carmen Schnaps were hungry. Though he should at the very least have a good bottle of wine and some nibbles ready for if she came back to his place.

Never before had two weeks passed so quickly for Flunker. But yesterday (Wednesday) at just before midnight, even though Thursday was already threatening Wednesday's existence, he was beset by impatience. He stood in front of the mirror in the light suit, chest out, belly in, and for an instant, saw her beside him. He sighed, hearing the clock strike only midnight.

He got through the next hours with half-hearted attempts to sleep, sudokus, and a bottle of beer, before finally dozing off at five. He was surprised and pleased that his alarm clock actually let him know when it was time to get up. Seeing as it hadn't had to do that for a long time. On his way to the station Flunker was hyper-aware of 'folk', and was amazed that no-one seemed to be taking any notice of him as he walked along in suit and tie. Since everyone seemed very absorbed in their own concerns, he tested out not giving a toss what they thought. The only thing that got noticed – and taken off him – was his hair shirt, which they somehow spirited away, so that on arrival at the station he went in with his head actually held high, and searched purposefully for Thomann's Bakery that had a branch here. There was enough time for a large pot of coffee. When he stood on the platform a little later and the train came in, the forceful Carmen Schnaps got out, spotted him, ran to him and, as though it was absolutely normal, kissed him on the mouth. Necking was for him even further back in the past than being roused by his alarm clock each morning. Flunker was distinctly aware of something else currently being roused. He took Carmen Schnaps's travel bag and for now carried it in front of his stomach, until it had gone down again. Carmen must have been taken the same way, because she was looking at him with strangely veiled eyes, their lids seeming suddenly swollen. She grabbed his right hand and pulled. He followed her. Where to, he didn't know, at first. When they had already gone almost right through the town on the high street, they took a turn into some allotments. After three or four forks in the path, she unlocked the wooden gate to a plot then locked it behind them. What happened next, bearing in mind the green streaks on Flunker's suit, is self-evident. The suit is lying beside him among the lettuce, and in the crook of his arm, the lovely creature is slumbering into the afternoon. And he suddenly realises that, while he no longer gives a toss what folk think, he wants folk to give a toss about the streaks on his suit. The thought of showing them off to folk makes him grin.

O snore, all ye faithful…

PIERS WAS WHISKING EGGS. The kitchen table was virtually smothered under the shells from three packs of a dozen eggs. A couple of shells were on the floor. Great heavens above, had he suddenly got a craze for baking? Was this the man who, with the children now gone, had so rejected Christmas that he spent the twenty-fourth of December either clearing out the cellar or clearing out his wardrobe? I was planning to go over to my daughter Carla's who lived just a couple of doors along and, with a husband and three daughters, would at the very least put up a little Christmas tree. I intended to have a nice time on Christmas Eve in the glow of their tree's lighted candles. Better than staying here with Piers banging about. I'd been doing this every year now for the last three or four years, not returning till after midnight, by which time there'd either be a bin-liner of old clothes beside the door or else a load of old junk overflowing from the dustbin. So what on earth was this egg-whisking about, today? I was so flabbergasted I couldn't get the question out. But Piers gave me the answer anyway. *Scrambled egg,* he said, and proceeded to get all four of our pans out of the cupboard, chop bacon and onions into them and set them on the oven. The jets weren't yet lit. I had to sit down.

With thirty-six eggs? The question arose, tremulous, from my throat, and hung in the air for all of half a minute until Piers opened his mouth.

I've put out an invite, he said casually, washing his hands.

Had he found himself a girlfriend, or what? It was already settled I was going to Carla's; did he see that as an opportunity to spring a revelation on me? We actually got on very well. We were both over fifty but we still had a bit of action, so to speak, and it was really quite good. I calmed down a bit. Any woman would be over-faced by eighteen eggs (I'd divided the quantity by two). So I breathed an almost apologetic little *Who?* into the bacon- and onion-laden atmosphere.

Brummer and his pals. Thought they shouldn't have to freeze their arses off today, for once.

Had I heard that correctly? The old codger was our 'neighbour', so to speak. The plot next door to ours didn't actually belong to him, but had been owned by his late lady-friend. Even when she was still alive Brummer had been a heavy drinker, but had nonetheless cut her grass, harvested the apples and cherries and made sure the shrubs got cut back. Six years had passed since Brummer had found his Irene dead behind the house. *Heart attack,* as he informed everybody he met, even today, whether they were interested or not. Since then the garden had gone to pot. Piers generously described it as having been *re-wilded.* In the middle of the wilderness was a little stone-built house with a shingle roof. In former times this had been regularly re-tarred and repaired, but after Irene died the unemployed Brummer completely let it go. In terms of maintenance, he never again lifted a finger. The first thing to happen was the water board turning off his supply. Then his electricity got cut off. Brummer would go for dumps behind his house, which we never commented on but found highly regrettable because we couldn't use the seating area behind our own place due to the pong. We did actually like the man, but he was beyond help. So we were glad that during the day he was off helping the Vietnamese fruit-seller at the local station, along with four or five other men like him, for which he got paid in bumper packs of bottled water that he brought home regularly on his bicycle. *Regular* being the important word, in terms of Brummer's wellbeing. Regular as clockwork, at six in the morning – by which time he would regularly be completely wasted – he'd head off on his bike, and would regularly set about his job of unloading and stacking the boxes of fruit and veg while regularly being shot disapproving looks by passers-by who noticed the glassy eyes of the man humping the satsumas. Then regularly at around six in the evening he would cycle back. I was often astonished at how he'd made it without incident through the traffic, but he obviously knew where he was going and came straight home. When he got off his bike he'd be staggering, and would take a very long time getting his key into the lock on the garden gate. If we were out barbecuing he'd come to the fence and be given a sausage or a burger. There had been only one occasion, shortly after we'd moved in, when Piers, who hadn't known what he was like by then, gave him a bottle. Moonshine, made by our Czechoslovakian friends. By the next morning the bottle was standing empty outside the front door of the little house. Piers then got the picture. Like me, Piers didn't drink spirits, but we'd accumulated quite a stock of such bottles, which he just left in the cellar gathering dust; I was always surprised he never got rid of them in one of his Christmas clear-outs.

To return to Brummer. The most I knew of his four or five pals was from the looks we'd occasionally given each other near the station. Oddly enough the prospect of them spending Christmas Eve in our rather nice home didn't worry me unduly.

I should have been putting my coat on to walk over to Carla's, but was procrastinating, which Piers noticed, and which made him smirk.

Honestly, though! Scrambled egg? I started to collect up the shells. In truth I was mentally wrestling between Carla and (I admit – I was curious) the invited guests. It was now close to five, the traditional time for most families to start exchanging presents. After church. They'd be kicking off shortly. My presents for Carla's kids were standing ready by the door in a big plastic carrier bag. I pulled on my boots. For the time being my daughter had come out on top. Outdoors it was bitterly cold. The first thing I was met with at Carla's was the stink of those little incense cones which I had never yet persuaded myself to like. With a tortured smile I watched my grandchildren getting their gifts. No, it was nice. But after an hour I felt so awful, I offered my apologies – happy at least that I genuinely wasn't lying: I was on the verge of being sick. Once outdoors the nausea was gone in an instant, and I immediately thought – our bodies are controlled by our minds. Looking all concerned, the family waved me off. I took off my woolly hat to let my head be cooled by the snow that was falling heavily. It did the job and, once home, I took off my coat and stood in front of the mirror with dripping hair. Seated at the kitchen table were six men. Piers had extended the table, having fetched up one of its two leaves from the cellar. It was once again the length it used to be when the children were still at home. The table was set with seven places. Damn it! Piers knew me so well. Can one's love for someone express itself in fury? Whatever: for a second that's what I felt, but then I quickly sat down in the remaining place at the head of the table. The men greeted me, bonded as one in their alcoholic reek. What told them apart were the odours of each of their bodies, which only came across once I'd got used to the alcohol fumes. Unlike Carla's incense cones, the body-odour of our five guests didn't make me want to gag. This surprised me at first, but by a sort of gradual metabolic adjustment, my awareness of it soon went altogether. I was glad, then, that I hadn't reacted to that initial overwhelming stench with an offer of the use of our bath.

The scrambled egg was ready in the pans. Piers broke up a fresh loaf of bread and brought a pot of tea to the table. Initially the men didn't have much to say and were eyeing the tea in their glasses with nigh-on embarrassment. Then, from the depths of his pants, Brummer drew out a bottle of GDR-era 'Goldie', a cheap, blended brandy from the good old days. In an instant, every man drew out something similar, and each laced his glass of tea with a toddy. Brummer proposed that with the downing of each glass, they pass the bottles along. Straight past us, of course. By the time the Goldie had made its first full round, tongues were considerably looser. The men had demolished the scrambled eggs and generous portions of bacon with great relish and were now enjoying the room's warm ambience. I was suddenly pleased there were no Christmas decorations in our house, meaning, there were no reminders that this was Christmas Eve and that, compared to what was going on elsewhere, it was abnormal. Its abnormality was passing unnoticed. That we were addressing each other in the familiar terms of lifelong friends was also not normal and yet felt entirely natural, and we knew it meant a great deal to Brummer. Furthermore, in this intimacy that had been so quickly reached, his pals, too, began opening up and telling stories about themselves. "Our" Gustav *(Nah then, lad!)* told how his foot would have totally rotted off last summer if a lady doctor hadn't come and had a word with him while he was having his weekly bath in the lake at Kaulsdorf. "Our" Herbert

(Nah then, Bert!) contended (taking out his false teeth) that just as nice a thing had happened to him as well, two years ago. This set Manfred chuntering. *Wots up, our Manfred?* He said he'd wanted to give blood to get the free breakfast afterwards, but when he got to the door of the mobile Donor Unit they'd chased him off. *They need blinkin blood, don't they?* He laced his tea with a shot of 'Timm's Bitter', a lemon-flavoured vodka from the old GDR days. I shuddered.

At around midnight, "our" Paul began a slow slide into a horizontal position. He moved from the kitchen to the lounge, spread a blanket he'd brought with him on the floor and lay down. I went after him to pull out the big bed-settee but I couldn't get him into it, he was already fast asleep. Instead of him, it was Brummer who came (slurring something about not having had such a nice night for a very long time) and lay down on the settee, facing the wall. I threw a blanket over him. Half an hour later, our Gustav followed him. There were two made-up beds ready and waiting in our guest-room, but our Fred and our Bert were too far gone even to pull back the covers. I went searching round the house and found two old cotton quilts in the loft which, after hurriedly beating out the dust, I spread over the pair of them. The men's snoring was deafening, and now and then a fart would burst forth like thunder-clap. Piers smiled, content. He fetched a bottle of red wine from the cellar, tipped it into a pan, peeled an orange, added cloves, cinnamon, nutmeg, cardamom and a little sugar, and set this on the hob. We drank the mulled wine in bed.

I so loved my Piers.

Balder & Sons

Last spring the Fizz Gallery offered me the opportunity to exhibit some of my pictures. The gallery is in G, the town I grew up in, in Germany's east, which in my childhood was still the German Democratic Republic. I set off, full of excitement because I hadn't set foot there for twenty years, having spent the last two decades over in west Germany finishing my schooling and then doing my degree. Would it feel familiar?

It hardly did at all. In fact I found the town to be greatly changed. The Renaissance-era town hall had been beautifully restored and the entire town centre had been pedestrianised. The quaint little buildings now housed bookshop and clothing chains, as well as a few medium-sized concerns, and even one of those Vietnamese-run household stores, full of the kind of unbelievable junk that middle-aged provincial housewives find so irresistible. Those buildings taken over by large retail chains had however managed, miraculously, to expand their premises to the rear, whereas the Vietnamese store was only as big – or to be precise, as small – as Balder & Sons, Stationers. I was amazed Balder & Sons still existed, considering that twenty years ago Herr Balder the elder had been over eighty and his sons well over fifty. On entering the shop I recognised the two of them straight away, perched there behind the old-fashioned counter, reading. Ortwin sprang up to attend to my needs. Though 'sprang' is taking it a bit too far. More accurately his eyes responded with sprightliness, whereas his body slowly and laboriously heaved itself out of his narrow armchair. His brother Erhard's hair was still combed forward into a fringe that was trimmed in a dead straight line across his forehead – the Bertolt Brecht look. He remained seated, not even looking up. I smiled, and at first didn't speak; just waited expectantly. Because of the silence, Erhard at last tore his eyes away from his book and looked in my direction. He recognised me, of course, since as a teenager I'd been in that shop every single day. I would go to play chess with old Herr Balder, who at the same time kept an eye on his sons from his look-out behind the counter, even when they were approaching pensionable age themselves, as though he couldn't trust them not to ruin the business. My own hair with its centre parting was no longer blond but carroty – an accident with henna last week – but it hung to just below my shoulders, exactly the same as back then, and proved to be the thing he recognised. After Erhard had come and said hello he wound a strand round his fingers. It took Ortwin longer, and he needed his brother's prompting before it dawned on him who I was. Before my mother and I emigrated in the mid-eighties, we had lived in this building, in the top floor flat under the roof with its one tiny main room and its even tinier side-room. I was born and raised there, on the floor above the – also tiny – three-room flat where the three Balder gentlemen had lived, which, in turn, was directly above the little shop on the ground floor. The house belonged to old Herr Balder. My mother had told me, way back, that his wife had died in the early 'fifties and that since then no other lady had ever crossed the Balders' threshold. It was odd how Ortwin and Erhard had not only accepted their father's hermit-like existence but actually joined in with it. From their three-person hermitage they had skippered the little shop through the waters of time, but time had not been good to them. Indeed the waters they were navigating today were no less choppy than twenty or forty years ago, when private ownership had been a matter of disgrace. While private ownership was nowadays far from a matter of disgrace, private ownership Balder-style was, as it had always been, modest, comprising no more than a draught-ridden little house with a small antiquated shop that could only continue to exist because there was no rent to pay, and which no doubt had folk queueing up to buy out the two resolute elderly gentlemen and pack them off to a luxury retirement complex. I was imagining with satisfaction all the unsuccessful overtures from potential buyers, then suddenly wondered how I could have got so lost in my thoughts when I realised that Ortwin had brought me a cup of tea, and Erhard had been asking questions and was now looking to me expectantly for answers.

I didn't want to let on I'd been imagining all this, and feeling such schadenfreude over the rejected buyers. *Pardon?* I said, casually as I could.

He still often comes out with your name, said Erhard.

I was immediately taken aback. Was old Herr Balder still alive? At over a hundred years old?

Where have you accommodated him? I asked, delicately, since they too were actually of an age when single gentlemen ought to be thinking about moving to a residence offering care facilities.

They looked at me uncomprehendingly, then at each other.

In the flat, of course, said Ortwin.

What – ours? I asked uncertainly.

No no – Erhard piped up: *Where you used to live was taken by a young man after you left, though we hardly ever saw him; he did pay his rent on time but of course that's not saying much, seeing as it was only fifteen marks back then anyway! Then after Reunification he left and we started using the flat as an attic. Father had so much old clutter but we couldn't throw it out, so we stored it up there.*

Aha. So they'd gained some space. Because a person as old as that needs a special bed; a commode… Was he still compos mentis enough to want to see me? I definitely wanted to see him, and so inquired as to whether he was receiving visitors.

They laughed, but their obvious embarrassment unsettled me. Erhard coughed. Ortwin said they'd have needed to clear up a bit beforehand, and the fact was, they hadn't had a visitor for so long it wasn't true, and they didn't even know if they'd be able to offer a drink or refreshments; they themselves always went across to the guest-house, the Pension Schubert, where that nice Frau Schmidt made them their breakfast, lunch and supper.

And… what about him? I asked in the same uncertain tone.

Oh, the little he eats, I can stock up in the supermarket and it lasts him easily three months, explained Ortwin.

Wordlessly I imagined a grizzled, emaciated geriatric whose existence was perhaps known to no-one; a man who, like a piece of wizened Christmas cake dropped long ago behind the bookcase, had passed from the memories of those who used to live round here in former times, while people who'd moved here more recently had never known him, and thus had not noticed his disappearance.

My uneasiness was growing.

I asked them how soon they might finish the tidying.

They both went red.

Not… not… not before tomorrow night, stammered Erhard.

We could just bring him downstairs though, don't you

think? Ortwin's suggestion served to release the iron grip that for the last minute or so had been tightening round Erhard's heart. And with all the businesslike efficiency they still had at their disposal, the duo headed upstairs, having asked me to keep any potential customers talking.

I looked round. The hidden contents of the many drawers were revealed on the cards inserted into the little slots on their fronts. I read off *Lead. Coloured. Ink.* And *A4, A5, A6.* Though there were brand names too: *Geha, Rotring* and *Pelikan.* The two tall shelving units against the wall were filled with boxes stacked in piles, neat and tidy, each bearing a label. *Calendars, fountain pens, blotting paper, erasers, brown paper, compasses, glue.* Just how it had been back then, under the old regime. Presumably the reason they kept this archaic system was that their father was still alive.

Unsurprisingly, no one did come into the stationery shop.

What I was more interested in was how they were going to get the old man down the stairs.

Might he still be good on his feet?

I heard the door close upstairs. There were no falling noises, no pushing or hard-breathing. They were coming down the stairs as quickly (or should I say slowly) as they had gone up.

I could hardly bear the tension.

They opened the door to the shop.

When I instantly burst out laughing, they were clearly startled. There, sitting on Ortwin's shoulder, was Coco! I'd completely forgotten Coco's existence. When I was little the only Amazon I knew about was a tanned, buxom woman who was good with a bow and arrow. Until Coco taught me better. It seemed male creatures, too, could be Amazons. Coco was an Amazon with a yellow beak. His life in an exclusively male household had made him suspicious of all females, hence my name had only ever come out as a screech of fury. *He still often comes out with your name,* so Erhard had said. Would things be any different now?

I couldn't stop laughing. Ortwin and Erhard looked at each other, perplexed.

Coco screeched my name, sounding furious indeed. When I'd at last calmed down, I saw him for what he'd always been: a green terrorist with misogynistic tendencies. An old feeling long since deleted from my emotional inventory now overwhelmed me: my sheer love for that parrot. What else could it be, this coach and horses galloping through my heart, making me choke up? With all due deference, I stepped back.

I didn't tell Ortwin and Erhard about the misunderstanding. Anyway they'd moved onto telling me in detail, and with ever greater animation and pleasure, about Coco's quirky habits: his love of television, but how watching TV would make him fall asleep while perched on one or other of their shoulders; how both his laughing and crying were so insistent that once he started up, you were forced to join in. However, his liking for a specifically human diet had been thwarted after they started having all their meals over at the guesthouse. He'd only taken to dry food very slowly; for the last decade though, since the death of their father who'd always cooked their meals, he'd had no other option.

Old Herr Balder had lived to be over ninety, and the way he'd looked after his sons had been more like a mother… I didn't want to think about the limited life of this man who, despite his own un-met needs, had nonetheless amply provided for the happy and fulfilled life that this Amazonian parrot had enjoyed.

At the end of that afternoon in Balder & Sons the Stationers, I bought some paints. Acrylics, in small white tubes. I now have a painting of Coco hanging above my desk. If I stare at it for long enough, the three Balder men pay me a fleeting visit. They stand there waving, guests in my here-and-now, but then in the blink of an eye, they become The Past.

Naked Eye Publishing
A fresh approach

Naked Eye Publishing is an independent not-for-profit micro-press intent on publishing quality poetry and literature, including in translation.

A particular focus is translation. We aim to take a midwife role in facilitating the translation of works that have until now been disregarded by English-language publishing. We will be happy if we function purely as an initial stepping-stone both for overlooked writers and first-time literary translators.

Each of us at Naked Eye is a volunteer, competent and professional in our work practice, and not intending to make a profit for the press. We see ourselves as part of the revolution in book publishing, embodying the newly levelled playing field, sidestepping the publishing establishment to produce beautiful books at an affordable price with writers gaining maximum benefit from sales.

nakedeyepublishing.co.uk

Lightning Source UK Ltd.
Milton Keynes UK
UKHW022210060422
401190UK00005B/313

9 781910 981153